LUCAS

LUCAS

TEXAS BOUDREAU BROTHERHOOD

By
KATHY IVAN

COPYRIGHT

Lucas – Original Copyright © September 2020 by Kathy Ivan

Cover by Elizabeth Mackay

Release date: September 2020
Print Edition

All Rights Reserved

LUCAS – Texas Boudreau Brotherhood

Opening a small town bakery, Jill Monroe feels Lady Luck is finally smiling on her. She's got everything she ever dreamed of, except the cowboy who won her heart. A new story has investigative reporter Lucas Boudreau stretched thin. Being home near his childhood sweetheart isn't helping. When unwanted attention escalate to threats, can Lucas gamble with his heart and still protect the woman he's always loved?

"In Shiloh Springs, Kathy Ivan has crafted warm, engaging characters that will steal your heart and a mystery that will keep you reading to the very last page." Barb Han, USA TODAY and Publisher's Weekly Bestselling Author

"Kathy Ivan's books are addictive, you can't read just one." Susan Stoker, NYT Bestselling Author

BOOKS BY KATHY IVAN

www.kathyivan.com/books.html

TEXAS BOUDREAU BROTHERHOOD

Rafe

Antonio

Brody

Ridge

Lucas

Heath (coming soon)

NEW ORLEANS CONNECTION SERIES

Desperate Choices

Connor's Gamble

Relentless Pursuit

Ultimate Betrayal

Keeping Secrets

Sex, Lies and Apple Pies

Deadly Justice

Wicked Obsession

Hidden Agenda

Spies Like Us

Fatal Intentions

New Orleans Connection Series Box Set: Books 1-3

New Orleans Connection Series Box Set: Books 4-7

Hello Readers,

Welcome to Shiloh Springs, Texas! Don't you just love a small Texas town, where the people are neighborly, the gossip plentiful, and the heroes are...well, heroic, not to mention easy on the eyes! I love everything about Texas, which I why I've made the great state my home for over thirty years. There's no other place like it. From the delicious Tex-Mex food and downhome barbecue, the majestic scenery, and friendly atmosphere, the people and places of the Lone Star state are as unique and colorful as you'll find anywhere.

My new series, the Texas Boudreau Brotherhood, series centers around a group of foster brothers, men who would have ended up in the system if not for Douglas and Patricia Boudreau. Instead of being hardened by life and circumstances beyond their control, they found a family who loved and accepted them, and gave them a place to call home. Sometimes brotherhood is more than sharing the same DNA.

This is Lucas Boudreau's story, and Lucas was a hard book to write. There are so many things going on in Lucas' life, trying to fit them all into one book seemed an impossible task. But while he's a complex character, Jill is the perfect heroine for him. She's spirited, loves her family regardless of all their flaws, and loves fiercely and with her whole heart. I promise she's going to keep Lucas' head spinning.

If you've read my other romantic suspense books (the New Orleans Connection series and Cajun Connection series), you'll be familiar with the Boudreau name. Turns out there are a whole lot of Boudreaus out there, just itching to have their stories told. (Douglas is the brother of Gator Boudreau, patriarch of the New Orleans branch of the Boudreau family. Oh, and did I mention they have another brother – Hank "The Tank" Boudreau?)

So, sit back and relax. The pace of small-living might be less hectic than the big city, but small towns hold secrets, excitement, and heroes to ride to the rescue. And who doesn't love a Texas cowboy?

Kathy Ivan

EDITORIAL REVIEWS

"In Shiloh Springs, Kathy Ivan has crafted warm, engaging characters that will steal your heart and a mystery that will keep you reading to the very last page."

—Barb Han, *USA TODAY* and Publisher's Weekly Bestselling Author

"Kathy Ivan's books are addictive, you can't read just one."

—Susan Stoker, NYT Bestselling Author

"Kathy Ivan's books give you everything you're looking for and so much more."

—Geri Foster, USA Today and NYT Bestselling Author of the Falcon Securities Series

"This is the first I have read from Kathy Ivan and it won't be the last."

—Night Owl Reviews

"I highly recommend Desperate Choices. Readers can't go wrong here!"

—Melissa, Joyfully Reviewed

"I loved how the author wove a very intricate storyline with plenty of intriguing details that led to the final reveal…"

—Night Owl Reviews

Desperate Choices—Winner 2012 International Digital Award—Suspense

Desperate Choices—Best of Romance 2011 –Joyfully Reviewed

DEDICATIONS AND ACKNOWLEDGEMENTS

I love it when fans tell me they wish Shiloh Springs, Texas, was a real place, because they want to live there. Trust me, if it was real, I'd be your next door neighbor, because I want to live there too!

To my sister, Mary, always helping me, encouraging me, and generally doing whatever it takes to get encourage me to get the writing done. Trust me, if she wasn't there prodding me, the books might never be finished.

To Chris Keniston and Barb Han, fellow authors and great friends. Our phone calls and Facebook chats helped keep me sane while I was figuring out all the foibles of Lucas Boudreau. Thanks, Ladies!

And, as always, I dedicate this and every book to my mother, Betty Sullivan. She shared her love of reading with me at a young age and I cherish the memories of the times we spent talking books and romance. I miss her every day and wish she'd been around to see my first book published, but I know she's smiling at the thought of her daughter, the author, writing the type of books she loved.

More about Kathy and her books can be found at

WEBSITE:

www.kathyivan.com

Follow Kathy on Facebook at
facebook.com/kathyivanauthor

Follow Kathy on Twitter at
twitter.com/@kathyivan

Follow Kathy at BookBub
bookbub.com/profile/kathy-ivan

NEWSLETTER SIGN UP

Don't want to miss out on any new books, contests, and free stuff? Sign up to get my newsletter. I promise not to spam you, and only send out notifications/e-mails whenever there's a new release or contest/giveaway. Follow the link and join today!

http://eepurl.com/baqdRX

LUCAS

By
KATHY IVAN

CHAPTER ONE

The road to hell might be paved with good intentions, but when it came to dealing with Patricia Boudreau, all bets were off. Jill Monroe couldn't quite figure how she'd become embroiled in Ms. Patti's latest scheme, or even why she'd shown up on the other woman's radar. Since nobody said no to the town's matriarch, here she was, waiting outside a desolate building in the rapidly approaching twilight.

Huffing out an exasperated breath, she cupped her hands around her eyes and leaned in closer, peering into the darkness beyond the huge plate glass window of the storefront. Dirty and grimy, and streaked with a greasy film she really didn't want to touch, she couldn't make out much. The building's interior sat shrouded in inky blackness and appeared more than a little spooky.

Guess nobody's here.

Taking a step back, she pulled the note from her pocket and checked the address again. She'd found it slipped under her apartment's front door when she'd gotten home from her job, the stark whiteness of the envelope standing out against her worn and faded chocolate-brown carpet.

Yep, she was in the right place, right time, but so far no sign of the woman who'd summoned her.

Wonder what Ms. Patti's up to now?

At least the interminable heat wave petered out overnight, and the temperature, while still warm, didn't feel like it was going to broil the skin from her bones. Texas in late summer meant rarely being outdoors during daylight hours—not even on a bet. Having the stifling heat of industrial-sized ovens cranked up high all day didn't create the same sensation as Texas humidity in the summertime. It's a lesson she'd learned working for a restaurant during her summer hiatus from school. She'd long ago decided she enjoyed her creature comforts far too much, which meant air conditioning running twenty-four/seven.

Today had been onerous, overly long, and she'd hated every minute of it. Driving over an hour each way for her day job ate up a huge chunk of her morning and evening hours, not to mention the wear and tear of her on-its-last-legs car. It was a used one she'd bought after graduation from college. She'd scrimped and saved, and sacrificed meals to scrounge up enough money for the down payment on an already eight-year-old rust bucket. She crossed her fingers every morning, praying it didn't give up the ghost and die on her daily commute. Add in the fact she felt like a glorified pencil pusher at the insurance company where she worked, with chances of advancement zilch, and her life was pretty much in the toilet. The only bright spot: her friend Tessa had moved to Shiloh Springs, and would be sticking around since she was engaged to the town's sheriff, Rafe Boudreau.

The edge of twilight ate away the remnants of what little daylight remained, cloaking the world around her in deepening darkness. Arms wrapped around her midsection, she tried her best to ward off the goosebumps spreading along her skin, ones that had nothing to do with a chill, but more an uneasy feeling of being outside alone. Almost all of the shops along Shiloh Springs' Main Street closed earlier, all their doors shuttered by eight p.m. Daisy's Diner down the street closed early on weeknights and the bookstore closed at eight sharp. Farther down the main drag, Jill saw the outside lights from the sheriff's station, so she didn't feel totally abandoned. If only Ms. Patti would get here and tell her why she'd wanted to meet in the first place, maybe she'd get over the eerie feeling riding her.

After what seemed like an eternity, headlights brightened the darkness, headed straight toward her, and Jill shielded her eyes against their sudden glare. Recognizing the highly-identifiable white Cadillac Escalade everyone in Shiloh Springs knew Ms. Patti drove, she breathed a sigh of relief. She watched it pulled to a stop in front of her, taking up nearly two parking spaces.

Ms. Patti's car was as distinctive as the woman herself. It seemed a strange dichotomy, this behemoth of a vehicle, wrestled into submission by the diminutive dynamo. But while she might be small in stature, her will and determination more than made up for her size. There wasn't a soul within a good fifty-mile radius who didn't recognize the pearly white gargantuan SUV as belonging to the town's unofficial matriarch.

The Boudreau family, a fixture in town for more years than Jill had been alive, was presided over by Patricia Boudreau. Deceptively tiny, she was a powerhouse in a petite package, and knew everybody and everything that went on in their little burb. She kept a watchful eye on the comings and goings around Shiloh Springs, and provided gentle nudges when needed. Ms. Patti was one of those women who got things done, and heaven help you if she decided you needed help, or if she believed you could accomplish things she felt would benefit her town. A force of nature, there was no stopping her once she got an idea in her head. It would be easier to stop a Texas tornado than try to ride rein on the Boudreau matriarch.

"I hope you haven't been waiting long." The smile Ms. Patti bestowed on Jill made all the waiting seem inconsequential. Jill couldn't hide her smile as she climbed out of the car, full of life and energy, even at the tail end of the day. Personally, her backside was dragging after a long day dealing with the idiots she worked with, clients who didn't have a lick of common sense, coupled with detours and construction on her homebound commute. All she wanted was a hot bath, a good book, and maybe a pint of her favorite chocolate-covered cherries ice cream. Yum.

"Not too long, Ms. Patti. What's going on?" Jill gestured toward the dark window behind her.

Instead of answering, Ms. Patti lifted the lock box attached to the door and punched in a code with an efficiency that bespoke familiarity. Standing aside, she gestured for Jill to precede her. Once through the door, Ms. Patti flipped a light switch, bathing the front part of the space in light. Overhead, the fluorescent bulbs buzzed and popped.

The space had seen better days. An air of tiredness clung to the white walls, which had yellowed with age and neglect. The terra cotta tiles on the floor were in pretty good shape, though a few had superficial cracks. Acoustic tiles covered the ceiling, although a few of the panels sat askew, giving it a forlorn, abandoned vibe.

Kinda like how I've been feeling recently.

But beneath the neglect, beneath the lack of cleanliness, there was...*something*...about the space that called to her. Something Jill couldn't put her finger on, but it seemed to whisper in the back of her mind she needed to be here. This raggedy, unkempt, hadn't been occupied retail space, which had sat empty for longer than she could remember, was meant to be hers.

"So, dear, what do you think?"

"Are you looking to insure the place? I can put you in touch with somebody at my office—"

"No. What do you think of the space for your bakery?"

A jolt of shock whipped through her, and she spun to

face Ms. Patti. "I don't understand. What do you mean, my bakery?"

"I know you've wanted to open your own place for a long time. You've got the skills, the talent, and the drive to make a success of it. I can feel it in my gut, and my gut is never wrong."

"Ms. Patti, the location is perfect, but I can't. I don't have enough money to afford the rent on a place like this, or to buy or even rent all the equipment and supplies I'd need to make a go of it."

Closing her eyes for a second, she wanted to scream. She'd been so close. Scrimping and saving every penny for the last three years, foregoing every luxury and sometimes even the necessities, and living on a shoestring budget, to make her dreams a reality, and one stupid decision wiped away everything. If she had it to do over again—she'd probably still give her brother the money. Having a deadbeat, always-falling-for-the-latest-scam brother alive and kicking was better than visiting him in the cemetery. Which is what would have happened if she hadn't bailed him out of his current jam, and wiped out her savings account in one fell swoop.

"I know, honey. I've got a business proposition I want to discuss with you, but I wanted you to see the place first, get your opinion. I might know my way around real estate, but I don't have your eye for what will work for setting up a viable, working bakery." Ms. Patti strode past her, walking with purpose and determination toward the back of the shop, and Jill followed along in her wake. A thousand questions tumbled around in her brain. What in the world was Ms. Patti up to now?

She flipped on another light switch, and pushed through a swinging door, revealing the back of the space, and Jill's mouth opened in shock. It was...it was perfect. Several long aluminum tables were pushed against one wall. They needed a good cleaning, but they'd make perfect work stations for mixing and kneading. A turntable for decorating cakes could fit on the far table. Two large racks were shoved into one corner, but they'd work for holding trays of pastries and cookies, or even loaves of bread. There weren't any ovens or cooktops, but she could picture them in her mind.

"Think this would work?"

"Ms. Patti, it's—it's perfect. It's almost like this whole space was made for a bakery. The front half could hold display cases, filled with cookies, doughnuts, and pastries. Maybe pies, too. You could set up a couple of small tables in front of the big picture window, where people can sit outside and eat. Maybe have a coffee station. If the weather's nice, maybe have a few tables and chairs out there. Add an overhang, an awning or canopy of some kind, for when it's really hot."

Ms. Patti's smile grew with every word, and Jill realized that the older woman hand suckered her right into her delusion. Because it was nothing but a pipe dream, always out of reach. Quashing down her feelings into a tiny ball, she shoved it deep inside, the way she did every time it seemed like it might happen. She was a realist, and she'd learned the hard way dreams didn't always come true, and not everybody got their happily ever after. Especially not her.

"Ms. Patti, I can't—"

"You know, I've never liked that word. Can't. It's like giving up without trying. If we don't make the effort, then can't wins." Ms. Patti studied her, her gaze intent, and Jill bit back the urge to run. She knew Ms. Patti didn't mean to hurt her, but she was, because dangling her life's dream before her right out of reach, was breaking her heart. Like her brother, Dante, had mere weeks ago.

"Before you say anything, there is a reason I wanted you to see this place. I wanted an honest appraisal of whether this location, this interior, could or should be utilized for a much-needed Shiloh Springs bakery."

Jill drew in a deep breath before answering. "The location is great. It's right in the heart of town, not far from Daisy's Diner, the bookstore, or any number of other great shops on Main Street. The back can be converted fairly easily to accommodate everything you'd need for a fully functional kitchen. The sales floor area has the potential for walk-in customers and even a small counter space where custom orders could be placed. You could have a shelf with pictures of wedding cakes, special occasion cakes, and specially designed orders. It's exactly the kind of place you're talking about."

"Excellent. That's what I wanted to hear." Ms. Patti reached forward and wrapped her arm around Jill's shoulder, and started leading her toward the front. "Tomorrow's Saturday. You don't have to work, do you?"

"Um, no ma'am."

"Perfect. Be at the Big House at noon. We'll have lunch and then talk about a proposition I'd like to share with you."

"Proposition?"

She stepped through the doorway and out into the humid night air. Ms. Patti turned and placed the lockbox back on the front door handle and pivoted to face Jill.

"We'll talk tomorrow. Now, I need to get home. Douglas is waiting for me." Ms. Patti's grin was infectious and Jill found herself responding. "He's cooking dinner, so I'm sure it's going to be an adventure."

"Sounds like fun."

Ms. Patti hefted her purse further up on her shoulder, and Jill wondered, not for the first time, how someone so tiny managed to carry around a bag that was nearly as big as she was, but somehow she always made it work.

"Do you need a ride home, hon?"

"No, thanks, Ms. Patti. It's only a couple of blocks, and I think I'll walk."

"You sure, I don't mind giving you a ride. After all, you came to meet me."

Jill shook her head. "The walk will do me good. Help me

clear my head from crunching numbers and writing policies all day. You head on home and have dinner with Douglas. Tell him I said hello."

"Good night, Jill. See you tomorrow."

She watched Ms. Patti drive away, and shook her head, before heading toward home. She couldn't help wondering what the other woman had in store for her tomorrow. Because once you found yourself on Ms. Patti's radar, she'd bowl you over like a tumbleweed in a thunderstorm, and you'd never know what hit you.

"Guess I'll find out tomorrow how my life's about to change."

Bad weather delayed Lucas' homecoming by a couple of hours. After leaving Fort Worth, he'd had to pull over a couple of times because the torrential rain made visibility impossible. His wipers hadn't been up to the job, even on the highest setting, but it wasn't like he was on a deadline, so he could take his time.

The decision to head home had been spur of the moment, even though he'd been back a few weeks ago to celebrate with Ridge and his pretty new lady, Maggie, and catch up with the rest of the family. Rafe and Tessa's wedding was still a few months away, but he'd never seen his brother happier. Antonio and Brody also seemed to glow, especially when around their newfound ladies.

Exhausted from investigating his latest story, the one he'd turned in the day before, he'd crashed for twenty-four hours straight. The investigative work for the story had turned ugly early on, and the more he dug, the harder it became to stay objective. He had to hand it to his brothers, because they had to deal with the scum of the earth on a regular basis. As an investigative reporter, he only came in contact with slimy characters when he was researching, making sure he had his facts straight, and that his sources were impeccable. This story, though, it got to him, crawled beneath his skin until he saw it, lived it, and breathed it even in his sleep.

Shaking his head, he realized he'd been so engrossed in his thoughts he'd missed his exit off the interstate. He backtracked through the south part of Shiloh Springs instead of heading straight to the Big House.

Everything looked the same as it had when he'd been a boy. Not a whole lot changed in the small town, and that's the way he liked it. He liked knowing even if he wasn't living here full time, when he came back home, everything stayed exactly as it had been when he'd left. Oh, sure, a few things changed. Shops closed. New ones opened. Folks moved away and new ones took their places. But the essence, the heart, of Shiloh Springs remained.

Silhouetted in his headlights, he spotted a woman walking, and immediately his chest tightened, his breath caught in his throat, because he recognized her.

Jillian Monroe.

Jill, the woman he'd known most of his life. They'd grown up together. Gone to school together. Shared a first kiss together. She'd been his first crush, all the way back in the sixth grade. He'd hated it when she'd gone away to college back East. Hated every minute she was gone, though he never admitted it to anybody. But when she came back, she was different. He couldn't put his finger on it. The laughing, friendly, loving Jill disappeared underneath a layer of silence, withdrawn and missing the spark that had always seemed to burn deep inside.

And she wouldn't talk to him. Oh, she never went out of her way to deliberately avoid him, but the spontaneity, the *joie de vivre*, her zest for life, disappeared. Slowing, he rolled down the passenger-side window, and called out to her. "Jill. Want a ride?"

In the dim light from the street lamps, she looked beautiful in an ethereal way, her skin glowing. Golden blonde hair framed the beautiful face he still saw in his dreams. He felt a tug inside his chest, the instinctive pull toward her that never went away.

"Lucas! You're home. I mean, welcome back."

"Thanks. Folks don't know I'm here, thought I'd surprise them."

She smiled. "You just missed Ms. Patti. She's headed home for date night with your dad."

"Huh. I forgot it was Friday night. Unless there's an emergency, they have a standing Friday night date. Been doing it for years."

"She mentioned Douglas is cooking tonight."

Lucas chuckled. "Well, unless he's fired up the grill, I bet he pulled a casserole or something out of the freezer and heated it up. I love my dad, but he can't cook."

"I kinda got that impression from your mother."

Tired of talking through the open window, Lucas put the car in park, and left it running while he climbed out. He stood in front of Jill, giving her a quick grin, and shoved his hands into his pockets. On the soft breeze, he caught the subtle scent of vanilla, and couldn't help wondering if she'd been baking up one of her wickedly delicious desserts.

"What has you walking down Main Street all alone on a Friday night?"

"I had a meeting with your mother, and I'm headed home."

"Momma didn't offer you a ride?"

She speared him with a glare, and he raised his hands. "Of course she offered. I decided to walk, clear my head. It's been a long day. Heck, it's been a long week."

"Yeah, it has."

"I should probably get home."

Before he stopped to think, he blurted out, "Why don't we go and get a drink? Catch up on what you've been up to. Like we used to—come on, Jill, say yes."

"Lucas, we really shouldn't…"

"Why not? Last I heard, there's nobody waiting for you at home. Me either. What's wrong with two old friends grabbing a drink and reminiscing?"

A long rumble of thunder rolled, loud enough to rattle the window in the shop beside them. A brilliant flash of lightning followed, illuminating the sky, filled with dark, ominous clouds.

"I need to get home before the storm lets loose."

Lucas sighed. He'd hoped she'd say yes. It had been far too long since they'd spent any kind of time together. The thought saddened him. They'd been closer than thieves when they'd been growing up, it hurt that they'd drifted apart.

"Yeah, you're probably right. But I insist you let me drive you home, otherwise, you'll be soaked before you get there."

Jill gave a shaky laugh, and ran a hand through her hair. "Okay, I give up. Take me home."

Lucas opened the passenger door and helped her in, then jogged around the front of the car and climbed behind the wheel. Her apartment wasn't far, only a few blocks. Before he'd made the turn off Main Street, fat raindrops were splattering against the windshield, increasing in ferocity with every second that passed. Soft country music played on the radio, almost a white noise in the background. He couldn't have said who was singing or even what song, his attention riveted on Jill sitting beside him.

She'd changed since the last time he'd seen her. His momma and dad held a get together at the Big House. Nothing special about this one he could remember. They did it all the time, because with a family the size of theirs, there was always something to celebrate.

He remembered Jill sitting together with his momma on the back patio. Dad had been manning the grill, ruling his domain with the determination of a general, and nobody got between his father and grilling meat. Jill wore a pretty yellow sundress with little straps on the shoulders. It had pretty blue and white flowers around the bottom, and he'd thought she looked beautiful. Like a breath of sunshine in an otherwise dreary afternoon. Of course, he'd been neck deep in an investigation for the story he'd just turned in. The one about human trafficking. Thinking about it turned his stomach, and he knew he'd barely scratched the surface.

By the time he'd pulled up in front of her apartment building, the rain was coming down in torrents. He could barely see the front end of the car through the windshield. No way was he letting her get out, she'd be soaked to the skin.

"Let's sit here for a minute or two, until it eases up."

Jill peered through the windshield, a tiny line appearing between her eyes as she squinted. It was cute. He chuckled, and she turned to face him.

"What's so funny?"

"You have the cutest little thing right here when you

squint." He ran his fingertip lightly across the bridge of her nose, watching the tiny line disappear.

"Cute? Lines on a woman's face aren't considered cute."

"Hey, I'm telling it like I see it. I guess cute is in the eye of the beholder."

"You're nuts, you know that, right? Only you would tell a woman she's got wrinkles and think it's cute."

He pulled back and placed his hand over his heart, feigning outrage. "I never said you had wrinkles. I said you had a tiny cute little squiggle mark. It's adorable."

Jill gave a playful slap at him, and he caught her hand and pulled it against his chest. Her gentle smile reached her eyes, and reminded him of the Jill he remembered, the laughing, bright light in his life. With a jolt that struck deep, he realized that he missed her. More than he'd realized, until this moment. When he'd made the choice to leave Shiloh Springs, he'd never once thought about what he left behind, instead focusing on his goals of writing, being the best journalist. Digging for stories, searching for the truth, and looking for his sister.

Instead, he'd left behind something precious, that intangible missing piece, and like a bolt of lightning, he realized what he'd been unwittingly searching for sat right in front of him. The silence lengthened as he studied her, noting the exact moment she withdrew from him. Not in a physical way. Sure, she pulled her hand away. But it was more, an almost invisible wall, erected brick by brick, and the twinkle left her eyes. An almost painful distance yawned between them, one that hadn't been there moments before, and he wondered what happened to make the once vivacious and heartwarming woman he remembered become this almost aloof stranger.

"The rain is letting up. I'd better get inside. Thanks for the ride, Lucas." She reached for the door handle, and he started to open his, ready to escort her to the door. "No, don't. No sense in both of us getting soaked. Let your momma know I'll see her tomorrow."

Before he could stop her, she climbed out of the car, and raced toward the apartment building's front door, and within seconds was out of sight. Lucas sat there with the engine running, watching the entrance and wondering why she'd darted like a scared rabbit.

Jill had made her first mistake. He was at heart an investigator, loved digging into a problem and coming up with the answers. There wasn't a challenge out there that he'd run away from, and whether she realized it or not, she'd thrown down the gauntlet.

Let the games begin.

CHAPTER TWO

J ill parked in front of the Boudreau house, and turned off the engine. Glancing in the mirror, she frowned at the dark shadows visible beneath her eyes. Even under a layer of concealer, she saw them. Great. That meant eagle-eyed Ms. Patti would surely notice them. She prayed the older woman didn't ask why. What was she going to tell her, that she'd tossed and turned all night, thinking about her son?

Climbing from the car, she straightened and strode purposefully toward the front door. It swung open before she reached the porch, and Douglas Boudreau stood silhouetted in the opening. A quick grin passed his lips as he walked out onto the huge front porch, and enveloped her in a hug. Not one of those wimpy, half-hearted ones most people used in greeting, either. Nope, this was a big ole bear hug, the kind her daddy used to give her. She blinked back the tears, wrapping her arms around him and squeezing him tight.

"My wife says you're to go straight through to the kitchen. I only stopped by for a second, gotta get back to the job. You two have fun." Releasing her, he continued off the porch and down the front steps, and climb behind the wheel of his oversized pickup. Douglas was bigger than life, and one of the sweetest men she'd ever met. His size belied an inner strength and character she only wished others could emulate.

She watched until he'd driven out of sight, then turned and walked into the Big House. She smiled, thinking about the name. Lucas had once told her his brothers came up with the name. Being foster kids, they'd looked on the Boudreau house as one step shy of prison, feeling like they were stuck there. The choice between staying with the Boudreaus or ending up in a group home really wasn't much of a choice. As they grew older, the name stuck. Most people thought the name referred to the size of the house, but the family knew the truth. Their own private joke.

Going through the opening to her left, she stepped into the kitchen. Ms. Patti stood at the counter, pouring glasses of iced tea. She smiled over her shoulder when she spotted Jill.

"Come in, make yourself at home, hon. Here, take these," she handed the two glasses to Jill, and then motioned to the table. Jill set the glasses down, and hung her purse over the back of a chair.

"What can I help with?"

"Nothing, thanks. Everything's ready." Ms. Patti pulled two brightly colored bowls from the fridge, loaded with fruit salad. The vivid colors of the cut fruit gleamed like jewels, and Jill's stomach rumbled. She had skipped breakfast, too anxious about this lunch meeting to care about eating. Suddenly she felt ravenous.

Placing the bowls on the table, Ms. Patti slid onto a chair and Jill seated herself across from her. Why'd she feel so nervous? Heck, she'd known Ms. Patti all her life, although they hadn't really been close until recently. Her family and the Boudreaus didn't move in the same social circles. It was only in the last couple of years she'd gotten to know the older woman better. Jill got invited to social functions at the Big House, probably because of her association with Lucas and a couple of his brothers when they were in school.

"Dig in. I hope this is okay?"

"It's perfect." Jill took a bite, the bright citrus taste bursting across her tongue. Umm, delicious.

"Have you had a chance to think about the property we looked at yesterday?"

Trust Ms. Patti, right to the point. She liked that about her. "I actually thought about it a lot. It'll take a lot of elbow grease to whip it into shape, but with the right tenant and the proper equipment, it'll make a great shop."

"Bakery." Ms. Patti's stare bored into her, hitting straight at her dream, as if she knew exactly where Jill's heart's desire hid. Her fantasy of owning her own business, being answerable to nobody for the day-to-day decisions, seemed like nirvana. Working in a never-gonna-get-anywhere nine-to-five job stole a little piece of her soul every day, and she couldn't see a way out. Not when Dante kept toppling her dreams like falling dominos.

"Sure, it's a great spot for a bakery. Great for foot traffic, and there's decent street parking. I didn't check behind the building, but usually you'll find a few parking spaces."

"There are," Ms. Patti answered. "So, you think you'd make a profit with the right management and people and equipment?"

Why does she keep saying you, like she's talking about me *running the business? Ain't gonna happen. Not now, maybe not ever.*

Jill laid her fork gently on the table. "Ms. Patti, what's going on? I assume you didn't call me out of the blue to ask me about space for a bakery."

"Jill, I rarely do anything without thought and planning. I think the last time I did anything spontaneous, I eloped with Douglas."

"Really? I'd call that spontaneous."

Ms. Patti's grin said it all. "Best thing I ever did. Not a single regret."

"That's awesome. But, again, why'd you want me to look at the property? I can't afford anything like it, at least not now."

"But I can." Picking up her glass, Ms. Patti sipped her tea, while Jill sat stunned.

What in the world? "Sorry if I'm being dense, but I don't understand."

"I have a proposition for you. Something I've been

thinking about for a while."

"A...proposition?"

"Let's call it a business proposal. I understand from Tessa you've always wanted to open your own bakery. True?"

I am so going to kill my bestie.

"Yes."

Ms. Patti smiled sweetly at Jill's answer. "I have firsthand experience with your products. All the cakes and cookies and other goodies you've made over the last few months, they're some of the best I've ever eaten. I'm also well aware of the time and effort it takes to make food look and taste good."

"Uh-huh." Jill tried to swallow past the gigantic boulder lodged in the back of her throat. She suddenly had an inkling of where Ms. Patti was headed, and it both terrified and intrigued her. Would working for Ms. Patti be so bad?

"Let me cut straight to the bottom line, then we can talk about the details, okay?"

"Sure."

"I want to go into a partnership with you and open a bakery. Co-owners. I'll handle the business and financial end of things. You'll handle running the bakery, hiring employees, and dealing with the day-to-day running the place. Interested?"

Jill knew her mouth hung open, but it felt like a semi had slammed into her at full speed, and she'd been tossed butt-over-bustle and landed on her head. Then again, that probably wouldn't have been as shocking as Ms. Patti's proposal.

"I...Ms. Patti...I'm not sure what I'm supposed to say. I don't have the money to go into a partnership with you. Opening something like a bakery takes a lot of investment cash, and at the moment I'm tapped out."

"I thought Tessa mentioned you'd been saving up to start a small shop."

Jill silently cursed her brother, because this was all his fault. If he'd simply managed to get his act together, she wouldn't have to look like a fool in front of Ms. Patti.

"I had saved a bit of a nest egg. Unfortunately, something came up and I had to use the money I'd set aside. Now I'm starting over." Because she knew darn good and well, despite all his promises, Dante would never pay her back. He'd need a job for that, and his prospects seemed slim.

"I understand. Still, I'm sure we can work something out."

"Ms. Patti, I don't think you understand. I appreciate your offer, honestly, I do, and it's the nicest, sweetest thing anybody's done for me in a long time, but I'm going to be straight with you. I'm flat broke. There's no way I could get a line of credit, much less a loan, to cover the expenses of renting the space, opening a business, getting the necessary equipment. Maybe in a couple of years, I'll be in a better situation, but—"

"Stop." Ms. Patti's voice held a firmness Jill recognized; she'd heard the other woman use *that* tone to Lucas countless

23

times when they were growing up. She stopped talking.

"You don't have the money now. Fine, we'll work around it. One thing you do have is a business degree and a brain. I wager you've already worked out what it would take to open the kind of place you've dreamed about, done a cost analysis, expensed out every item to the last detail. Am I right?"

Keeping her lips pressed firmly together, Jill nodded.

"I want to see everything you've got. I've given this a lot of thought, and Shiloh Springs needs an upscale bakery. I'm tired of our folks having to rely on supermarket birthday cakes, or having to order from Austin to get anything custom. We might be a small town, but there's a need, a niche market, going unfulfilled. We, you and I, are going to fill the void."

"Ms. Patti, did you get the part where I have no money?"

"We can draw up a business agreement, wherein I will provide the initial funds to get the business up and off the ground. Since I have no doubts this endeavor will be a rousing success, we will stipulate in the contract repayment of the loan will come from the profits after all expenses are covered, including a modest salary for you and whatever staff you hire. Once the loan is paid back, all future profits will be divided equally, fifty-fifty."

Jill's breath caught in her throat, her mind whirling with everything Ms. Patti was suggesting. Could she do this? Did she even dare consider it?

"I don't know what to say. It seems like everything in your agreement is geared in my favor. If you're putting up all the capital investment, shouldn't your share of everything be much higher?"

Ms. Patti reached across the table and patted Jill's hand. "I'm not doing this just for you, hon. It's for Shiloh Springs. Everybody benefits when—not if—the bakery takes off. I haven't got a single doubt we'll be making a profit." She leaned back in her chair and gave Jill a wink.

"Now, how about you show me the photos of all your cakes? Tessa tells me they're spectacular."

Without another word, Jill pulled up the photos and handed her phone to Ms. Patti. As usual, whatever Ms. Patti wanted, she got. And right now, she wanted to go into business with Jill.

Could life get any sweeter?

Lucas stretched and sat up higher in the saddle. He'd gotten up before dawn and headed to Dane's, needing to do some physical labor. Maybe if he broke a good sweat, he'd get his mind off Jill and her midnight blue eyes, or the hint of sadness he'd glimpsed in them the night before. Dane immediately put him to work, riding the pasture looking for strays. After the long, wet night, the morning sun beating down against his shoulders felt good, and he rubbed his hand along the back of his neck, shaded by his hat. The day might turn into a scorcher later, but for now it was perfect—because he was home.

"You gonna tell me why you showed up without a word? It's not like you to turn up like a bad penny. And don't tell me you planned on coming home yesterday, because Momma or Dad would have mentioned it."

"Turned the finished story in to the editor. Decided I needed a break, both physical and mental." He paused for a moment, considering his words. "Bro, this one turned ugly fast. I've seen some horrific things digging for info, but this story got to me."

Dane pushed his hat further down on his forehead, and kept a light touch on the reins as they walked the horses back toward the barn. Lucas wasn't sure he was ready to discuss the gory details he'd unearthed while researching human trafficking. Not yet. It was still too fresh, too close. "When you're ready to talk, I'm here."

"I know. And I appreciate it. I needed to step away from it for a couple of days. The things I saw...don't know I'll ever get some of those images out of my head."

"I get it. You've never been one to simply skim the details and not dig deep to find the truth. Makes you good at your job. But I'm guessing it's hard to separate the reporter from the man. Most people never see, never imagine, some of the stuff you've encountered. Give yourself a break."

The swaying movement of the horse beneath him eased

him like a lullaby, the rocking motion soothing and peaceful. He'd needed this more than he wanted to admit. Being home on the ranch helped ground him, push all the ugliness aside, at least for a while.

"Anything new on the search for Renee?"

Lucas grimaced. "I followed up on the lead Dad told me about last time I was here. Unfortunately, by the time I got to Cincinnati her trail had gone cold, but I did find one thread I'm following. It's another longshot. I'm trying not getting my hopes up."

He didn't want to admit it, but when his dad told him they'd found Renee, he hadn't wanted to believe it. Not at first. Too many years had passed. Too many dead ends. Too many false promises. He refused to let this latest clue get his hopes up. Unfortunately, no matter how hard he tried quashing it, a tiny grain of hope still persisted and blossomed no matter how hard he tried to ignore it.

"You'll find her. Someday, you're going to look and she'll be there. Don't give up."

Lucas drew in a deep breath, listening to his brother's words. Aching for them to be the truth. He'd loved his baby sister, adored her from the moment his parents brought her home from the hospital. Spotting the tiny tuft of hair on top of her head, the color the same as he saw in the mirror every morning when he brushed his teeth, she'd been his joy. He wondered what she'd look like now. A grown woman, she'd be in her twenties, maybe with kids of her own. But he'd never forgotten her, not for a single day. The welfare system had failed them when they'd placed them into different locations. After that, there'd been nothing but an avalanche of disinformation, missing records, destroyed files, and cover-ups.

"I'll never give up on finding Renee. I made her a promise when they took her, and I'll keep it, if it's the last thing I do."

"Anything you need, I'm here. We're all here for you. We're family, and Renee is family too. Blood doesn't matter to a Boudreau."

"Except I'm not a Boudreau. I'm an O'Malley."

Dane reached over and snatched the reins out of Lucas' hand, slowing the horses to a complete stop. "I don't care what your legal last name is, you moron. You're a Boudreau, same as the rest of us. Everybody understands why you've kept the O'Malley name. We respect it, and the search for your sister. Douglas and Ms. Patti have always understood why you didn't change it when you came of age, never questioned it. Regardless, you are as much a Boudreau as I am, or any one of the rest of us. Being a Boudreau is about more than carrying the same blood. It's about choosing your family. Sticking beside each other, no matter what life throws at us, and being there. We're brothers by choice. Sometimes I think it makes us a heck of a lot closer than blood relations."

"Sometimes I feel guilty about not changing my name.

All the rest of you did it without hesitation."

"We didn't have anybody who cared enough to want us, not the way Dad and Momma did—do—you know what I mean. Other than Ridge and Shiloh, you're the only one who had somebody who cared about what happened to you. Renee didn't have a choice; she was snatched out of your arms, and you were too young to do anything about it." Dane tossed the reins back to Lucas. "If I'd had family who'd cared, even a little bit, I'd have done the same. But nobody cared whether I was a Lockhart or a Boudreau—except Douglas and Patricia Boudreau—and me."

Lucas blinked rapidly, blaming the bright sunshine for the excessive moisture in his eyes. Dane was right. Then again, he usually was. "It drives me crazy sometimes—not knowing what happened to her. I know she's out there someplace. I feel it here." Lucas pointed to his chest. "I'd know if she was gone. But I find it strange nobody's been able to find her. I've looked for years. Shiloh's looked. Antonio's used his resources with the FBI. Ridge had a couple of his computer hackers, excuse me, computer experts try to find any trace of her. But no matter what direction we take, we fail."

"Dad's got his army buddies looking, too."

"Yeah. Okay, time to stop feeling sorry for myself. You ready for lunch? Bet Momma has something waiting for us."

"Sounds good. Let's take care of the horses and wash up."

"Race ya!" Lucas chuckled as he left Dane in his dust, already feeling happier.

Coming back to Shiloh Springs was good for his soul. He'd talk to his dad later, tell him what he'd found in Cincinnati. But any way he looked at it, it was good to be home.

CHAPTER THREE

J ill stared at the papers scattered across her table, chewing on the end of her pen. She'd been working on spreadsheets for the last two hours, and at this point couldn't make heads or tails of anything. All she could concentrate on was her talk with Ms. Patti earlier.

Can I really do this? I've always dreamt of owning my own bakery, but I never imagined having a partner. What if I screw up? There's no guarantee it'll make a profit, and I'd never forgive myself if I lost all Ms. Patti's money.

She picked at the sticky note she'd put on her cost analysis sheet, staring at the dollar figure she'd written. It was so much money. When she'd fantasized about having her own place, she'd anticipated starting out small. Taking orders for a couple of custom cakes. Maybe catering a few parties, and building her way through word of mouth around town. Thinking about having an actual storefront? It seemed an impossible pipe dream.

"Maybe I can talk with Daisy, see about providing cakes or pies for the diner. Or maybe some breakfast muffins and Danish for the morning crowd." Tapping her pen against the table, she stared at the large mirror on the wall, not really seeing herself reflected; instead, her mind whirled with the possibilities. Ms. Patti had opened the floodgates and now the ideas wouldn't stop flowing.

She jerked at the knock on her door, and shook her head. "I'm getting jumpy in my old age." Tossing down the pen, she walked over and opened it.

"Hey, Sis." Her brother, Dante, leaned in and brushed a kiss against her cheek before pushing past her into the apartment. Jill rolled her eyes, because it didn't surprise her. Dante always did what he wanted, when he wanted, and nobody and nothing stopped him. Probably why he was always in trouble. She couldn't begin to list the number of times she'd pulled him out of one scrape or another. Sometimes those problems were itty-bitty and she handled getting him out of a jam without too much fuss. Other times, Dante was neck deep in alligators and sinking fast, and she'd end up bailing him out. Which explained her current predicament.

"Please tell me you're not in trouble again."

Dante feigned a hurt expression, which only lasted a few seconds before he chuckled. He clasped his hands against his heart, and gave a long, exaggerated sigh. "Me? In trouble? Can't a guy drop by to see his big sister without her thinking he's in a jam?"

"Not usually."

"Sheesh. I promise I've kept my nose clean, Sis. I told

you I would."

Jill blew the bangs out of her eyes, before walking back to the table, and began gathering up her papers into a messy stack. Better to not let Dante seem them or he'd feel guilty about taking all her savings. Okay, taking wasn't the right word. He'd given a solemn promise he'd pay her back, though she wasn't holding her breath. After all, she couldn't have her brother getting his kneecaps broken, even if he deserved it.

Dante handed her the single rose in his hand.

"Thanks, that's really sweet of you."

He shrugged. "Wish I could take the credit. Found it on the mat in front of your door."

"It's not from you?" She glanced at the long-stemmed red rose, turning it in her hand. "Did you see a card?"

"Nope, but then I really wasn't paying much attention. I picked it up when I knocked."

Jill headed for the front door and opened it, looking down at the carpet. She didn't spot a note. How strange. Who'd send her a rose without a card? Closing the door, she walked over to the table and laid the flower next to her computer.

"What're you up to?" Dante grabbed one of the pages from the stack, and she tried to snatch it back, but he stutter-stepped back a couple paces and held it out of reach. "Work? It's the weekend, Jilly. You know, time to unwind, have a little fun?"

"Gimme. Unlike some people I know, I need my job. And no, since you asked, it's not from the office. It's mine."

"Cool." He glanced at the page, his jovial expression turning serious. "This is for the bakery. Before I took your life savings and screwed up everything."

Jill closed her eyes and counted to five. Some days five was enough, although when he got her riled, it took a full ten count to rein in her temper.

"Look, Dante, we've been over this. No sense beating a dead horse."

He solemnly handed the page back, then turned away. "I can't believe I'm such an idiot. I never thought I'd lose so much. My luck had to change, I felt it. I swear I'm never gonna play again."

"Dante, I love you, but don't make promises you can't keep. Unless you're willing to get help, I can't—I won't—bail you out again." She gave a bitter laugh. "I couldn't even if I wanted. There's nothing left."

"Jilly, please, I promise…"

"Stop. Just stop." She placed the paper back onto the table, and cupped her brother's face between her hands. "I can't do it anymore. I know you mean what you say now, but I can't take another empty promise. You're old enough to stand on your own two feet and take responsibility for your actions. If you're going to continue throwing your money away and racking up more debt, don't come to me with your hand out. Me being your piggy bank stops now.

We've all got a breaking point, and I've reached mine. Dante, you are my baby brother and I adore you to pieces, but it's over."

He jerked back, and she let her hands slowly fall to her sides. Did any of what she'd said even penetrate his thick skull? If she could, she'd force him to go to Gamblers Anonymous, get him into counseling, anything to break his addiction. But every time she brought it up, he stormed away angry and bitter, blaming her for being a tightwad who didn't know how to have fun. What did he expect? She'd had to play the grownup from the time she was in her teens, because as much as she loved her parents, they weren't the most responsible people either. Her dad changed jobs like people changed socks, and her mother, bless her heart, was a throwback to more gentile times, when Southern women stayed home, and the man ran the household and took care of the family. Too bad her dad hadn't been the responsible type.

"It's only money, Sis. It's not like I wagered your firstborn child. I said I'll pay you back." He fisted his hands at his sides, and shot her a look filled with confusion and a touch of guilt. "It's part of the reason I came over. Wanted to let you know I got a job working at Frank's Garage. He's taking me on part-time, and he's gonna teach me about engine repair."

"Really? Dante, that's wonderful!" Jill wrapped her arms around him, pulling him close, and wondered when he'd gotten so much bigger than her. She still thought of him when he'd barely reached her shoulders, with skinned knees and hair always in need of a trim. "I'm happy for you. It's a good start."

He grinned down at her. "Yeah. I start Monday. If things go well, and I learn quick, maybe it'll lead to something full time."

Giving him a final squeeze, she stepped back and studied him. He really had changed in the last several months. Taller, broader across the shoulders, he had the same blue eyes she did, and blond hair, though his was a shade or two darker. Maybe if she stuck to her guns this time, with a little bit of luck, he'd turn his life around for good.

"Anyway, I'm outta here. Unlike some people who are sitting at home working on boring paperwork instead of going out and having a good time on a Saturday night, I've got a date." The grin he shot had her rolling her eyes, and she set her hands in the middle of his back and gave him a little shove.

"Get out. Have a good time."

Reaching for the doorknob, a knock sounded on the wood, and she jumped, her hand against her chest. Pulling the door open, she bit her lip to hide her shock at seeing Lucas on her doorstep.

"Hi, Jill."

"Lucas, what are you doing here?"

His slow smile sent little tingles along her spine and

straight to her toes. That little dimple in his cheek, the way the left side of his mouth quirked a little higher than the right did something to her. Got her all hot and bothered.

"I thought maybe we could get that drink we never got around to last night." The low husky timber of his voice, his slow Texas drawl, made her knees go weak, and she clung to the door before she collapsed into a puddle at his feet.

"Hey, Lucas! Good to see you. I hadn't heard you were back." Dante reached out and shook Lucas' hand, before cutting his gaze toward her. She could practically read his thoughts, from the quirked brow to the question in his eyes. Questions she had no intention of answering, because it wasn't any of his business.

"Got in last night. I'm taking a short break before starting my next story. Ran into your sister last night, right before the storm hit."

"And you came to take her out? Cool. She needs to get outta this apartment." Dante grabbed her purse off the hall table and thrust it into her hands. "She's been working way too hard, and needs a break. Go on, Sis, have a good time."

"Dante, I have to finish—"

"There's nothing that can't wait until later. You work too hard as it is. Go, have fun. Relax." Dante made a shooing motion with his hands. Knowing there was no way to gracefully decline Lucas' invitation, she stepped past him into the hall. She couldn't help noticing the subtle scent of his aftershave, and those jittery butterflies in her stomach started doing the samba.

Oh, boy, this is wrong on so many levels. I'm gonna need to be on my toes, because he smells really good, and he's got a killer smile. One drink. I can handle one drink. Make a little small talk. Who am I kidding? I am in so much trouble.

"Jill?" Lucas waved a hand in front of her face. "Everything okay?"

"What? Oh, yeah. Sorry. I was making a mental check list in my head of things I still need to get done." Of course, she wasn't about to tell him what was on the list. Like his gorgeous eyes or his dimple, or the way his shirt clung to his muscles, or…

"See what I mean? She really needs to take a break. All work and no play, Jilly, is gonna make you an old maid."

"I'll old maid you, you little punk!" She took a playful punch at Dante's arm, wincing after her fist made contact. "Ow!"

"Ha! That'll teach you to pick on somebody your own size. Lucas, my man, good to see you, but I've got a date. I'll call you, Sis!"

Jill watched her brother saunter down the hall toward the stairs and disappear out of sight. She could feel Lucas' gaze watching her, and she glanced down at what she was wearing. Thankfully she hadn't changed out of the clothes she'd worn earlier when she met Ms. Patti. The dark blue jeans and navy and white blouse were casual, but still nice enough for going out.

"You don't have to do this if you don't want to, Jill. Dante kind of forced your hand and didn't give you a choice. But I will—give you a choice. I'd like it if you'd join me for a drink. I thought we'd head to Juanita's. Maybe sit out on the patio, listen to the band."

"Juanita's sounds awesome. I could use a margarita."

There it was again, his slow sexy smile.

Oh, yeah, she was a goner.

Lucas held out Jill's seat, watched her slide gracefully into place, before walking around and sitting across from her. The night was warm, but not unbearably so, and they'd opted to sit on the patio at Juanita's. He'd chosen it because it was the best place in Shiloh Springs to get Tex-Mex, and they usually had some good music, played by live local bands. They alternated between country and soft rock, and the patrons loved it.

After giving the waiter their drink orders, he leaned back in his chair and studied her. It had been impossible not to pick up on the tension between Jill and Dante when he'd arrived, although they'd both done their best to cover. He read people; it was part of his job. Most people tended to lie given half a chance. But little nuances, subtle signs, were easy to find if you knew what to look for. He did.

"Momma said you were at the house today. I'm sorry I

missed you."

"I met your mother for lunch. There was some business she wanted to discuss." Jill shook her head, a bemused expression crossing her face. "Your mother is certainly full of surprises."

"That's a fact. I learned a long time ago to simply roll with the punches, because when Momma wants something, there's no stopping her. Is it a secret, or can you talk about it?"

Jill picked up the napkin and carefully spread it across her lap before answering. "She wants to go into business with me, a partnership. To open a bakery."

"Really? That's great! You've always wanted your own shop. I remember when we were in school, it's all you talked about." He grinned and patted his stomach. "I loved being your test monkey when you experimented with all those recipes. You did all the work and I got all the rewards."

Jill laughed and Lucas relaxed a bit more. He loved hearing her laughter. Loved seeing her face glow with warmth and happiness. The strain from the prior night was gone.

"You gotta admit, some of those were disasters. Remember the black walnut brownies?"

"Hey, it wasn't my fault it turned out you were allergic to their pollen."

Jill chuckled. "It never dawned on me, either. I can eat walnuts without a single problem, but I will never again crack open a walnut in the shell. I couldn't see for two days because my eyes swelled shut."

"Well, it tasted good. I really miss those almond short-bread cookies you made with the candied cherries. I've never had anybody else make those since."

"Those were a total fluke. I'd baked some homemade fruitcake for the holidays and had some of the candied cherries left over. I decided to toss them in the cookies at the last second."

"They are still my favorite cookie, even after all these years."

"Thanks. They're not hard to make."

He almost choked on his beer at her words. "Easy for you to say. You actually have a gift in the kitchen. Some of us can't boil water."

Jill chuckled again at the memory his words evoked. "I remember your momma wanted to take a strip out of your hide when you forgot you'd turned on the stove and put the pot on the stove without putting water in it. She loved those kitchen curtains before they were flambéed."

"In my defense, I was thirteen years old and easily distracted."

"Yeah, yeah. Seriously, though, I'm not sure what to think about Ms. Patti's offer. It's the opportunity of a lifetime, but I don't feel right accepting."

"Why not? Momma's a shrewd businesswoman, and wouldn't offer if she didn't believe you'd make a profit."

Jill shifted in her chair and took a sip of her margarita,

eyes half-closed, a look of bliss crossing her face. A slight pink tinge colored her cheeks, and in the ambient golden light from the patio, she practically glowed. He drew in a deep breath and fought down the urge to walk around the table and pull her into his arms. Which was crazy. She was his friend. His confidant. His high-school crush. Why was he suddenly having all these feelings roaring to the surface about wanting to hold her? To kiss her?

"I was going over the numbers when Dante showed up. Profits and loss, cost analysis, projected equipment and supply expenses. Lucas, your mother's already picked out the location! Granted, it's perfect, but I feel like I'm in over my head and going down for the third time."

"Never gonna happen. I bet you'll be in the black within a year of opening. Guaranteed."

"Ugh, don't say bet." She shook her head and reached for the bowl of chips in the middle of the table, took one and swiped it in the queso. "I don't believe in gambling."

"It still sounds like an excellent opportunity, one you're more than capable of taking on and succeeding. What's really holding you back?"

Toying with the napkin on her lap, she kept her eyes lowered. It made it a little harder for him to read her, but he could tell *something* bothered her, made her hesitate to take the leap toward her dream job. It was more than fear of failure. He knew Jill well enough to know she'd throw herself head first into any business, especially something she'd wanted most of her life. Yet she hesitated.

"I've dreamed about this," she whispered softly. "Every time I think it's within my grasp, something bad happens, and it all falls apart. I'm beginning to think I'm cursed."

Reaching across the table, he grasped her hand, squeezing it. Her gaze flickered toward him for a second, before she lowered her eyes. "Jill, you're not cursed. Scared maybe. Starting a business is a big step, something not everybody has the guts to undertake. But I know you. The you who's strong. The you who's a fighter. You can do this, if you really believe.

"I think that's what scares me. If it was just me, investing my own money, I'd jump at the opportunity in a heartbeat. But it's not, it's also your momma, and by extension the rest of your family."

"Nonsense. We believe in you." He stroked his thumb gently across her knuckles, felt the softness of her skin beneath his touch. "I believe in you."

"I...I don't know what to say."

"Say yes. Tell Momma you'll do it. Then work your magic and you'll have customers flocking to your bakery in droves. I'll be first in line the day you open. I promise."

She drew in a deep sigh, her eyes closed. When she finally opened them, he read her answer shining through.

"I'll do it."

CHAPTER FOUR

S potting his editor's name on the caller ID, Lucas answered on the second ring. A surge of excitement zipped through him. He'd submitted a concise summary of his notes for an in-depth article to him earlier this morning, wanting Chuck's input on the strength of his new idea.

"Hey, Chuck."

"Boudreau. Good job on the human trafficking article. Evocative, yet thought-provoking. Made me sick to my stomach a couple times, but that's what good writing ought to do. You hit your mark, got your facts straight. We need copies of all your documentation. Once this article hits, readers will be outraged, and the feds are gonna come down on us like a ton of bricks. I need facts to back up your findings, nice solid proof to hand over."

His boss chuckled, and Lucas pictured him sitting in his cubbyhole of an office, the credenza behind his desk stacked halfway to the ceiling with folders and papers, a disaster waiting to happen. The man was a tried-and-true Texan, with a deep drawl and a tendency to talk in countrified cliches, but woe unto the reporter who dared add a single one to his writing.

Chuck's mind was a bear trap, waiting for the unsuspecting writer to take a wrong step and then SNAP. He pictured him leaning back in his chair, arms folded behind his head, his ever-present half-glasses perched on the end of his nose. Nothing got past Chuck. If you didn't cross every T and dot every I, he'd tear your head off, his scathing comments flaying the literary skin from your hide.

"Everything's in my safe at the apartment. I'm out of town, but I'll get it to you ASAP. Did you get the notes I e-mailed you this morning?"

"Yeah. I'm not sure there'd be enough interest in the story. It doesn't have the same—*zing*—I'm used to seeing from you. *Illegal gambling?* Who cares? Anybody who wants to toss their money down a rat hole can find a legit casino within driving distance nowadays. Or play the lottery. Those are all legal."

"Chuck, I'm not talking penny-ante stuff. Money being raked in by these illegal gaming rooms is used for sex trafficking, human trafficking and drug running, which ties back into my last story. The penalties imposed when they're caught is laughable. It's considered a misdemeanor at best, and the people running the clubs get a fine or maybe a slap on the wrist. I did a little digging, and some of these places take in upwards of a hundred thousand dollars a day. And that's just the tip of the iceberg."

Chuck let loose a whistle. "I hear ya. But it's still not big news. People honestly won't care because it doesn't impact them. Not directly."

"That's part of the problem. It does impact them, they don't realize how much. Sometimes hundreds of thousands of dollars gets channeled away from the poorest communities, and tossed back into the hands of the cartels. People sell their food stamps for a chance at playing slot machines or electronic poker, hoping for a pot of gold at the end of the rainbow to solve all their financial woes. Others cash paychecks or social security checks and immediately head for these illegal gaming rooms and spend countless hours there—until all their money is gone. Then they're stuck trying to figure out how to make it through until the next check."

Lucas could cite facts and figures until he was blue, but if Chuck didn't want the story, he'd shelve it—for now. Yet his gut told him to fight. There was something here, beneath the surface, and he itched to dig deeper. He knew where a half dozen or more of these game rooms were in the Dallas-Fort Worth area. Could be there were more located in the suburbs. Maybe even Shiloh Springs. The thought sickened him. Gambling for many ended up more than a harmless habit; it was a sickness, an addiction with no sure-fire cure.

"Boudreau, I can tell you've got a burr under your saddle, and ain't giving up until you find it and pluck it out. I'll give you two weeks. Two. Weeks. Not a minute more. Get your facts straight, prove this is something bigger than recreational fun and maybe—and it's a big maybe—I'll pass it along to the big guys."

Lucas let out a silent sigh, and felt his grin growing. If he hooked Chuck, and it sounded like he had, he'd get the green light. Now to figure out who to talk to around Shiloh Springs, find the closest club, and a way to get in the front door.

Jill ended up face-to-face with Ms. Patti the next morning. After church services, she'd found herself corralled and shuffled into a car with Rafe, Tessa, Antonio, and Serena, headed for the Big House and Sunday supper. She had every intention of calling Ms. Patti first thing Monday morning, and telling her she'd decided to accept her offer. Instead, she found herself seated on the back patio at the Boudreau home, holding a plate overflowing with fried chicken, mashed potatoes and gravy, and biscuits hot from the oven slathered with rich honey butter.

Lucas sat beside her on the love seat, with Rafe and Tessa directly across on an identical matching couch. Her world seemed like a whirlwind, spinning out of control, and she was the kid twirling around in circles, balance all out of whack.

"Did I tell you the florist says she can do the colored baby's breath?" Tessa grinned at Jill, her gaze filled with mischief. "Picture it: Dark pink roses and the barest blush of pink in the baby's breath, tied with silver ribbons. It's going to be simply gorgeous."

"And with that, I'm outta here." Rafe placed a kiss on his fiancée's cheek, and stood, holding his half-empty plate. "I love you, but I'm in desperate need of some testosterone. All this wedding talk—sorry, I'm taking the afternoon off. Lucas, want to go join Dad and talk football and monster trucks?"

"Be right there."

Lucas leaned toward Jill and whispered, "Want me to stay?"

Shaking her head, she gave him a smile. "Go. Tessa and I have some catching up to do anyway. Have fun."

"I'll give you a ride home when you're ready."

"Thanks."

As Lucas walked away, Tessa switched seats, plopping down beside Jill with a heavy sigh. "Thank goodness. I knew wedding talk would make Rafe head for the hills. He's been really sweet through all the planning, but he's a guy. He can only take so much of what he calls 'girly stuff' before his eyes roll back in his head and I've lost him."

Jill pulled Tessa against her side in a one-armed hug. "You two are perfect for each other. I'm amazed I never thought to invite you to visit Shiloh Springs whenever I came home on break. You'd have met him sooner."

"Things worked out in the end. I got my guy. Beth's

found her true love. Looks like you're the only one left who needs fixing up."

Jill shook her head vigorously. "No thanks. Remember my last fiasco? I've sworn off guys. They're all liars, cheaters, married, or gay. Think I'll pass. Besides, I'll have my hands full soon, and won't have time for dating."

Tessa shifted on the seat, turning to face her. "Girlfriend, what are you talking about?"

"I can't say yet. Not until I talk to Ms. Patti, but I promise it's all good news."

Tessa studied her, and the intensity of her gaze reminded Jill of a scientist studying his latest find under a microscope, and not liking what he saw. "It's not like you to keep secrets. We tell each other everything. You sure you can't give me a tiny hint?"

"Tomorrow, I promise. Until then, my lips are zipped." Jill pantomimed the motion, her shoulders shaking with laughter at Tessa's pout.

"You girls doing alright over here?" Ms. Patti asked as she sat on the couch across from them. "Need anything?"

"I'm good."

"Me, too," Tessa added.

"Great, because I need to take these off." Ms. Patti slid her feet out of the heels she'd worn to Sunday service, giving an audible sigh. "Don't tell anybody, but my feet were killing me. Give me a pair of flats any day. Or tennis shoes. Heels are torture devices surely invented by a man."

"Or the devil," Tessa chimed in.

"Same thing." Ms. Patti grinned at Jill's shocked gasp. "I've lived in a predominantly male household all of my adult life. Trust me when I say, there are times they are one and the same."

Jill looked at Tessa, who had her hand over her mouth, stifling her laughter and her own burst forth. How could you not love Ms. Patti? The woman was a Shiloh Springs treasure, and Jill adored her. Why had she hesitated at the thought of working with the woman? She'd keep her on her toes, keep her motivated, and keep her focused on succeeding. All things she wanted and needed, because there was no way she planned on failing.

"I'll do it," she blurted out before she could stop the words.

"Do what?" Tessa gave her the oddest look, and Jill simply grinned, because now she'd said the words aloud, there was no taking them back.

"Excellent. It's the right decision." Ms. Patti nodded once, as if she hadn't expected any other answer.

"What decision? She's going to do what?" Tessa's head ping-ponged back and forth, in a vain effort to follow their conversation. "Somebody better tell me what's going on before I explode."

"Should we?" Ms. Patti's grin had Jill's lips curving upward, along with the frustrated expression on her best friend's face. While she'd love to keep toying with her, she knew Tessa might actually explode if she didn't find out what was going on, so Jill decided to let her off the hook.

"Ms. Patti and I are going into business together. We're opening a bakery."

"What! Oh, Jill, that's awesome!" Tessa started bouncing in her seat, her hands wrapped around the sides of her plate. Within seconds, the plate was on the ground, and her arms were around Jill, squeezing her tight.

"Can't…breathe…"

"Too bad. This is amazing news! I'm so excited. You're already doing the cake, but now I can have you do all the other stuff for the wedding reception and for the cocktail hour, and I won't feel like I'm imposing and being a jerk, and—"

"And take a breath, hon, before you pass out." Ms. Patti leaned back against the cushions, a serene expression on her face.

"I promise your wedding day feast will be the best one ever," Jill promised. "We have a lot of details to work out, but Ms. Patti already scouted out the perfect location, right on Main Street. It's going to be a lot of work—"

"But you're up to the challenge, I know. You've never backed down from anything. I'm so excited! This means you get to quit your awful insurance job, right?"

"I hadn't really thought that far ahead yet. I mean, I only made the decision last night. Yeah, once we've signed all the papers, I guess I'll be turning in my notice."

"Yay!"

Tessa stood and practically flew across the patio, straight into Rafe's arms. He caught her and spun her around, her feet leaving the ground, and she leaned toward him, whispering what Jill assumed was the big news. Rafe's eyes met hers over the top of Tessa's head, and he smiled.

"Guess it's not going to be much of a surprise, not with blabbermouth over there spilling the beans." Jill watched her best friend, feeling so much love for the vivacious woman. They'd been best friends ever since meeting in college, and stayed in touch after graduation, even though they'd been half a continent apart. She'd been the one to mention the opening at the elementary school, which prompted Tessa's move to Shiloh Springs.

"There's no such thing as secrets in this family." Ms. Patti moved from the couch, to sit beside her. "Besides, we're your biggest supporters. Especially Lucas."

Jill felt a surge of heat blast her cheeks at the mention of his name, remembering all-to-vividly her steamy dreams from the night before. The ones in which Lucas played the starring role.

"Lucas is a good friend."

"Yes, I suppose he is." Ms. Patti reached over and squeezed her hand. "How about we meet at my office in the morning, and go over the details? I took the liberty of having a contract drawn up, and you'll need to go over it thoroughly. Have your own attorney look at it, and we'll make any changes necessary."

Jill looked down at her half-eaten plate of food, her mind reeling. She'd really done it—agreed to a business partnership with none other than Patricia Boudreau. She'd taken the first step in the pursuit of her ever-elusive dream. And it felt good. No, it felt great!

"I'll need to call my office, and let them know I'll be late—no, I'm going to take a personal day. I haven't taken a day off in two years, so it shouldn't be a problem."

"Good idea. I don't want you feeling pressured or rushed in any way." She grinned at Jill before continuing. "If I'm being honest, I can't wait until we're up and running. Have you thought of a name?"

"Name? Oh, well…not really."

"I'm sure you'll come up with the perfect name, once all the real work starts." She looked past Jill's shoulder and then shrugged. "I think the word has spread. Prepare yourself, they're coming."

Within a few seconds, Jill found herself surrounded by a throng of grinning Boudreaus, all congratulating her on her upcoming success. She couldn't help marveling at all the support the brothers poured her way. When her gaze caught Lucas', he nodded, a huge grin on his lips. Warmth suffused her, reinforcing her decision. He moved to stand beside her, clasping her hand in his, and she closed her eyes for a second, savoring his touch.

This wouldn't last. He'd head back to DFW in no time,

and she'd go back to mooning over him from Shiloh Springs. At least she'd have her new business to keep her mind and body occupied, because her heart knew the truth. No matter how much she might wish otherwise, Lucas Boudreau wasn't meant to be hers.

CHAPTER FIVE

Lucas pulled into a parking space in front of the sheriff's office the next morning. He'd decided to check in with Rafe, and ask him a few pointed questions about the possibility of illegal gambling in Shiloh Springs or any of the surrounding towns. Something about this story needed to be told, though he hadn't found the right angle yet. He needed a hook, something to make people care about the importance of closing these places down. A true perspective on the people who ran the illegal gambling halls, most with connections to organized crime or the big drug syndicates, and how they preyed on the less fortunate.

Sally Anne sat at her desk by the front door, the phone to her ear. She waved at him as he walked past, and pointed toward the back. Giving her a wink, he headed down the hall toward Rafe's office. His brother sat behind his desk, frowning at a piece of paper. Whatever it was, he wasn't a happy camper.

"Hey, big brother, what's got your britches in a bunch?"

"Huh...what?"

"You're scowling at that paper like you want to light it

on fire. Problems?"

"Nothing I can't handle." Rafe pulled open the middle drawer of his desk, and shoved the page inside, slamming it closed with a little more force than necessary.

Yeah, right. Guess I'm gonna stick my nose in big brother's business. See if it's something I can help with, before I head back to DFW.

"What brings you by?"

Lucas sat on the chair across from Rafe, and tossed his hat onto the one beside him. He rarely wore his Stetson in the city, but there was something about being home which made it feel right, in a way that tugged at his soul. Made him a little homesick every time he left it behind.

"Wanted to pick your brain, if you've got a few minutes."

"Sure. Want some coffee before you start?"

"No, thanks, I'm good. Had a couple cups before I left the Big House."

"Momma's taking good care of you, I bet. She'd like nothing better than for you to move back to Shiloh Springs. I heard her talking to Daddy the other night about wanting all her boys back home. Bet she'll be subtle about it, but she's surely coming up with a plan to make it happen, so watch your back."

Lucas chuckled at his brother's warning. "Duly noted. She mentioned Heath came home for a bit. He didn't mention it when I called him."

Rafe grinned like he hid a huge secret. "He showed up out of the blue around the time Beth's ex escaped from prison. Evan Stewart's sister was visiting Beth at the time, and Heath took one look at Camilla Stewart, and you'd think he'd been hit with a sledgehammer."

"You're kidding. Heath Boudreau, the man who swore he wasn't going to ever get married? The man who thinks women—other than Momma, of course—are lying, duplicitous schemers, finally met his match? She must be something special."

"Picture a woman the exact opposite of Heath. He's huge, works a demanding job with the ATF, rides a Harley, and doesn't have a suave or sophisticated bone in his body. He's more beers, bikes, and heavy metal. I'm still shocked he isn't covered in tattoos. Camilla is all polished charm and elegance. One of those never-a-hair-out-of-place women who'd pick ballet over baseball. When those two clashed, it was a sight to see. We're talking Fourth of July fireworks."

"Sorry I missed it."

"All water under the bridge now. Probably wouldn't have worked anyway. He works in D.C. and she lives in Charlotte. Doubt they'll ever cross paths again." Rafe grabbed his coffee mug and took a long swallow. "Anyway, what can I help you with?"

"I'm looking for information for my next story. I've got the basic info, facts and figures, but I want the dirt. The ugly, dark side of illegal gambling in Texas. Who it affects, what kind of toll it takes on the family when a loved one goes too far, and ends up over their head in debt."

"Thinking about exposing the seedy underbelly, showing people one of the dirty little secrets folks ignore, huh? Texas is one of the strictest states with regards to illegal gambling. They've cracked down in the last couple of years, especially around Houston and South Texas. The area around Victoria got hit pretty hard. They'd close down one gaming club and two more would pop up in their place."

Lucas nodded. "I read about that while doing my research. It's not considered an epidemic yet, but more and more of these places are popping up all over the country. If something isn't done to bring the truth to the forefront, there'll be no stopping it. Hundreds of thousands of dollars pass through these gaming clubs daily, most of it coming from people who can't afford to take the hit. We're talking a multimillion-dollar illegal industry, and it's still classified as a misdemeanor offense." Lucas could feel the bottled-up rage in the pit of his stomach, thinking about all the poor unfortunate souls who'd been sucked in with the allure of easy money. Prey for the cartels and Mafia, it made his blood boil.

"Which is why they get away with it most of the time. It's a slap on the wrist, maybe probation, or if there's jail time, it's minimal. Usually it's a five hundred dollar fine."

Lucas leaned back, watching Rafe closely, and could see the lines of frustration bracketing his mouth. Guess he wasn't the only one worried about the growing need to eradicate this blight. He also noted the dark circles beneath his brother's eyes.

"You look tired. Everything okay?"

Rafe drew in a long breath, and let it out slowly. "Yeah. The wedding's been a pain. Don't you dare tell Tessa I said that. Most of the time it's fine, and all this planning, looking at dresses and flowers, makes her happy. Momma, too. Personally, I'd have been thrilled to stand up in front of a justice of the peace, but she deserves to have the whole shebang."

"It's more than the wedding, though. Talk to me. What's going on?"

"Really, it's—"

"If you say nothing, I'm coming around this desk and punching you. You know I can read you like a book. Now spill."

Instead of answering, Rafe opened the drawer and pulled out the paper he'd shoved in there earlier, and handed it to Lucas. It was a letter, and as he scanned its contents, the madder he got, until his hands shook.

"Is this a joke?" He bit the words out, jaws tight.

"Afraid not. There's a petition being circulated through the county to recall me as sheriff, and hold a special election for my replacement."

"That's the stupidest thing I've ever heard. Nobody in their right mind could think you've done anything wrong, much less egregious enough to call for your removal from office. What are their allegations?"

"Bro, it's a petition, they don't have to state a specific reason. All they have to do is collect enough signatures, and present it to the right people and call for my ouster as sheriff."

"What a load of—"

"Yeah, well, you're gonna keep your mouth shut, you hear me? Nobody, and I mean nobody, hears about this. Especially the family. I do not want Tessa or Momma getting wind of this. I'll handle it."

Lucas stood and paced the small space in Rafe's crowded office. Six steps, turn, six more steps, turn. He was surprised steam wasn't pouring from his ears. Nobody with half a brain could think Rafe wasn't doing a good job running the sheriff's department. He was the best sheriff Shiloh Springs had seen in twenty years or more. No way was he going to let this stand, not without a fight.

"Any idea who's behind this?"

"Not a clue. Doesn't matter. If people don't like the way I'm running this office, they've got the right to kick me out and elect somebody else."

Each word landed like a blow to his heart, and Lucas felt every one with the ferocity of a physical punch. He knew how much being sheriff meant to his brother. From the time he'd joined the Boudreau clan, he remembered hearing about Rafe. About the accident that claimed his mother's life, leaving him virtually alone in a strange town with nobody. Not until Douglas, working as a volunteer fireman, stepped up and claimed Rafe as his own son. From that day forward, Rafe's goal focused on becoming an integral piece of Shiloh Springs. Part of the community who'd welcomed him. To give back in a tangible way, and help others the way he'd been helped. Now some idiot with a piece of paper and a grudge thought they could take it all away from him?

Not in this lifetime!

"I'm gonna find out who's doing this, and they're going to wish they'd never messed with a Boudreau brother."

Lucas started for the door, but Rafe was around his desk and blocking the entryway before he'd taken more than a couple steps.

"You're not doing anything. I mean it, Lucas. You're going to keep your mouth shut and let me handle things. This is my problem, and I'll deal with it. Don't make me regret telling you."

Lucas turned and flung himself onto the chair. "I don't like it. And I've got a pretty good idea who's behind it. You do, too. Don't tell me it didn't cross your mind the minute you heard about the petition."

Rafe leaned against the doorjamb, arms crossed over his chest. "Of course I thought it. Richard and Julie Calloway have been a thorn in my side since the day I took the oath of office."

"Do they really think messing with the Boudreaus is

gonna make Ridge and Shiloh come running back to them with open arms? The Calloway's destroyed any chance of reconciling when they disowned our brothers' biological mother, and tossed her out when she was pregnant. Didn't want anything to do with their grandsons when they moved back here as kids. Now they expect Shiloh and Ridge to simply welcome them with open arms? They're both idiots."

"But they are within their rights as citizens."

Lucas simply stared at Rafe, reading the quiet determination in his face. His brother was hurting, because like it or not, this petty attempt by the Calloway's was a slap at his pride. An undeserved condemnation of one of the finest men Lucas knew.

"I won't say anything to the family, but I can't promise I won't try and figure out what they hope to gain from this stupidity."

Rafe sighed and straightened, walking around to his chair behind the desk. "I know. And I'll get some numbers for you, for your research. Let me know what you need, and I'll pass it along."

"Thanks. Call me if you need anything."

"Get out of here. Go see Jill, I know you want to."

Lucas chuckled at his brother making kissy noises. "Bro, that's not a good look on you. Save it for Tessa."

"Yeah, well, tell me you're not heading over to see Jill the minute you leave here, I dare you."

Lucas started whistling and headed toward the front door, his brother's laughter echoing behind him.

CHAPTER SIX

Jill stood in the center of the shop she'd visited with Ms. Patti, and spun slowly in a circle, taking it in. She'd spent a good chunk of the morning at Ms. Patti's real estate office, going over the lease agreement, and looking over the contract for co-ownership of their bakery.

Their bakery.

Hearing the words in her head made her giddy. The dream she'd cherished for most of her life was finally within her grasp, though she hadn't anticipated having a partner. She didn't mind, because she knew Ms. Patti was an honest, aboveboard, and honorable woman.

"I can't believe it," she whispered, her hand stroking softly over the door between the front of the shop and the back kitchen area. It was really happening. Glancing into her bag, her fingertips skimmed over the contract Ms. Patti gave her. Insisted she take to her lawyer. Once she signed on the dotted line, they'd be in business.

She grabbed the pen and pad she'd slipped in her purse earlier, and jotted down a couple of notes, then walked into the back. Better to get the biggest list done first, because getting the right equipment was a make-it or break-it proposition. There were a couple of good places in Austin she could check for rental equipment, or maybe they'd have some used they'd be willing to sell, if the price was right.

First thing, she'd need to get in here and do a thorough cleaning. Whoever had been the last occupant obviously hadn't done a deep scrubbing before they left. The floors beneath her feet held enough dust it looked like it had snowed indoors. Cobwebs decorated the light fixtures, and clung to corners of the ceiling.

"Gotta remember to bring a ladder."

"What do you need a ladder for?"

Jill screeched, spinning around at the sound of Lucas' voice, hand pressed against her chest. She hadn't heard him come in. Her fault because she hadn't locked the front door behind her.

"You scared the living daylights out of me."

"Sorry. I thought you heard me."

"Guess I need to put a bell over the door—or one around your neck," she joked, watching the corners of his mouth twitch.

"If I get a vote, I pick the door." She jotted the word "bell" on her list, along with ladder and cleaning supplies. Decided to add fresh paint to the list, because the walls hadn't seen any in decades.

"Congratulations. Momma said you signed the lease this morning, and your attorney's looking over the partnership agreement."

Jill couldn't help the smile she knew beamed on her face. "I can't believe it! I'm going to have my own bakery. It's...I guess it hasn't sunk in. That's why I stopped by here. Ms. Patti gave me the keys, and I thought I'd start a list of what needs to be done. What we need to order. It's overwhelming—in a good way."

Lucas looked around, and she wondered if he could see it the way she pictured in her mind. She didn't want anything too schmaltzy or juvenile. Nothing too upscale. No, she wanted a place where everybody felt like they were welcome to walk in, look at what she had ready for sale fresh each morning, and pick out something delicious.

"I like it." He pointed toward the front. "You've got enough space for customers not to feel crowded. With some elbow grease and a couple cans of paint, it's going to be something special."

"That's what I think, too. The whole place needs a good cleaning, from top to bottom. Which is why I mentioned the ladder." She pointed toward the light fixtures. "Cobwebs and about an inch of dust clinging to those."

"I'm sure Dad has one out at the house he'll lend you. And I volunteer to help with whatever you need, at least until I head back home."

Jill tried to maintain her smile, though it took everything she had because at the mention of him leaving, going back to DFW, it felt like she was losing her best friend all over again.

She'd mourned when he moved away, though she'd never admit it out loud.

"I'll take you up on your offer. It's going to take an army to whip this place into shape."

"You can do it, I have total confidence."

"Tell me again after we've put in some long hours whipping this place into submission. Until then, I've got a lot to do, including turning in my notice at the insurance company."

"I can honestly say I'm happy about that. I worried about you making the long drive every day to a place you hated working. I know, I know, people have to work jobs they hate every day—but you shouldn't have to, Jill. You have a gift, and people need to know what you're capable of."

She ducked her head, and mumbled, "Thank you."

Lucas' finger tilted her chin up, and he stared at her, studying her face. "I mean it. You're something special, and deserve to have your dreams come true."

There it was again, that silly *thump, thump* inside her chest racing at his touch. Her lips parted and she felt breathless. It seemed like everything around her shifted into slow motion at his touch.

"Thank you, Lucas. I want that for you, too. Happiness, wherever it takes you." Because she knew it wasn't here in Shiloh Springs. It never had been, or he wouldn't have left, leaving her behind, with her heart broken, without a backward glance.

Breaking their stare down, she took a hesitant step back, and clutched her pad to her chest. *Think about work. Think about everything it's going to take to make this a success. Don't think about Lucas walking away again. You know he's not here to stay. Keep things light. Have fun, but don't risk your heart— never again.*

"Alright, I've got to get busy figuring out what needs to be done and what needs to be ordered. I also need to call my attorney, and fax him a copy of the contract."

"You are going to sign it though, right?"

She nodded her head. "Your mom wants me to have my lawyer look it over, and make any changes he suggests. Smart businesswoman, she knows more about how things are done at this stage than I do—but I'm a quick learner. I'm finally going to be able to put my college degree to good use."

"Guess that means you don't have time to grab lunch with me? Daisy's has smothered pork chops this afternoon. Sure I can't tempt you?"

Oh, boy, can you tempt me. No, bad Jill. No Lucas for you.

"Thanks, but I really want to get a handle on things here. Another time?"

Lucas nodded, his smile a little sad. "Sure. I'll talk to you later."

She watched him turn and walk out the front door, with a sinking feeling in the pit of her stomach. Dwelling on the past wouldn't do her a lick of good, because that only led to heartache. Squaring her shoulders, she placed her purse on the empty table against the wall, and clicked the end of her pen.

Time to get busy.

After leaving Jill, Lucas decided to head to Santa Lucia. Ridge spent most of his days there now when he wasn't working on expanding his security business. All his brother's time and energy since turning his back on the DEA had been laser focused on building up the elite reputation he'd established for Sentinel Guardians, the company he started right after leaving the army. He'd occasionally used it as background for his DEA ops, but now he planned to build it bigger and better. While it had an excellent reputation in Texas, Ridge wanted to grow and expand his base, and with the people he contracted, Lucas had no doubt within the next few years, Sentinel Guardians would be one of the premiere security specialists in the nation.

It still chafed Ridge hadn't told him about working undercover for the DEA. It stung he'd kept it secret. He understood the reasoning, but didn't make it hurt any less. On the bright side, though, Ridge had found the girl of his dreams, and along with expanding his business, he was building a life with Maggie White.

Pulling up to the gate fronting Maggie's land, Lucas

pressed the button, notifying the house somebody was at the gate. In less than thirty seconds, he heard Maggie's voice.

"Can I help you?"

He leaned closer to his window, making sure the camera could identify him clearly. "Hey, Maggie, it's Lucas. Is Ridge around?"

"Lucas! He's out in the garage. Come on back, I'll tell him you're here."

The iron gates swung inward, and Lucas drove through, heading for the front of Maggie's house. A large circular drive dropped him at the front door, and he killed the engine and climbed out. This was the first time he'd been here, and he was impressed. Large double doors graced the entrance, the front façade built with Texas limestone. Landscaping was tastefully done, unobtrusive yet highlighting the features of the estate.

"Hey, bro, what brings you here?" Ridge walked around the side of the house, casually dressed in jeans and a T-shirt. He'd left his hair loose, hanging a little past his shoulders, instead of tying it back, which he normally did when he was working.

"Had a bit of free time this afternoon, and thought I'd drive over. See how the other half lives. This," he waved toward the house, "is pretty spectacular."

"It is. Maggie's pretty proud of the place, and I've been hanging around enough it's starting to feel like home."

"I've gotta say, I never expected you to fall so hard and

fast. I'm beginning to think there's something in the water, because my brothers are dropping like flies stuck in the honey pot."

Ridge slapped him on the shoulder. "You should try it. Being in love, it's a feeling like no other. When you find the right woman, it's worth everything." With a grin, Ridge swung the front door inward.

Lucas shoved past him, giving Ridge a playful elbow to the gut. His brother grunted, and followed close behind. Lucas spotted Maggie in the kitchen. She waved as she filled glasses with ice.

"Lucas, welcome to my home. Make yourself comfortable. I'm fixing something to drink. What can I get you?"

"Whatever you're having is fine."

"Lemonade it is. What brings you by?"

Lucas grabbed one of the barstools, and perched on the edge, facing her. "My plans got sidetracked, and I had some time to kill this afternoon. Figured I'd catch up with this big lug." He pointed over his shoulder at Ridge. "I'll probably be heading back to DFW in a few days, and thought I'd spend a couple hours with him before I leave. Since most of the time he's hopping between here and his office, this seemed like the best way to pin him down for a chat."

She grinned and Lucas could see the appeal she held for his brother. There was an openness in her impossible to ignore. "Well, I've leave you to it. I'll be in the office if you need me. Chance has been running me ragged, getting this foundation set up. I'm up to my eyeballs in paperwork."

"And you love every minute of it." Ridge grabbed her around the waist as she walked past, brushing a kiss against her cheek. "Holler if you need anything."

"Have fun, guys."

They watched her until she disappeared from view, and Ridge turned to him. "Grab your glass and let's go out on the patio. It's shaded and I could use the fresh air."

Lucas followed him out, and took in the amazing outdoor space behind the house, and again felt a surge of happiness for his brother. Ridge practically lived here anyway. Maggie had invited him to move in, but Ridge insisted he was going to woo his beloved. He hadn't officially proposed yet, but Lucas knew it would happen any day. Seeing the love they shared almost made him wish he had somebody.

His thoughts immediately sprang to Jill. Pretty Jillian Monroe, the girl he'd had a not-so-secret crush on all through middle school and high school. Shy until she got to know you, once you'd become part of her inner circle, she was the most outgoing, charming, vivacious, and funny person you'd ever meet. And he'd been the idiot who hadn't realized what he had—until he'd tossed it away.

"Dad told me the lead for Renee didn't pan out. I'm sorry."

Lucas sat in the cushioned chair, sitting his glass on the small table beside it. "It wasn't a total bust. The information was solid. The woman Dad's buddy found could be her. Elizabeth Reynolds is the right age. Right hair and eye color. Driver's license photo and social media pics look like they could be her. Problem is she's not at the address in Cincinnati any longer."

"Forwarding address?"

"Nope. The apartment complex said she left without notice. She was on a month-to-month lease, and forfeited her deposit, so they didn't think anything about it. Mail was returned to the post office, no forwarding address given. The manager of the place said there wasn't much mail anyway, only bills. Nothing personal or private."

"Let me put my guys on it. I hired a computer expert—"

"Hacker," Lucas coughed to cover his word.

"Don't knock it. She's the best I've ever seen. I swear she's got magic in her fingers when she's finessing a keyboard. If there's a record out there, anywhere, a single thread, Destiny will find it."

"I'll e-mail you the new info I've got. Whoever this person is, even if she's not my sister, she's running from something or somebody. Three name changes in the last two years. Four relocations in that same time period. Indianapolis, Chicago, Evansville, and Cincinnati."

Ridge leaned against the wall, and stared into the distance. "Definitely sounds like somebody with something to hide. I'll get Destiny on it ASAP. Who knows, even if it turns out this Elizabeth Reynolds isn't Renee, maybe she needs help."

"Your area of expertise, bro. I'm a simple reporter."

Ridge choked on the lemonade he'd swallowed. "Right, just a reporter. How many awards have you been nominated for again?"

"Hmm, eight? No, nine. Which kind of brings me back to why I wanted to talk to you, except now I've got to go; I have someplace I have to be. Give me a call tomorrow?"

Ridge moved away from the wall as Lucas stood. "You've got it. It's really good to have you home."

Lucas shrugged. "Wish I could stay longer, but I'm probably going to be moving around a bit for this new story. Waiting to hear from Chuck."

"How is the old geezer?"

"Ornery as ever, but the man's a genius at making my work shine, so I put up with him." They walked to the front door and Lucas pulled Ridge in for a hug. "I've missed you."

"Miss you, too. Why don't you think about coming back to Shiloh Springs? You can work from anywhere, as long as you have internet and Wi-Fi. I know it'd make Momma happy."

Lucas didn't want to admit he'd been thinking the same thing recently. More and more frequently, if he admitted the truth. He missed his family, his friends. Missed the feelings that came with being home. A stark apartment in a city full of strangers had been his life for the last few years. That and his search for Renee, which got harder and harder with each passing day. He'd never give up, but he'd become disheartened with the endless search and never finding her.

"I'll think about it."

Ridge followed him out to the car, and Lucas climbed inside.

"Don't give up hope, bro. We'll find your sister—our sister."

Lucas paused for a moment, absorbing Ridge's words. He'd never thought about the fact when he found Renee, she'd be getting a whole new, ready-made family with a passel of older brothers.

"Thanks. Talk to you tomorrow."

He pulled away, watching Ridge in his rearview mirror. Ridge was right, he couldn't—wouldn't—give up. One day he'd find his sister and make his family complete.

Smiling, he turned the car toward home.

CHAPTER SEVEN

Tessa plopped herself down on Jill's sofa, slid off her shoes, and gave a happy sigh. She'd shown up out of the blue, bringing a bag filled with tacos, guacamole and chips, and a six pack of long necks. Passing the whole thing to Jill, she'd maneuvered past her, stating she'd brought dinner because she knew Jill wouldn't bother to fix anything after putting in a long day.

"I have been on my feet all day, and I'm pooped. The little darlings ran me ragged."

"You love every minute of it," Jill shot back, unloading the food on her small table.

Tessa grinned. "I do. But teaching all day, going home to do the lesson plan for the next day, and work on wedding planning is wearing me out. Rafe's a doll about all the meetings, scheduling venues, and tastings, but honestly, I'm at the point where I'd as soon elope to Vegas."

Jill motioned her over to the table, and sat two plates on its wooden top. "Baloney. You've wanted a white wedding ever since I've known you. Remember, I saw all those bridal magazines in your dorm room with the turned down pages, complete with sticky notes."

"I know. I never realized how much work goes into planning a big, fancy blowout. Thank goodness for Ms. Patti. She has been a godsend." Tessa reached and grabbed two tacos, putting them on her plate. "I am getting the best mother-in-law in the world. How did I get so lucky?"

"You fell in love with her amazing son. Gaining the perfect mother-in-law is an added bonus." Jill reached for the guacamole bowl, and Tessa smacked her hand.

"What?"

Tessa gave her a hard glare. "I know you saw her today. How'd it go?"

"Sheesh, can't I even fix my plate before the twenty questions start?"

Tessa pointed her taco at Jill. "You'll be lucky if I stop at twenty. I've got a million of 'em. Did you sign the contract?"

She shook her head. "I will, but I'm having my lawyer look over it first. Ms. Patti insisted. I did, however, sign the lease for the bakery."

"Yes!" Tessa clicked her bottle against Jill's. "I am so happy for you. You know I'm going to be your biggest customer."

"You better be. Oh, you need to stop by and see it, Tessa. I don't think I could have picked a better spot. It's on Main Street, not too far from Daisy's Diner and Gourmet Grounds. Plus, the sheriff's station is right down the street, so that'll make people feel safer. Dusty has a sweet tooth, so I can probably count on him keeping me in business."

Jill took a huge bite out of her taco and nearly swooned as the taste of spicy beef and tomato burst upon her tongue. She'd been too nervous to eat before she met Ms. Patti, then she'd gone by the new store. Only now did she realize she'd forgotten to eat all day. Taking another bite, she practically inhaled the rest of her taco.

"Wow, you must've been starving. Glad I decided to bring dinner."

"Thanks. I kinda got busy and forgot to eat." She took a quick drink, and reached for the guacamole. This time Tessa let her grab the spoon without swatting at her.

"I've made a list of stuff I'm going to need right away. All the big things. We're establishing a line of credit with a restaurant supplier in Austin. And I'm probably going to need to hire a cleaning crew, because the shop's been empty for a while, and it needs a ton of TLC."

"You know you've got a handy-dandy cleaning crew, ready to chip in and do whatever you need?"

Jill shook her head, catching on quick to what Tessa suggested. "No, they've already done more than enough. I'm not asking the Boudreaus for more help."

Tessa started to answer, but paused when she glanced at her phone. Swiping her finger across the screen, she laughed and handed the phone to Jill. "Guess again, sister."

The text message on Tessa's phone was plain enough.

TELL JILL TO SET ASIDE SATURDAY MORNING.

DOUGLAS AND THE BOYS WILL MEET HER AT 8 A.M. AT THE BAKERY, READY TO WORK. THEY'LL BRING ALL THE CLEANING SUPPLIES. SHE SIMPLY NEEDS TO SUPERVISE.

She immediately burst into tears. Was there anything Ms. Patti couldn't do? Now she'd solved another one of Jill's problems, before she'd even realized it was one.

"Hey, none of that!" Tessa jumped from her chair, and squatted beside Jill, wrapping her arms around her. "I know she tends to take over, but she never means it in a malicious or mean way. Never, ever. She simply sees a situation, figures out what needs to be done, and then makes it happen."

"I know." Jill wiped at her damp cheeks. "I adore her. It's just…everything. I'm feeling overwhelmed and honestly a bit scared."

"Welcome to my world. Remember when I first moved here? I adored my family, but once you've met the Boudreaus, been around them for any length of time, you realize they are like a force of nature. In the best possible way, of course."

"I never expected to be part of their world. You are because you're marrying into the family. The only connection I had to them was Lucas, and that ended a long time ago."

Tessa leaned back in her chair. "You know, for as long as I've known you, even back in school, you never once mentioned Lucas."

"Sure I did." *Didn't I?*

"Nuh-uh. Not even once. What's going on with the two of you? And don't tell me nothing. The few times I've seen you together, there's a sizzle between you that's more than an old school crush."

Jill shoved a chip in her mouth, needing a second before answering. She hadn't deliberately kept her past with Lucas a secret. It simply hurt too much when he'd moved away, and then she'd left for Duke. Throwing herself into her courses, she'd been able to keep the memories at bay, at least for a little while. She swallowed down the chip, which suddenly tasted like cardboard.

"I'm not sure where to start. Lucas and I have known each other forever. We went to school together. For a while, we were close."

"How close—like boyfriend and girlfriend close? Or more bosom buddies close?"

Trust Tessa to go right for the heart.

"Both. Neither. He was my best friend, the one person I told everything. I had such a crush on him in high school. We hung out together all the time. Lucas was…special."

A tiny smirk appeared on Tessa's lips. Jill rolled her eyes, and shoved another chip in her mouth. The guacamole was really good. She'd have to ask Tessa where she got it.

"Special. Is that synonymous for you had the hots for him?"

"Gutter, meet Tessa."

Tessa swatted her arm. "Shut up. You know what I mean."

"Yes." Jill felt the heat flooding her cheeks, knew she was probably bright pink bordering on tomato red, but there wasn't anything she could do about it. She'd always blushed at the slightest provocation, and being fair-skinned, it was a trait she'd dealt with her whole life.

"And?"

"Lucas was my first kiss. I'd gone to his house after school, and he kissed me in his mother's gazebo."

Tessa squealed and threw her hands in the air. "I knew it! There's still something there, right? Because I have to tell you, he watches you when you're not looking. And those looks definitely aren't the platonic 'she's an old school chum' kind, if you ask me."

"Really?"

"Yes, really. The bigger question here is—how do you feel about him now? Do you still want him?"

"There's not an easy answer, Tessa. We don't even live in the same town anymore. Too much time has passed. We're different people, not the same kids from high school."

"Doesn't matter, those are merely obstacles in the path of true love. It's how you feel in your heart that counts. Do you love him?"

Jill fought the urge to run and hide, because Tessa was asking her all the questions she'd already asked herself. The answer both scared and exhilarated her, because once she said the words out loud, there'd be no more hiding from the truth.

"Yes. I love him."

"I knew it! So, what are we going to do about it?"

Jill shook her head and pushed away her plate. "Nothing. It broke my heart when he moved away. You and I both know long-distance relationships don't last. Besides, getting ready to open the new bakery is going to take up all my time. I don't have it in me to deal with the upheaval of juggling a new business and keeping my heart from breaking again."

Tessa sniffed, blotting at her eyes with her napkin. "I know I'm playing matchmaker, but I want you to be as happy as I am. You're my bestie; you should be getting married, opening your bakery, having babies. I want you to have it all."

Jumping up, Jill wrapped her arms around Tessa, who gave a watery chuckle. "You're overflowing with happiness, aren't you? Right now, the bakery is enough. More than enough if I'm going to make it a success. I have to pour all my energy and concentration into it. Anything else, especially a man, is a distraction I can't afford."

"But—"

"No. Don't go getting any crazy ideas, either. I know you. Leave Lucas alone. He'll be heading back to Fort Worth soon, and off to his next investigation. Living his life the way he wants to—so leave it alone."

"Fine. But doesn't mean I have to like it."

Jill started picking up the plates and carrying them to the sink. She paused for a second, closing her eyes, and letting the loneliness wash over her. It didn't matter what her heart wanted, her mind told her she was making the right choice.

"Want some dessert? I've got ice cream."

"What flavor?"

Jill spun around and glared at Tessa, hands on her hips. "You mean there's more than one?"

"Not as far as you're concerned. Chocolate-covered cherries it is."

Jill laughed at Tessa's antics, knowing her friend was doing her best to cheer her up. And it was working.

"Two bowls coming right up."

Lucas studied the notes he'd made, outlining the things he'd figured out so far. All the facts and figures about gambling in Texas, compiled into several handwritten lists. It astounded him how little was actually known about a multimillion-dollar industry operating beneath the legitimate radar. Where the money went. How much was actually won and lost by the people desperately tossing money at a pipe dream that most likely would never pan out.

Legal lotteries were huge business. The Texas Lottery, established in 1992, had generated over thirty billion dollars in revenue, with those funds going to education, veteran services, and other state programs. Winners, big and small, accounted for over sixty-four billion dollars in prizes. Billions with a capital B. He'd known the numbers were big, but those were only the ones from Texas. Add in the rest of the country, and you're talking mind-boggling numbers.

But something still didn't add up. That extra instinctive zap he got when he was on the right track for a story. It hadn't happened yet, and until it did, he was barking up the wrong tree. Should he do it from a lost revenue perspective, how it was taking money away from the people who could least afford it? Or maybe do it from a more personal angle, an in-depth interview with somebody who'd been personally affected by illegal gambling? How it affected not only them, but those around them. Their families. Their friends.

Zap. There it was. He'd been looking at the story from the wrong perspective. Sure, the money side of things was important. It was a given that a huge chunk of the money from these illegal gaming establishments didn't make its way back into the legitimate coffers to help out communities, schools, and citizens. No, organized crime made a fortune on the games of chance. Had for decades, even before little mom and pop shops sprang up in every county, every town. Drug cartels gained huge profits by running these sites, and funneling the money back into human trafficking, among other things. It was perverse and ugly.

But did the Average Joe, reading about the facts and figures, get anything beyond the details? They looked at the astronomical numbers, the amounts of money being tossed around, and their eyes glazed over, because they couldn't imagine seeing that kind of money in their lifetime, and then they moved on to the next thing to read. There was no personal impact. No discussion of how it affected their community, because maybe somebody they knew, somebody they sat beside in church on Sunday, was caught in its clutches.

What if he told people about its impact on one person's life? How they got started. How they found themselves falling deeper under the allure of making a fast buck. The excitement and adrenaline of the win. The agony and despair at losing. Make it personal. Make them hurt when it impacted the wife or husband, their brother or sister. How they hid their addiction. Define the danger it presented to one lone individual, and how it inevitably spread to include those they loved.

Lucas looked up from his notes, realizing he'd written over three pages of questions needing answers. Yes, this felt right. The personal angle, the lure to get people caring about what was happening, because once you tugged on their heartstrings, you motivated them to make changes.

Picking up the phone, he called Chuck. If he pitched this right, he'd get the okay, because this went beyond a simple investigative piece. It was more than an information dump of facts and figures; it was about an epidemic sweeping the nation.

Now he needed to find the subject of his expose, his person of interest. Somebody with firsthand experience of the rise and fall, the lies and deceit this insidious disease carried. But who?

CHAPTER EIGHT

"Wow, Sis," Dante turned slowly, examining what she'd accomplished. "I can't believe how much you've done. I'm really proud of you."

"Thanks. I can't believe it's happening. I've got a couple of bruises where I've pinched myself, to make sure it's real."

Dante's arm came around her shoulder, and Jill leaned her head against him. For the last several days, she'd worked every spare second, whipping the new bakery space into a semblance of order. Unfortunately, her old boss held her to the two weeks' notice she'd given. She found herself driving back and forth to work at the insurance company, slogging away at the mundane number crunching. Knowing it was temporary, her heart's dream within her grasp, made it bearable. Although her tail dragged, she worked late into the night every night, cleaning, scrubbing, and painting, until she fell into bed exhausted. Only to repeat the entire process the next day.

"You deserve this." He sighed and squeezed her tight, brushing a kiss against her forehead. "I know it's my fault you never got the chance to do this sooner. If I'd gotten my act together, stayed away from Junior and his guys, you'd already have the bakery."

"Dante, you made a mistake." At his raised brow, she chuckled. "Okay, fine, you made a bunch of mistakes, screwed up more times than I can mention. But you haven't gone back, right?"

"Nope. I promise I'm steering clear of the whole gang."

"Good. I know it's hard, but it's for the best. You've got a problem, but I swear you're doing the right thing. No more poker. No more slots. No gambling at all. It's the only way you'll stay clean."

"It's harder than I thought. I spent almost every day with those guys. Nights in their garages playing Texas Hold 'Em or blackjack. Sometimes we'd go do some slots and video stuff. Smoke a little weed. Getting high and gambling aren't a good combination, and I got in over my head. Gotta tell you, I never knew those guys were part of an illegal ring. They're my friends. We played friendly games for penny ante stakes—until we moved things to the club. Then everything escalated."

"Don't do it again, and we're square." Jill shuddered at the memory of the large men who'd met her at the door of her apartment several weeks ago. They'd demanded payment of Dante's poker debt. Holding her bruised and broken brother draped between them, it would've been obvious to a blind man he'd been roughed up. More like beaten to a bloody pulp. Bruises and bloody streaks decorated his face.

Even now, she remembered the stark terror in his eyes. The reality of what he'd done filled her with disgust and loathing for the monsters preying on the weak. And her brother was weak.

Dante had looked pathetic, held between two large men smelling of stale beer and greasy fast food. They'd stood behind a man, obviously their leader, her brother's body drooping, his legs unable to hold his body's weight. The middle-aged man, dressed impeccably in a navy suit and blue and white striped tie, called the shots from the way the others never made a move without his approval. He wasn't tall, probably the same height as her, but he'd exuded an aura of power impossible to ignore. His dark hair was swept back, accentuating the sharp angles and craggy planes of his face. If he'd been smiling, or even showing a modicum of civility, he might have been considered attractive. Instead, goosebumps leapt to attention all over her, and she knew he was dangerous. It was impossible to tell much about him, though he'd barked out an order in Spanish when one of the goons holding Dante backhanded her brother across the face.

His eyes, though, she remembered those. They'd been icy cold. They contained an eerie empty blackness, devoid of any spark of life within their obsidian depths. Whatever soul he might have possessed had long since been lost, because there wasn't a whiff of humanity visible. A shiver raced down her spine at the memory.

Money. Everything came down to money. The grim-faced leader calmly explained to Jill her brother was beholden to him, owed him a debt. A rather large sum he'd racked up, and he was late paying it back. Dante's pleading look from swollen and bruised eyes tugged at her, but she'd sworn she wasn't giving him any more money. Over the last several months, he'd been hitting her up for small amounts. Fifty here, a hundred there, but she'd finally wised up and cut him off.

Until that night.

"Jill?"

She shook her head and took a step back. "Sorry, I was thinking about how much more I've gotta do to get this place open." Grinning up at her baby brother, she noticed how tall he'd gotten. When had her little bro grown up?

"Well, I'm here. How can I help?

"Wait, you're serious? You're volunteering to work? Okay, who are you and where is my real brother?"

"Don't be a dork. I'm a pretty decent worker. At least, that's what Frank says. If business keeps picking up, he's going to give me some more hours."

Jill hugged Dante, squeezing extra hard, because this was the best news. "That's great! I am so proud of you. You've really turned things around."

Dante's expression turned serious. "I had my eyes opened the hard way. When they threatened you, threatened our folks—Jilly, I know I'm a stone-cold idiot. I'll never be able to say I'm sorry enough for what I put you through, but at least I can be your muscle around here. You know, since you're so puny."

"I'll puny you," Jill quipped, taking a playful swat at him.

"Seriously, Sis, I've got a few hours. Put me to work."

Giving him a playful push, she pointed him toward the back, which still needed the most work. During her late night work-a-thons, she'd focused most of her attention on fixing up the public area. The equipment supply place in Austin couldn't get the ovens or industrial refrigeration units to her for another two weeks, so she'd directed her energies into cleaning and sprucing up the area people would see first.

The kitchen area, on the other hand, needed a heavier hand. Ms. Patti was coming on Saturday and bringing along Douglas and 'extra hands', as she'd put it. Jill knew that meant one or more of the Boudreau brothers would be corralled into doing all the heavy lifting. But with Dante here, she might as well let him reach the things she couldn't. Like those giant cobwebs on the light fixtures and in the corners, and running a broom over the highest parts of the walls. They needed a good cleaning before any painting could be done.

"Uh, maybe I spoke too soon. It's gonna take a miracle worker to get this ready."

"Well, it'll only get done if we do it. There's a ladder leaning against the back wall, next to the door. Grab it, and let's get busy."

Dante gave her a jaunty salute. "You're the boss."

And didn't that have a nice ring to it? Jill smiled, hands on her hips, and looked around her tiny kingdom.

He's right. I am the boss, and I'm going to succeed. Nothing and nobody is going to stop me. Look out, Shiloh Springs, because I'm about to rock your world.

Friday afternoon, Lucas pulled up in front of Frank's Garage. He'd been partway to the Big House when he'd heard the sputtering and sizzling sound, one he recognized. The water pump was going out, and he'd babied, begged, and pleaded with his car to make it to town. Parking in front of one of the open bays, he climbed out and headed toward a pair of coverall-encased legs beneath a car with the hood raised.

"Frank?"

"Be with ya in a sec," came the gruff reply from beneath the car.

Lucas headed toward the tiny one-room office, where Frank did all his billing. There were two metal folding chairs sitting beneath the one window, currently covered with blinds. A blinking neon sign flashed over a metal desk, stacked high with papers and folders, with no rhyme or reason and most definitely no organization Lucas could fathom. Digging in his pocket, he pulled out enough money to grab a Dr Pepper from the machine, because he knew

Frank's be-with-ya-in-a-sec could mean anything from a couple of minutes to half an hour, depending on how much cursing came from the garage.

He got lucky, because it was only five minutes before Frank ambled into the office, wiping his hands on an oily cloth. A huge grin broke across his face when he spotted Lucas.

"Long time, no see. How's the big city treating ya?"

"Can't complain. I'm home for a visit, and it sounds like the water pump quit."

"What are ya driving these days?"

"Same thing I'm always driving, Frank. The old Impala you gave me when I turned eighteen."

Frank chuckled and then started to cough. Lucas rushed across the space and thumped him on the back a couple of times. He didn't like the sound coming from his friend. Watched the older man run his hand across his mouth, and give an almost imperceptible wince.

"Can't believe you still got her. She's a beaut. You better be treating her good."

"Like a princess. She's got her own parking space in a garage, so she's out of the elements, and I make sure she's kept in tiptop condition. But she's over twenty years old, so normal wear and tear happens."

"Lemme take a look see. Water pump, huh?"

Lucas followed Frank out to the Impala and popped the hood. He bent over and took a look, and then a deep breath.

"Well, looks like you're right. I gotta check to see if I've got the part in stock. If not, I'll have to get it from Austin, and it might be tomorrow before it gets here. You okay with that?"

"Not going anywhere, so it's fine."

Frank closed the hood, and ran a hand over it lovingly. "She's looking good. Glad you're taking care of her. Grand lady she is, treat her right and she'll be on the road for another twenty, maybe thirty years."

"And if I have my way, she'll still be mine. You know I love the old gal." Lucas patted the hood lovingly. "I remember the summer we worked on her together. She wasn't much to look at, but by the end of August, she was purring like a kitten with a belly full of cream. And since that television show has an Impala in it, you should see the looks my baby gets when I turn her loose on the streets."

Frank gave a gruff laugh. "Don't tell anybody, but I watch that show, so I can see the cars. Especially the ones the old guy has in his junkyard."

Lucas bit his cheek to hold back his laugh. He'd guessed Frank would know about the cult classic supernatural show. It was a little bit quirky—like Frank himself.

"Need a lift? Dante should be back any minute, and he can give ya a ride."

"Dante? You mean Dante Monroe?"

Frank nodded and headed back for the office. "Yeah, he's been helping out around here part-time. Kid's a bit flighty, but he's got a good heart. Heard he had a bit of a problem in the past, but he's buckled down and got his head on straight."

Lucas thought about Jill's little brother. He hadn't seen much of him since he'd been back this time, except once at her place only in passing. Dante had encouraged his sister to go out with him.

"I'm good. I'll call and have one of my brothers pick me up."

"Alrighty. I need to get back under that one." He gestured toward the foreign sedan he'd been working on when Lucas pulled up. "It's a righteous mess. I wish people took care of their cars, but most of 'em today think of cars as disposable. Mess one up, get another." He shook his head, laid on the mechanic's creeper, and slid under the sedan.

Lucas headed to Frank's office, pulling his cell out of his pocket. Which brother should he call? Before he could decide, a white Toyota pulled up and parked beside the garage. Dante jumped from the driver's seat, a paper sack in one hand. Tall and slender, he'd matured a bit since Lucas left Shiloh Springs. He hadn't kept tabs on the younger man; it hurt too much to think about anything connected with Jill.

"Hey, Lucas! That your Impala out front? She's really something!"

"Thanks. Got her from Frank when I turned eighteen. Have had her ever since."

"What's wrong with it?"

"Water pump went out."

Dante nodded. "Frank will get her fixed right up. Gimme a second, I've got to let Frank know his food's here."

"No problem. I need to call one of my brothers to give me a ride."

Dante stopped in his tracks and looked over his shoulder. "I can take you wherever you need. Besides, I'd like the chance to catch up a bit. It's been a while since we talked."

Zap.

"Sure. Thanks, I'd appreciate it."

Lucas wasn't sure why his instinct was screaming for him to take the ride from Dante; all he knew was it hadn't steered him wrong yet. Now all he had to do was figure out what triggered his investigator's radar, and the only way to do that was to talk.

With Dante.

CHAPTER NINE

J ill looked up at the sound of the front door opening, and watched as a stream of Boudreau men walked through, arms loaded with cleaning supplies, buckets, mops, brooms, and about every other cleaning supply she could imagine. She didn't even try to hide her grin, and directed them to where they could unburden themselves of all the goodies. Trust Ms. Patti to be true to her word, because she'd sent enough help that the bakery could be cleaned from top to bottom with ease.

"I can't thank you enough. There's a ton of work still, and I honestly can't imagine how I'd get it done without y'all pitching in."

Douglas strode over and placed his hand on her shoulder. "We're more than happy to help out, Jill. My wife said she'd be along in a bit. She had a client meeting, and this morning was the only time available. Happens that way more often than not. Folks working Monday through Friday end up having to do all their outside meetings on the weekend. We'll manage fine. Point out what needs doing or fixing, and we'll get started."

"The kitchen area needs the most work. Follow me." She led the way through the doors separating the front of the bakery from the kitchen, and Douglas, Liam, Shiloh, Brody and Chance followed.

"There's a ladder by the back door. Dante got the cobwebs down the other night, and brushed off the walls for paint. Over there," she pointed to a stack of boxes piled against the far wall, "are new light fixtures I need to get installed. Is that something you can handle? Otherwise, I'm going to call in an electrician to put them in."

"No problem, Liam and I can handle the light fixtures. All I need to know is where you want them, and where your breaker box is."

Jill pointed to the electrical panel on the back wall, and Douglas nodded once. Taking the small notepad out of her pocket, she jotted down the light fixtures by name and where she wanted them installed. Handing the list to Douglas, he gave her a smile and walked over to Liam. Heads bent together, they talked for a few minutes, then Liam grabbed the ladder and lined it up beneath the first fixture.

Jill spun around to find the rest of the Boudreau men standing in the open doorway or leaning against a wall, watching her. Waiting for instructions. Chance was busy unloading the boxes of cleaning supplies. Every time he bent over a box, more stuff was added to the growing stack on the table, until it held a mountain of rags, sponges, soaps, bleach, degreaser, and even steel wool.

"Sorry I'm late." Lucas shouldered past Brody, and walked over to stand in front of Jill. Her heartbeat sped up until it felt like her heart would burst from her chest. Lucas' absence had been the first thing she'd noticed when the others came into the bakery, and for a fleeting second, she'd wondered if he would show up.

"Hi."

"Looks like Momma rounded up everybody who could make it. Course she promised to feed us, so that's a pretty big incentive."

"Feed you—of course. I brought stuff. For you. I mean for everybody."

Okay, stop talking. You're babbling.

Spinning around, she rushed through the door, with Brody and Shiloh moving out of her way, and darted into the front of the bakery. She'd left a big box of goodies there, knowing she'd be feeding a bunch of hungry men. Reaching for the box, a pair of masculine hands grabbed it first.

"Let me help you." Lucas' amused tone told her he knew he made her nervous. Of course, she hadn't seen him since she'd admitted to Tessa she was in love with him.

"Thanks. You can put it on the other table, beside the one where Chance unloaded the supplies."

Lucas carried the box, and as soon as he put it down, she started unloading it. The last two nights after she'd gotten home, she'd been baking like mad. It was the least she could do to show her appreciation. There were dozens of cookies, lemon bars, which she knew were Douglas's favorites, brownies and even those almond shortbread cookies with the cherries. The ones Lucas mentioned were his favorites. She'd also made a batch of peanut butter fudge, cupcakes, and blueberry and banana nut muffins. Enough to feed an army—it might be enough for a few hungry cowboys.

Paper plates, napkins, and plastic forks joined the food, and she put the empty box on the floor beneath the table.

"Everybody dig in. I'm gonna run across the street to Gracie's and grab some drinks for everybody. Back in a second."

"Thanks, Jill." Brody barely got the words out around a muffin, and she didn't even attempt fighting her grin. A chorus of happy thanks filled the air, and warmth grew inside her. This was what she was meant to do, provide a little sweetness, a little happiness through her concoctions.

"Hang on a sec, Jill. I'll go with you, help you carry stuff." Lucas matched her stride for stride. They crossed the street and walked past a couple of shops until they reached Gracie's Grounds Coffee Shop. Gracie Medeiros had moved to Shiloh Springs a couple of years back from San Antonio and opened the place. Jill knew she'd have business crossover between the two shops, since Gracie's provided hot drinks and she'd be providing sweets for those with a hankering for something to munch. It was an ideal match, and she needed to meet up with Gracie, and see if they could work out something beneficial to both their businesses.

"Hey, Gracie."

"Lucas! What a nice surprise. I heard you were back in town." Gracie came from around the counter and gave him a hug. Jill resisted the urge to reach out and grab the petite brunette by the hair and yank her out of Lucas' arms.

What is wrong with me? I don't act like this, not about any man and especially not about Lucas. He's not mine, no matter how much I wish I could change that.

"I'm taking a quick break. Turned in my last assignment, and thought I'd come home and visit with my family." He looked around at the crowded bistro tables, and chuckled. "Guess I don't have to ask how you're doing. The place gets busier every time I come by."

"Things are going well." She finally seemed to notice Jill standing quietly by Lucas' side. "Oh, hi. Good to see you, too, Jill. Didn't mean to monopolize Lucas, I was surprised to see him. What can I get you folks?"

"We've got a pretty good size order. Go ahead and handle the customers at the counter first."

"Okay. Come on up to the register when you're ready."

"Thanks, Gracie."

After she walked away, Jill studied Lucas' face, wondering if there was something between the two. Before she could think of a polite way to ask, without seeming all stalker-like, Lucas nodded toward Gracie's back.

"She helped me out on a story. About a year ago, she put me in touch with her ex. He's a cop in San Antonio. Gave me some surprisingly good intel."

"I wondered how you knew her so well. She opened the business after you moved to Fort Worth."

"Actually, Rafe introduced us on one of my visits home."

"Oh."

"I think he was trying to play matchmaker. Didn't work, since Gracie's got her eye on somebody else. Never would tell me who it was, though."

As long as it's not you, it's all good.

Once the crowd cleared, Jill placed an order for enough coffee for the entire group over at her bakery, and made an appointment to talk with Gracie in a couple days.

Grabbing their order, along with all the little extra cream and sugar packets, they headed back across the street and into the back. Jill's mouth dropped open when she spotted the table and what was left on it—which was basically a couple of oatmeal raisin cookies, one brownie, half a banana nut muffin, and crumbs. It looked like a swarm of locusts descended while she'd been gone.

"What happened?"

Shiloh shrugged, though the twinkle in his eyes belied his solemn expression. "We were hungry."

"Dude, couldn't you have saved me something? I mean, I brought you coffee."

"There's still stuff—oh, guess the vultures already picked the bones dry."

"Can we help it if Jill's the best baker in town?" Chance

reached into the box and plucked out one of the cups. "I'll probably be in here every morning once you're open, Jill. I'll have to add an hour to my daily workout, but it'll be worth it."

"Um...thanks?" Placing the box with the coffee on the table, she started handing out cups, placing creamer and sugar on an empty place by the box. "Glad you enjoyed the food."

The sound of a throat clearing behind her caused Jill to spin around, and she spotted Ms. Patti standing inside the doorway with an amused expression. "Thought you boys were supposed to be cleaning."

"They certainly cleaned me out," Jill quipped, pointing to the table, with its wadded-up napkins, paper plates, and remnants of the Boudreau's feast.

"I can see that."

"Okay, guys, coffee break's over. Back to work." Chance passed coffee to Shiloh and Brody.

"Right, like they've even started yet," Lucas whispered, making Jill smile.

"Now they've been fueled up and ready to work, I know we're going to get a lot accomplished today."

"But I didn't get anything. I knew I should have snagged some of those cookies."

"You snooze, you lose, bro." Shiloh saluted Lucas with his cup.

Jill patted Lucas' arm, and whispered, "Don't worry, I

saved some especially for you."

"You're the best." Leaning in, he kissed her on the cheek, and then grabbed a cup of coffee for himself. "Put me to work, boss lady."

"I'm thinking all of your brothers better get busy, too." Ms. Patti hefted her ever-present bag higher on her shoulder, and the boys scattered, grabbing the buckets and rags. Satisfaction lit her eyes, and Jill snickered behind her hand, watching grown men cower in the face of a five-foot nothing woman.

"Can you teach me that?"

"Hang around my boys long enough, you'll pick it up naturally."

Ms. Patti pushed back her sleeves, and put her hands on her hips, eyes surveying the room. "Douglas and Liam already started on the lights. Shiloh and Chance can deal with scrubbing the floor in the front. Lucas and Brody, I need you to run an errand."

"Of course, Momma. Whatever you need." Brody walked over and placed a kiss on his mother's cheek. Jill loved how all the Boudreaus freely expressed their affection and love for each other with little gestures and felt a bit envious. That wasn't something they'd done in her home when she'd been growing up. Oh, she never doubted her family loved her and each other, but spontaneous displays just didn't happen. An occasional hug was about the extent of any physical outpouring.

"Jill, did you make the order at the hardware store?"

"Yes, ma'am."

"Brody, you and Lucas head over to McAnaly's and pick up Jill's order. Do you have your truck? Otherwise, borrow your daddy's."

"I have mine. We'll be back in a bit."

They left, coffee cups in hand, and Ms. Patti turned to Jill. "I didn't get a chance to tell you, but I like what you've done with the place so far. Have you come up with a name yet?"

"I've been toying with a couple of things, but haven't really settled on any one yet. I kinda like Sweet Temptations or How Sweet It Is."

"Oh, I like that. How Sweet It Is. Reminds me of an old Marvin Gaye song. Douglas and I danced to that song forever. I think we wore out the album." She began humming the tune, swaying a little with the melody. Almost immediately, Douglas crossed the room and wrapped his arms around Ms. Patti from behind. It was an incongruous sight, to see this mountain of a man holding his petite wife in his arms, swaying to an old classic.

"You're singing our song." He closed his eyes and hummed along with her, his expression so full of love it brought tears to Jill's eyes. Watching these two, their love stronger than ever after all these years, gave her hope maybe one day she'd be lucky enough to have something of her own.

"Love you," Jill heard Douglas whisper to his wife, before taking her hand and spinning her out in the prettiest dance move, before twirling her back into his arms.

"Love you too, cowboy."

The moment seemed suspended in time, and Jill turned away, not wanting to intrude on the magic. The sound of splashing water and masculine chuckles caused her to turn, and she saw Chance and Shiloh watching their parents, while Liam leaned against the ladder with an indulgent expression.

"Back to work, sons." Douglas turned Ms. Patti loose and walked over to the partially unpacked box holding the light fixture. Between him and Liam, they'd already managed to hang one. Guess that explained why the kitchen area lights were turned off. There was enough sunshine spilling through the big glass block windows to see by, but Jill couldn't wait until they got the other three installed.

Grabbing a bucket, she filled it with soapy water and joined in the cleaning. Half an hour later, Brody and Lucas came back, loaded down with the buckets of paint, drop clothes, rollers, brushes, and the other stuff she'd ordered. Nibbling on her thumbnail, she hoped her business partner liked her choices, because once they started slapping paint on the walls, it was a done deal. Besides, she'd already ordered the artwork, and the sign with her logo design was simply waiting on the bakery's name.

Which they'd just chosen, she realized.

"Got everything you wanted, Jill. Mr. McAnaly said if

you need anything else, he can whip it up in a jiffy. His words exactly."

"Thanks, Brody."

"Boys, stack everything in the front, and then grab some supplies. We're going to finish up the cleaning today. Tomorrow, we paint!"

Jill fist-bumped Ms. Patti's raised hand, and everyone laughed, before hunkering down and getting to work. It was going to be a long day.

CHAPTER TEN

It was later than he'd hoped by the time Lucas caught up with Dante. After spending all day working at Jill's bakery, the place shone from top to bottom. His back ached from scrubbing windows, especially when he'd had to climb a ladder to reach the upper ones. But it had been totally worth it to see the expression on Jill's face when they'd finished. He had to admit, the place cleaned up well, and even with his limited imagination, he could picture it as someplace he'd want to spend time.

Except he wasn't going to be in Shiloh Springs long enough to enjoy the ambience or the baked goods.

He hadn't bothered going home to change, opting instead to keep on the battered and worn T-shirt and jeans he'd worn all day, figuring where he was headed, they'd help him blend in better than fancier duds. He pulled his car up alongside Dante's beat-up pickup, right on the outskirts of Shiloh Springs' county line and Burnet County. The area wasn't heavily populated, and what few buildings remained were rundown, vacant, or had for rent or for sale signs in their windows. The place was little more than a strip mall which had seen better days. A smattering of cars populated the pitted parking lot, most like their locale, weatherworn and ancient.

The passenger door opened and Dante climbed in, a baseball cap tugged down low over his eyes, a gray sweatshirt covering his torso. He probably wouldn't draw a second glance from passersby, if there'd been any.

"You sure you want to do this?"

Dante scrubbed both hands across his face, never looking at Lucas. "Tell you the truth, I'm scared. I haven't seen or talked to Junior since I promised Jill I'd quit going to his poker games. Dude, I've been cold turkey since. But it's like an itch you can't scratch, the urge to play one more hand. The promise Lady Luck will smile on you, give you the pot of gold you've always dreamed about." He sighed, long and drawn out. "This sucks."

"I'll figure out another way." Lucas reached for the ignition, and Dante grabbed his hand.

"Don't." He took a ragged breath. "I can do it, just gimme a second."

Lucas worried he might be asking too much of the younger man. He didn't want to be the reason Dante got sucked back into the life, even if he swore he could handle it. Putting anybody in danger went against Lucas' personal code of ethics, and he wasn't about to let Dante walk straight into this particular lion's den. Not if there was the slightest chance there'd be trouble.

"I can figure out another way to get the info."

"Dude, I volunteered to do this. I want to take these guys down. For you, this is all about a story, exposing the ugly side of gambling to your readers." He sat up straighter in his seat. "For me, it's a way I can prove to Jill—to myself—that I've changed."

Lucas reached into the center console and pulled out the recording equipment he'd borrowed from his brother. Ridge wanted to come along and make sure there weren't any problems or glitches, but he'd had an emergency at the last minute. Truthfully, Lucas thought his brother wanted to keep an eye on him and make sure he didn't screw up. *Once a big brother, always a big brother.*

The mic was small enough he doubted anybody would notice it, even if they frisked Dante. He had Dante pull the drawstring out from the hoodie, before sliding the mic into the opening where the drawstring would normally go. Unless somebody grabbed the guy by the collar, they'd never spot it.

Lifting the recorder, he turned it on. "Say something so we can test the mic."

"What do you want me to say? Testing one, two, three?"

Lucas played back the few brief words, and they came through loud and clear. Fingers crossed, distance wouldn't be a factor or distort the quality, though Ridge assured him it shouldn't be a problem. He used this particular model in his surveillance work, and Lucas trusted his judgment.

"You know what to do, right?"

"Easy. Go in, talk to Junior. Tell him I've got a buddy who wants to play. Give him your name—"

"Not my real name."

Dante shot him a glare which could have peeled the flesh off his bones. "I'm not an idiot. You're my friend, Luke, visiting your sister from North Carolina, and wanting to hook up in a nice friendly local game."

"Good. I'll answer easily to Luke since it's close enough."

"He might balk at first. Junior can be real picky about who he invites in. Tends to be super-suspicious of strangers."

Lucas nodded. "Which is why I need you to vouch for me. Once I'm in the game, you're out. You do not play. I'm not going to be the reason you break your word to your sister."

"Not a problem, buddy. Let's get it over with. He's gonna want to get in touch with you, kinda feel you out before he gives the okay. You good with that?"

"Yeah, I expected as much. You might mention you noticed I had a wad of cash, if you can work it into the conversation without looking obvious. Give him the number I had you put in your phone. It's a burner, so he can't track it."

"And you're gonna be out here, in case things go south?"

"I'm not going anywhere, and Rafe is a phone call away."

Dante scrubbed his palms against his jean-clad legs and nodded. "Alright. Here goes nothing."

He climbed from the car and headed toward a weather-beaten and worn storefront with the windows blacked out in places, and covered with yellowed newspapers in others. The unlit sign out front proclaimed it to be Henderson's Hardware, although a battered for rent sign in the window told its own story. Dante's shoulders were hunched, and his posture resembled that of a defeated, down-on-his-luck man, and not the young, full of life guy he knew.

Dante rapped three times on the glass front door, each spaced out and deliberate. After two beats, he knocked two more times in quick succession, and then shoved his hands into his pockets, head bowed. He stood there more than a minute, and Lucas couldn't detect any movement from inside the darkness. After what seemed an eternity, the front door opened enough for Dante to slide through.

Now all he could do was sit back and wait.

Jill finished tying the last bag of trash, and carried it out the back door, tossing it into the dumpster. Back inside, she stopped and looked around the kitchen. The amount of work they'd accomplished was astounding. Everything shone beneath the artificial lights, the floors were spotless, and the metal tabletops gleamed.

Ms. Patti promised they'd be back tomorrow after church to start painting. Things were progressing quicker than Jill thought possible, but then again, they usually did when Ms. Patti got involved. The woman could move mountains if she wanted, by sheer determination and stubbornness if she set her mind to it. And for some inexplicable reason, she'd turned all that focused attention on Jill.

Tomorrow, she'd bring in the custom artwork she'd commissioned from her friend, Harper. The peach, cream, and green colors she'd chosen for the walls and trim might seem an odd choice for a bakery to others. Most of the more contemporary ones she'd seen in the big cities like Austin and Dallas tended more toward primary, bright pops of color, eye-catching and festive. Those worked well for their clientele, but her gut felt they were too modern, too hip, for Shiloh Springs. Instead, she planned a relaxed atmosphere, a little bit country but with a contemporary appeal. A place people could walk into and relax with friends. Which she hoped was reflected in her friend Harper's art work. She also planned to have framed portraits of her baked goods along a display wall, with pretty green frames to match the trim paint. Seeing the actual cakes, pies, and other sweets in living color would hopefully encourage orders. At least that was the plan.

With an official name for her bakery, Harper could finish the design she'd come up with for the bakery's sign. Jill wanted a large chalkboard display as the backdrop behind the glass-fronted counters, with the bakery's name in the center, and hand-drawn cupcakes, cookies, macarons, and other edible goodies drawn with chalk and then sealed for a rustic yet charming image. She'd seen something similar when she'd been in Dallas, and had fallen in love with the simplicity and timelessness of the design. When she'd shown it to Harper, her friend immediately sketched the perfect display piece, everything but the bakery name.

How Sweet It Is. Jill smiled, recalling Ms. Patti and Douglas dancing in the center of the kitchen to a song only they could hear, confirming once again the name was the ideal choice.

Locking the back door, she grabbed her purse and turned off the lights in the kitchen, and pulled the keys out of her pocket. Giving the place a final onceover, she grinned, an almost giddy feeling racing through her. It finally felt real, things were falling into place, and she was getting everything she'd ever wanted.

Well, not quite, if she was honest. She didn't have the man who still held her heart. The one she'd never gotten over, no matter how hard she tried. Lucas had captured her heart when she'd barely understood what love meant, and even though he wasn't in the picture, not in any tangible way, she'd never been able to forget him, and probably never would.

"Stop daydreaming about the one that got away. You can't go back and change the past, any more than you can lasso the moon. Be happy with what you've got right in the palm of your hands, and hold on tight."

"Who are you talking to?"

Jill screamed and spun around, hands balled into fists, the keys sticking out between her fingers, feet in a fighter's stance. She'd taken self-defense classes a couple of years ago, when she'd been working late hours and going out to her car in a dark parking lot made her leery. Looked like some of those moves had stuck. She relaxed when she realized it was only Dusty Sinclair.

"You scared me half to death. What are you doing here?"

"I saw the lights on, and figured I'd better check things out. I heard you rented this space. Congratulations."

"Thanks. I'm still pinching myself, because it feels a bit surreal that in a few weeks I'll have a bakery."

Dusty grinned and pushed his cowboy hat a little farther back. "Well, I'm looking forward to it. Don't get me wrong, Daisy's Diner makes a mean breakfast, but nobody can touch your baked goods. I'll be in line opening day, I guarantee."

"Thanks, Dusty. I'm really looking forward to seeing what I can do with the place. The equipment will be here soon. Paint's going on the walls tomorrow."

"Need any help?"

Jill shook her head. "Ms. Patti's pretty much got it covered. She's corralled all her sons and Douglas, and they'll be here after church. With all those hands, it shouldn't take long."

"Well, good luck. I'll keep an eye on things when I'm

doing my rounds."

"Appreciate it."

"You need a lift home?"

Jill studied Dusty closely before shaking her head. They'd gone out a couple of times when he'd first moved to Shiloh Springs, and while he was a good man, somebody she trusted implicitly, she'd quickly figured out there wasn't a spark. As a friend, she wouldn't hesitate to call on him. Anything more simply wasn't in the cards. He was such a sweet guy, and she refused to lead him on or give him false hope.

"Thanks, I'm good."

"Alright. I'm on duty tonight, so if you need anything, give me a shout."

"I will. Thanks again for checking on the place."

"No problem. Take care, Jill."

After Dusty left, she turned off the lights and locked up. One of the things she liked about the new bakery space was its proximity to her apartment. Within walking distance, that alone would safe her tons in wear and tear on her old rust bucket of a car, not to mention gasoline costs. Turning toward home, she watched the sporadic headlights of the passing cars as she walked. It wouldn't take more than fifteen minutes to reach her apartment, and it was a gorgeous night. Nary a cloud overhead, the stars twinkled like the backdrop for a painting. Small town at nightfall, the perfect place.

She wasn't sure why, but she'd barely walked a block

before being overcome with the strangest feeling, like somebody watched her. Looking around, she didn't spot anybody. The lights on either side of the front door to the sheriff's department gleamed, illuminating the sidewalk for several feet. Yet she still felt uneasy. Not scared exactly. More like alert with a desire to be extra cautious.

Shaking her head at her vivid imagination, she walked past the sheriff's office, intent of keeping a tight rein on her thoughts. Halfway down the block, the tiny hairs on the back of her neck stood straight up, and she clutched her purse closer on her shoulder. She couldn't shake the feeling of being stalked. Hunted. And like prey, the fight or flight instinct kicked in. Adrenaline raced through her, spiking her anxiety and quickening her breathing.

Refusing to let fear dictate her actions, she sped up. But she also wasn't a fool and standing in the middle of the sidewalk with nobody around wasn't the brightest idea either.

She'd barely taken two steps when she heard it. Footsteps behind her. Like a deer caught in the headlights of an oncoming semi, she froze. There it was again—the tap, tap of heels against concrete. Her heart raced and she swallowed down the lump of fear lodged in her throat.

Refusing to act the coward, she whirled around, intent on confronting whoever was stalking her. Only there was nobody there. The sidewalk behind her stood empty, the illumination of the streetlights and from the sheriff's office the only things between the bakery and where she stood.

I'm an idiot, jumping at shadows, letting my overactive imagination run rampant. Who'd want to follow me?

Turning, she started back toward home, though the night no longer held the same beauty it had earlier. That sense of safety had disappeared and her anxiety ratcheted higher. Her pace increased with every step, until she was practically running by the time she turned the corner toward her apartment. Racing past the closed shops, she sprinted the last hundred feet to her apartment, and shoved the key into the door.

Sliding the deadbolt into place, she leaned her back against the door, the breath soughing in and out of her lungs. Eyes closed, she took steadying breaths, willing her heartbeat to slow.

She didn't understand what had spooked her or why, but she did realize one thing. Tomorrow, she was driving to the bakery.

From the shadows he watched, noted the exact instant she realized someone was following her. Her rigid posture. Hands gripping her handbag closer to her body. Cataloging every movement, he noted every nuanced action. He replayed every moment in his mind over and over, memorizing each detail later.

He'd watched her most of the afternoon and into the evening. Saw people traipsing in and out of the place on Main Street. Of course, he recognized the Boudreaus instantly. Pillars of Shiloh Springs, easily identifiable, though he rarely ventured into their beloved town. He wondered how Jill ended up on their radar. She didn't seem the type to catch the notice of the high and mighty Boudreaus. Jill's family wasn't from the same social class, didn't breathe the rarified air of the high and mighty Boudreaus.

Her footsteps quickened as she walked farther down Main Street, and his lips quirked up in a smirk. She was heading home. The place she felt safe. Would it surprise her if she knew how fragile that safety was? Would her heart race, her breaths quicken, when she realized her sanctuary had been breached before without her knowledge? Oh, he'd been careful the last time he'd visited. She never knew he'd been inside her sacred space.

But he remembered every single detail. The scent of the candle beside her bed. The brand of lotion she lovingly spread on her body each night. The feel of the sheets that touched her body with an intimate caress while she slept burned into his subconscious.

Oh, he'd been tempted to take a souvenir, a memento, something tangible and tactile he could hold in his hands whenever he thought about Jill. He remembered how strong she'd been standing up to him, her eyes flashing, contempt a visible, almost physical thing. Her brother hadn't been a challenge; no, he'd been little more than a debt to be collected. But Jill Monroe? She was a prize worth pursuing. And he intended to capture the prize.

She belonged to him.

CHAPTER ELEVEN

Lucas kept the recorder in his hand with ear buds in, listening as Dante was greeted by several people inside the old hardware store. Great location, but if people thought it was an actual hardware store, then he was Godzilla.

Most of them sounded genuinely glad to see him. The sounds in the background were muffled, almost unintelligible, the occasional whirring ring of slot machines or video poker blaring through the headphones. He shook his head, wondering why people would toss money into the electronic one-armed bandits. Sit there and plunk in coins, one after the next, hit the button and watch the wheels spin, hoping for a miracle.

It was a losing proposition, because anybody who'd done a lick of research knew they rarely paid out anything over small amounts. Enough to make the player feel like they'd hit a jackpot. Maybe it was the lure of the bright flashing lights, or the blaring winner's siren song of the sound effects. Maybe it was all the people who'd quickly gather around, rush up to congratulate the man or woman who'd won fifty or a hundred bucks, after putting at least that much or more into the machine before the big payoff. Far as he knew, those machines never paid out the big prizes. Like everything else, they were rigged because the house always walked away with the lion's share of the profits.

So far, he hadn't heard Dante mention Junior's name. Guess he hadn't spotted the other man yet. Junior ran this particular enterprise on the outskirts of Shiloh Springs County. Dante had been quick to explain Junior operated this gaming club and one other, on the other side of Santa Lucia, but he wasn't the head honcho. He didn't have a clue what the big boss' name was, though he'd had a couple of run-ins with his next in command. From the sound of it, Dante had been on the wrong side of this guy's enforcers a time or two.

"Dante, long time no see. Heard you got banned, couldn't come back to the club."

"Junior!" Lucas heard the rustle of clothing, figured the men were doing that macho-hug thing guys did. At least the mic continued functioning, because the background sounds came through.

"Yeah, I had to play it cool for a while. My sister blew a gasket when she found out. But, it's all good, coz she paid up, covered my debt. If I don't get into the hole again, everything's aces."

"Boss wasn't happy when you didn't pay. Told me to turn you away if you showed your sorry behind around here. Orders are orders, man. You understand."

"Wait, Junior! I figured the big guy wouldn't want me hanging around, but I know how to make things better."

"How're you gonna do that, bro? It's gotta be something huge, because you're banned."

"Look, there's this guy I know, he's new in town. Name's Luke. He's here visiting his sister. Guy's from back east, North Carolina I think, but that's not important. Anyway, his sister is friends with Jill, so I've seen him around a lot. Get this, dude. I overheard him asking Ike at the diner about finding a game. Ike practically laughed him out of the place, but I mentioned that I could maybe hook him up—for the right price. Junior, the dude's got a wad of cash big enough to choke a mule. Says he doesn't trust credit cards, and is paying for his trip with cash."

There was a long moment of silence, and the knot in Lucas' stomach seemed to double in size with every heartbeat. Dante had played his part perfectly, sounding eager, but not overplaying his hand. Would Junior take the bait?

"I don't know. Sounds kind of sketchy. I've got enough problems with cops sniffing around. Probably have to relocate soon, too."

"Man, I know his sister. She's cool and squeaky clean. And Luke's into real estate or something like that. He ain't no cop."

"Well, bringing in some new blood would make the boss man happy, that's for sure. How long's your friend sticking around town?"

"Couple of weeks at least. He's here celebrating his sister's engagement. I think all the wedding foo-foo stuff is driving him over the edge, and he needs something to kill time until the official engagement party or something."

Lucas shook his head. Dante was going off script, and making stuff up. Good thing this was being recorded, so he didn't screw up all Dante's hard work when Junior called. Sounded like Junior might be interested, which was a step in the right direction.

"You gonna vouch for him? Boss will hold you responsible if the dude welshes."

"I'm telling ya, Luke's got deep pockets and he's itching to play. You want to check him out? I got his phone number."

This was it. Either Junior took the dangled bait or Lucas would have to figure out another way, another angle, to get into the gaming club. He could probably find a dozen or more places like this in Dallas-Fort Worth, but his gut told him it was important to gear his story here in Shiloh Springs.

"Yeah, gimme this Luke's number, and I'll call him."

"Cool." Dante rattled off the number for Lucas' burner phone.

Okay, Dante, you've done your job, now get out of there.

"If the big boss gives the okay, are you playing tonight?" Junior's voice crackled through the mic, a bit of static obscuring the sound. Lucas kept sending mental pushes at Dante to get the heck outta Dodge.

"Can't tonight. I wanted to tell you about Luke, and make sure I'm still welcome here. Tomorrow's payday, so I'll be here. Did I tell you I got a job?"

Lucas heard laughter at Dante's words, and closed his eyes, hoping the kid wasn't overplaying his hand. He wasn't ready to have to ride to the rescue if things got ugly.

"Tell you what, Dante, you show up tomorrow and bring your friend. What's his name again—Luke?"

"Yeah. I can do that."

"Good, good. I have to get back to the paying customers." There was a moment of silence, before Lucas heard the other man's whisper. "Don't screw this up, man. Boss won't stop at beating you half to death next time, you hear me?"

Lucas could practically hear Dante swallow. "I hear ya. See you tomorrow, dude."

After that, all Lucas heard were the sounds of the make-shift casino, the bells and whistles of the slots, and a raft of voices, garbled and muffled in the earbuds. It took a few interminably long minutes before Dante finally walked out the front door, and headed straight for him. He slowed perceptibly when he reached the bumper of his pickup, parked next to Lucas, and whispered, "I'm getting in my truck. Meet me in the parking lot at Juanita's."

Lucas watched the taillights of Dante's truck until they disappeared from view, and then waited another three minutes before heading out of the parking lot, toward his meetup with Dante. He double checked, making sure nobody tailed Dante.

Less than twenty minutes later, he pulled into Juanita's parking lot. Dante's pickup sat at the back of the lot when Lucas arrived. He climbed from his truck, and walked over to lean beside Lucas' open window.

"Looks like you're in."

"You did good, Dante. Even when you improvised, you thought fast on your feet. Story is plausible, especially since you didn't give Junior a last name, so he can't really check up on me." Lucas watched the young man's chest puff up at his words of praise, and wondered if he'd ever been that young.

"You want to go in, grab a beer?"

"I can't tonight. I want to get some notes down while it's still fresh in my head. Rain check?" Lucas was itching to get back home, and make plans for the next evening. The thrill of investigating, delving into the story, rode him hard.

"No problem."

"Dante, are you sure you can handle this? I can head over there tomorrow on my own. You've laid the groundwork, and Junior knows I'm coming. If you want to step back—"

"I can do it. I won't take more than fifty bucks with me, that way I can't get in over my head." Dante's eyes met Lucas' directly. "This is my personal demon, and I'm dealing with it every day. Jill's counting on me to keep things together, and I'm not going to let her down."

"I'll front you the money; it'll come out of my expenses. And I'll explain everything to Jill. I'm serious, man, you feel the slightest bit of pressure, or think you're being pulled back in, you're out of there. Immediately."

"Can I tell you something? You gotta swear not to tell anybody, not even Jilly."

Something in the younger man's voice had Lucas straightening in his seat. Whatever he was about to say might change everything.

"You've got my word."

Dante kind of shuffled his feet, almost like a little kid, and Lucas was again reminded of how young he really was. Barely twenty-one, but sometimes he seemed a lot younger. Was he wrong for dragging Dante into this?

"I've been going to Gamblers Anonymous meetings." He held up his hand when Lucas started to interrupt. "I had to, because I never want my sister to deal with the backlash of my problem ever again. She gave up everything she had to dig me out of the bottomless pit I'd crawled into, and I will never—*never*—put her through that again. I may be stupid, but I'm not a big enough idiot I don't realize I'm not the only person who's affected by my actions."

"I'm glad you decided to get help. Even more reason to step back. You're not going tomorrow, I'll handle this."

"Nope. One thing the meetings taught me about is honesty and taking responsibility for my own actions. I've learned there are no shortcuts. First thing I had to do was admit I have a problem. Trust me, there's nothing easy about doing that, especially when you've got illusions of grandeur, thinking about all the things you'll do once you've hit that big jackpot. It's like an alluring whisper in the back of my mind, a promise of so many good things I could do if I played one more hand. Bought one more lottery ticket. With that kind of money, I could change my world."

Lucas heard what Dante said, but more importantly what he wasn't saying. He'd acknowledged he had a problem, which was a huge first step. He was being honest with himself about the hold gambling had on him, on his life. Opening his mouth, Dante cut him off again.

"Recovery isn't a fast process. There's no magic bullet. I realize I'm going to be dealing with this for the rest of my life. Have to be alert for any backsliding, because it could spell disaster for my recovery. But I can and will do this, because there's too much at stake. My parents—Jill doesn't have a clue how many times I've hit them up for money." Dante grimaced and took a deep breath. "I'm ashamed. Ashamed of what I've become. I almost cost Jilly her dream. Now, she's got a second chance, and I can't let myself fall into the abyss again."

"Which is why you're out now. I swear, if you'd told me this before, I'd never have asked you to head back into that hellhole. Tomorrow night, I'll go to the club alone. We'll work it where you call Junior, let him know something came up and you can't make it, but you've given me directions. That'll get me in the door. I'll do the rest."

Dante scrubbed his hands across his face, before leaning

further in Lucas's window. "I feel like I'm letting you down, too. It's like being caught with one foot on either side of a giant divide; one step either way and I'm going to fall."

"You're not letting me down. I'm still going to need a ton of information for this story. You're the main focus. We'll expose illegal gambling for what it is, the dirty little secret that's a multi-billion dollar industry hurting those who can least afford it. All the while, cartels and mobsters and wannabe thugs are lining their pockets with the money hardworking people risk every day. You don't have to actually go back underground to tell this story. Man, you *are* the story."

Dante scrubbed a hand over his eyes, and Lucas had the sneaky suspicion he was holding back a bellyful of emotion. No way was he letting Dante risk his newfound recovery. The plan should still work, and if it didn't, they'd come up with something else, because Dante was officially out.

"People need to know how easy it is to get sucked in. It doesn't take much, because it's so easy. I even won a few times. Nothing huge, but when you've got nothing to begin with, a couple grand makes you feel like a king."

"I'm still going to hit you up for information. All the personal stuff, how you found out about the gaming, the different levels of people, leading all the way to the top. Everything you tell me will be confidential, I swear. Nobody will know who you are, or where you live. I'm not going to mention Shiloh Springs by name. There'll be no way for anybody to identify you. I'm going in alone tomorrow. Your physical part in this is done. Over."

Dante's whole body seemed to wilt, and Lucas finally understood how stressful this had been on him. There weren't many men who'd step forward and risk a lot to expose corruption. Especially when it meant admitting his addiction, his shame, to have it splashed across headlines nationally. Lucas was positive this story would be picked up. The expose would resonate with readers and hopefully with those who could make changes.

"What if Junior gives you a hard time?"

"Let me handle Junior. I know his type; I've dealt with them before. You leave him to me, and I'll get him to lead me to the big boss."

"Be careful, Lucas. These guys play dirty, in more ways than one. If you cross them, they won't let you walk away unscathed."

Lucas turned on the ignition, then reached through the window and grabbed Dante's forearm in a firm but gentle grip. "Watch your back. And take care of Jill."

Dante drew in a deep, ragged breath. "I will. Can you call me tomorrow, so I know everything goes okay? Otherwise, I'm gonna freak."

"I'll call." He reached into his pocket and pulled out a couple of twenties and handed them to Dante. "Go have that beer, it's on me."

Dante gave him a quick grin and grabbed the money.

"That I can do. Talk to you mañana."

Lucas watched long enough to see Dante enter Juanita's place before he pulled out onto the road and headed toward home. Between the recording and what Dante had admitted to about Gamblers Anonymous, he had a lot to think about.

Tomorrow night was the first step. If he was smart, careful, and a little bit lucky, he'd get enough evidence not only for his story, but for Rafe and the district attorney to close the places down. While it was a mere drop in the bucket when it came to illegal activities, at least he'd feel good about getting it out of his home town.

But first, he had plans that had nothing to do with games of chance, and everything to do with a pretty baker name Jill.

CHAPTER TWELVE

Jill double checked the deadbolt on her door for the fifth or sixth time. She lost count, but her heart rate had finally slowed down enough she could catch her breath. Tossing her purse on the console table by the front door, she walked over and plopped down on the sofa, and did a few deep breathing exercises.

I'm being paranoid. Nobody was following me. It's my imagination playing tricks, that's all.

When her cell phone rang, she gave a little yelp, her hand against her heart, then laughed at her reaction. "Great, now I'm jumping at the phone."

She walked over and dug her phone out of her purse, smiling when she spotted Lucas' name on the screen.

"Hi."

"I'm driving home, and thinking about you. I needed to hear your voice."

Curling back up on the corner of the couch, she snuggled against the cushions. "I'm glad you called. Helps take my mind off other things."

He must have heard something in her voice, or maybe

her tone, because when he spoke it was all gruff and serious sounding. "What other things? Is anything wrong?"

"Nothing's wrong. At least, I don't think anything's wrong."

"What's that mean exactly?"

"It's probably nothing. I got a little spooked walking home from the bakery. You know that feeling you get when it seems like somebody's watching you? Only I didn't see anybody."

"You're okay?"

"I'm fine. The deadbolt's on the door. Although I swear I'm driving to the bakery tomorrow."

"I'm coming over."

Her eyes widened, and she blinked a couple of times before she managed to sputter out a reply. "Why? I mean, that's very sweet, but unnecessary. It was dark and my imagination played tricks on me. Nobody followed me home. Why would they?"

Lucas sighed. "I forget sometimes how things are different here than where I live. In the city, you never walk anywhere at night. Nine-one-one is your friend, and you'd probably have it on speed dial."

Jill chuckled. "If I called 911 here, Sally Anne would never let me live it down. I guess I was a little jumpy because Dusty stopped by the bakery and startled me. He saw the lights on and was double checking that everything seemed okay. I didn't hear him at first, so I'm guessing my nerves were still a little rattled, and made me jump at shadows."

"If you're sure, because I can be there in less than five minutes."

"That's sweet, Lucas, but really, I'm fine. Are you coming by tomorrow after church?"

"Absolutely. Momma's rounding up everything, and we'll knock out the rest of the cleanup and painting in no time."

Jill looked down and saw her free hand still trembled, and balled it into a fist. Everything she'd told Lucas was the truth; she probably was jumping at shadows, but the adrenaline high still rode her. What she needed was a hot bath and a good night's sleep, and she'd forget all about boogeymen stalking her through the streets of Shiloh Springs.

"Good. Monday they're going to be delivering the glass-fronted display cases, and Harper is working on the store's sign. It's going to be amazing. Wait until you see it."

"I'm looking forward to it. Whatever you've chosen will be perfect, I'm sure."

"Thanks. I—I better let you go. I'm going to take a hot bath and then grab some shuteye. Tomorrow's going to be a long day."

"Goodnight, Jill. Sweet dreams. Promise you'll call if you need me for anything."

Jill hesitated for a brief second. "I promise." She crossed her fingers at the half-truth. If there was a problem, she'd called the sheriff's office, because she wouldn't let herself get used to having Lucas ride to the rescue. He'd head back to Dallas-Fort Worth soon, and she wasn't about to risk her heart again. It had already been broken once, and she didn't think she could handle having it shattered again, because this time she knew she wouldn't be able to pick up the pieces and start over.

"Jill?"

"I'm fine. I've double checked the locks and the windows. Go home and get some rest. Good night, Lucas."

She disconnected the call, leaned her head against the cushions, and closed her eyes. All she could do was take things one day at a time, until he left Shiloh Springs. Thank goodness, she had the bakery to keep her busy and her mind focused on something besides Lucas.

Lucas booted up his laptop and opened his e-mail program. There was the usual junk, all the unsolicited nonsense that he had to wade through and delete before he got to the actual important stuff. There was an e-mail from one of his buddies who worked on the West Coast, who needed a reference. No problem, he could handle that in the morning. Another one from his brother, Heath. Immediately, he grabbed his cell phone and dialed, because knowing his brother, he'd still be awake, even with the time difference.

"Evening, Lucas." Heath's grinning face appeared on his phone, and Lucas returned his grin. It was good to see his brother smiling, because he'd seemed weary to his soul the last time he'd seen him.

"Howdy, bro." Lucas put the full effect of his Texas drawl into his greeting, drawing out the three syllables into a much longer sentence, and was rewarded by his brother's chuckle. "What's up with the cryptic e-mail?"

"I wanted to talk to you."

"I got that. But did you have to make your e-mail sound like it was life or death? All you had to do was pick up the phone, you know."

"I talked with Dad. He told me the lead he and his buddies gave you on Renee came up empty."

Lucas leaned back, and closed his eyes, pinching the bridge of his nose before opening them to stare at Heath. "Yeah. Wasn't a total bust, but she'd already moved on by the time I could check it out. I'm trying not to lose hope, but sometimes…"

"On the plus side, you know she's still alive and kicking. That's good news, even if you're still on the hunt."

"If this turns out to be her. We still aren't one hundred percent sure. Anyway, what'd you want to talk to me about?"

Heath shrugged, his big shoulders filling the lower half of the phone's screen. "That's the thing, I wanted to talk to you about Renee. When Dad told me about the lead he'd gotten, he gave me the name your sister used, but I couldn't remember it."

"Elizabeth. Elizabeth Reynolds. That's the name she used in Cincinnati." Lucas swallowed past the lump lodged in his throat when he gave Heath his sister's name. Not that he gave a fig about what she called herself. All he wanted was to find her, make sure she was safe and happy. Let her know she wasn't alone in the world, and if she'd have him, he'd be a part of her life.

"That's it! I knew it sounded familiar." Heath grinned, and Lucas felt the corners of his mouth tic upward in response. "One of the newbies and I were working a case together. Nothing big, the kid's still wet behind the ears, and needed a chaperone, you know what I mean?"

"Sure. I remember when you were the wet-behind-the-ears-punk."

"Stuff it, bro. He transferred to the DC office from Portland, Oregon. Been here about three months. Anyway, we're sitting in the car, staking out this place where they were moving illegal alcohol shipments, and he starts talking about this girl he'd been dating back home. Get this, her name was Lizzie Reynolds. Cute little redhead with green eyes."

Lucas' heartbeat raced in his chest, beating so fast he thought he might be having a heart attack. What were the odds? Was it possible that Heath's Lizzie Reynolds was the Elizabeth Reynolds he was looking for? Could it be?

"Before you say anything, hang on, okay?"

"Why?" Lucas bit out the word.

"I got Chuck to show me a picture of his gal pal. I gotta say, bro, she looks a heck of a lot like you. A more girly version, but pretty darn close."

"Heath—"

"Check your text messages. I sent you something."

Lucas heard the familiar tone beep, and pulled up the screen. The photo was a little grainy, but the tight squeezing around his heart spoke louder than any words. *Renee.* There wasn't a shadow of doubt Lizzie Reynolds was his baby sister, Renee O'Malley.

"Bro, did you get it?" At Heath's worried look, Lucas chuckled, though it had a ragged and slightly watery sound.

"Yeah, I got it. It's her. Heath, that's Renee."

"Son of a biscuit! I knew it!" Heath's triumphant yell reverberated through the cell phone. His brother's colorful turn of phrase made Lucas laugh, because for such a big man, at six foot five, and two hundred and twenty pounds, he refused to curse. Swore he'd learned his lesson the hard way when Ms. Patti washed his mouth out with Lava soap. Instead, he came up with a variety of old-fashioned terms and euphemisms whenever he needed to replace his swear words.

"Your buddy, Chuck, was it? He got an address for Lizzie?"

"I wanted to make sure it was her first before he gave me the information. He did mention she seemed like a bit of a loner. Didn't have a lot of friends, far as he knew. He met her at the gym in their apartment building, and struck up a friendship. So, yeah, he's got an address. If he won't give it up, I'll simply dig it out of his records, coz I can do that." Heath's eyes lit with amusement before he sobered. "This is it, bro. If you want or need me to go with you, say the word, and I'll be right by your side."

Warmth built inside Lucas at his brother's offer and he remembered the conversation he'd had with Dane. His brother was right. Being a Boudreau meant more than sharing blood. They were brothers through choice, and at times like this it made his decision all the sweeter, knowing his family had his back no matter what.

"Thanks, I can't tell you what it means to hear you say that. Talk to your newbie, get the address and text it to me. I'll let you know my plans after I've checked some stuff out."

"Will do. I'm only a call away. I've got a good feeling this time, bro. You're finally gonna find your sister."

"I'm trying not to get my hopes up, but this feels right. I'll talk to you soon."

"Wait, hold on." Heath leaned in closer to the screen. "A little birdie told me you're seeing Jill Monroe again."

Lucas' laughter burst forth. "Tell Nica to mind her own business."

Heath's laughter mingled with his own before he disconnected the call. His mind raced through all the possible scenarios, yet with each one he still felt hope growing. After all these years, was it possible he'd finally find Renee?

Closing his laptop, he leaned back against the couch cushion and closed his eyes. Tomorrow, he'd start looking into this new lead, but for now, he'd think about Jill, and maybe check into whether she had a mysterious stranger following her.

CHAPTER THIRTEEN

Jill raced home after church long enough to change from her nicer outfit into a pair of paint-splattered jeans and a T-shirt, and pulled her hair into pony tails on each side of her face. Grabbing her bag, she sprinted toward her car, stuttering to a stop when she noted it listing to the left.

Glancing at the front driver's tire, she instantly spotted the problem. It was flat. She squatted down and ran her hand over the black rubber. It felt spongy beneath her fingers. Standing, she wiped her hand on her jean-clad leg, and turned toward the rear of the car, intent of getting out the spare. Only then did she spot the rear tire was flat, too.

Hands on hips, she stared at the second tire, and pondered her luck. Seemed like today kept going from bad to worse. First thing this morning, the hot water hadn't worked right, and she'd ended up having to rush through a cold shower in order to be on time for Sunday services. Fine, she could deal with that. Then her car, which had seemed okay all the way to church, or at least as all right as it ever was, started making odd noises on her way home. The old rust bucket, as she called it, made strange wheezing sounds whenever she accelerated over thirty most of the time, and rattled and shimmied at any speed over forty-five, but she hadn't noticed anything wrong with the tires. Now she stood starting at two flats.

"Can this day get any worse?"

"Got a problem, Jill?"

Jill spun round, a hand across her racing heart, and stared at Douglas Boudreau. She blew out a shaky breath, thankful he'd shown up, even if she hadn't been expecting him. Too bad he'd scared a couple of years off her life.

"Sorry, you startled me. And, yes, I've got a bit of a problem." She pointed toward the car. "Two flats. Guess it isn't my day."

"Let me take a look. Maybe you ran over something in the road and didn't notice at the time. Happens that way sometimes."

"Thanks, Douglas." She watched him squat down beside the car, and feel around the wheel, exactly as she'd done moments earlier. He moved with ease for such a large man, and gave a final check of the rear tire before standing.

"I can't see anything which might've caused them to go flat from looking at them. I'll give Frank a call. I'm sure he can get you fixed up pretty quick."

"That's okay," she protested, "I'll call Dante. He's working with Frank now. I'm pretty sure he can change the tires, get me a couple of retreads until—"

Douglas's large hand on her shoulder stopped the rest of

her words, and he squeezed gently. "You've got enough on your plate, let me handle it. Ms. Patti sent me by to help you with some food. She mentioned you were bringing refreshments for the boys."

Jill slapped her palm against her forehead. "The food! I don't know what's wrong with me today. I completely spaced out about the stuff I was bringing. It's still in the apartment."

"Good thing I showed up then."

"I swear I can't seem to remember anything recently. Between the forgetfulness and my overactive imagination, I'm probably going to end up talking to myself."

"Tell you what," Douglas' smile was like a beam of sunshine straight to her soul, filled with a warmth and compassion, a balm to her frazzled nerves, "let's get the food and anything else you need loaded into my trunk, and you can call Dante on the way. Sound like a plan?"

"You, sir, are a lifesaver."

Douglas walked her back to her apartment and within a few minutes, they'd loaded up the boxes Jill packed earlier, along with the cooler filled with drinks. She must've really been distracted to have forgotten something she'd worked on all morning before church. Shaking her head at her own folly, she climbed into the passenger seat, and gave a final glance toward her car. It looked forlorn and a little pathetic, listing to the side with the two flat tires. It kind of reminded her what her life had been like up until recently.

Before she knew it, they'd arrived at the bakery. Douglas pulled around the block and drove down the alley behind the storefronts, and parked at the back door. Jill sat a little straighter in the seat and looked around. She'd been in and out of the back door multiple times, but she'd never really paid much attention. Seeing it now, she grinned. If she drove to work, she'd have her own parking here in the back, and wouldn't take valuable real estate away from paying customers who wanted to park in front. Plus, it was only a few feet from the back door to the parking space. It gave her a feeling of safety and relieved the secret fear that had taken hold of her the night before. No more worrying about strangers following her.

"I talked with Liam. He's going to install a couple of lights back here, the kind that'll come on at dusk and turn off at dawn."

"Thank you. Tell him to send me the bill, and I'll..." Her words trailed off at Douglas' scowl. Wow, that wasn't an expression she'd seen on his face before, and honestly? She didn't want to see it again, especially directed at her.

"We don't charge family."

There it was. The royal Boudreau decree. She'd been accepted as part of the Boudreau clan, something she'd never imagined in her wildest dreams, and the warm glow deep in the pit of her stomach spread upward until her whole body felt encased in happiness.

"Thank you, Douglas."

His single nod told her more than mere words how he felt, and she waited quietly, still a little stunned at his pronouncement, while he strolled around the car and opened her door. Clicking his key fob, the trunk slid open, and he walked over to the bakery's back door and gave a couple of hard raps. Only a few seconds passed before it swung inward and Chance stuck his head through the opening.

"Dad?"

"Come help me with these boxes. Jill, you go ahead inside, we've got this covered."

Knowing she'd been dismissed, she smiled at Chance and walked inside, marveling again at how much they'd accomplished the day before. The overhead lighting fixtures illuminated every inch of the kitchen, which was spotless. The floors shone beneath the glow, clean as a whistle. They wouldn't stay that way for long, not with all the work still to be done, but for the moment, everything seemed perfect.

Voices from the front drew her, and she pushed open the door between the kitchen and the front area, and spotted Ms. Patti, Antonio, Serena, and Nica spreading canvas tarps on the floors. Tessa was taping the edging around the windowsills, and Rafe teased her about how she was doing it wrong. Her hand flew to her mouth to hold back her laugh when Tessa threw the roll of tape at him.

"If you think you can do a better job, do it yourself, hotshot."

He caught the tape one-handed, and grabbed Tessa

around the waist, pulling her in for a quick kiss, before taking over where she'd left off.

"Jill, good, you're here. I think we've got everything pretty much ready to go. All you need is to point out where you want what colors, and let's put these lazy people to work." Ms. Patti gave her a wink, amusement coloring her gaze.

"Right, gotcha." She pointed to the can of light cream-colored paint. "This color is going on all of the walls except that one." Indicating the one wall between the bakery's front and the kitchen, she picked up a can of the peach-colored paint. "This color is going on the dividing wall, as a backdrop accent color behind the shop's sign."

"Oh, I like that color." Nica picked up the can and examined the splotch painted on the lid. "It'll go great with the sage green color. Where are you using it?"

"The green is for the beadboard wainscoting and the baseboards. Also for the trim around the windows."

"Nice color choices," Ms. Patti added with a smile. "Not that I'd expect anything else. I've always said you have a lovely sense of style and color."

You did? I never knew that.

"I'm not sure what I expected. Whenever I think about a bakery, I'm always thinking trendy, bright colors, primary colors like red, and blue, and yellow." Serena picked up a roller and an empty paint tray and gave Jill a smile. "I like this better. Sometimes all the overabundance of color makes it a little too, I don't know, frenetic? Doesn't make me want to linger because it's too overwhelming to the senses."

Reaching around Jill, she grabbed the can of peach paint from Nica. "Gimme. I'm going to start on the back wall there."

"Hey, wait! I was going to work on that one."

Serena grinned at Nica. "You snooze, you lose, sister!" At the disappointed expression on Nica's face, she relented. "Grab a paintbrush. You can cut in the edges while I roll, how's that?"

"Deal."

Douglas and Chance came through the kitchen entrance, arms loaded down with boxes, and Chance also carried the cooler. Ms. Patti immediately took charge, directing the men on where everything should be placed. She winked again at Jill, then began assigning jobs, delegating like a Marine Corps drill sergeant who'd brook no backtalk. Not that she got any. Everybody knew when Ms. Patti was in the room, she was in charge. Well, everyone but Douglas. There wasn't a single doubt he was the family's patriarch, who ruled with a firm yet loving hand. He was simply smart enough to step aside and let Ms. Patti do her thing, while he smiled indulgently. The love shining in his eyes spoke more eloquently than any words, and Jill envied their shared affection and devotion.

Within minutes, everybody knew what their job was and dug in with an exuberance that defied description. Paint started going up on the walls, while Tessa carried a bucket of hot soapy water outside, and began scrubbing the big window out front.

"Where do you need me, Ms. Patti?"

"We'll be in the back, dear. I want to go over our list, make sure we've covered all the bases, and everything you need has been ordered."

"Hang on a sec, darlin'." Douglas walked over to stand beside his wife, his large stature nearly dwarfing her. "Jill had a bit of an issue before we got here." He looked at her, brow quirked, as if silently asking if she wanted him to say anything.

"Thanks for reminding me. I better call Dante and have him pick up my car."

"Car trouble? Douglas, why didn't you call Frank?"

"Jill wanted to call her brother to handle it. He's working at Frank's garage now, and I didn't want to overstep."

Ms. Patti's hand on her arm startled Jill for a second. "Is there anything we can do? Shiloh's car's up at the Big House if you need a loaner for a bit. He's back in San Antonio, I'm sure he won't mind you borrowing it."

She couldn't help but be touched by the offer. "It's nothing mechanical. Just a flat tire. Dante will have it fixed and back to me by this evening, I'm sure."

Douglas cleared his throat, but didn't rat her out, which she appreciated. "Good thing you sent me along to help her. I found her in the complex's parking lot."

Ms. Patti's hand cupped his cheek, and she smiled. "Thank you, honey." Turning, she met Jill's gaze. "You go ahead and call Dante, and get your car handled. We've got this. Take your time. Nica, stop playing around. Serena doesn't need a peach-colored streak in her hair." With that, she was off across the room, whispering something to her daughter.

"You didn't want my wife to know about you having two flat tires?"

Jill ducked her head before answering. "It wasn't intentional. I said flat tire, and then I realized if I corrected myself, it would make it sound like a bigger deal than it really is."

She could almost feel Douglas studying her, weighing her words. Darn it, he was one of the most astute men she'd ever met, and one of the best judges of character. She needed to somehow divert his attention, or he'd get suspicious that it was more than simply running over something in the road. Which it probably was, right? Nobody had messed with her car. There was no reason they would. Like nobody had followed her the night before.

"Jill, you want to tell me what's really going on?" His deep voice held concern with an underlying thread of steel which refused to be ignored. She couldn't help wondering how many times his sons had heard that exact tone when they'd been growing up. And since he seemed insistent, she wasn't about to lie to him. The Boudreaus had been good to her, and she wasn't about to do anything to tarnish their trust.

"I...it's probably nothing. I thought somebody was following me last night after I left here. It's silly, because I looked and there was nobody around. Just an overactive imagination working overtime."

"Did you call Rafe?"

She shook her head. "Honestly, it's nothing. Dusty even stopped by last night when he saw the lights on. Nobody would have been hanging around if they saw a deputy talking to me, right? Oh, I did mention it to Lucas last night when he called."

"He wasn't concerned?"

Jill felt a blush heat her cheeks. "He wanted to come over and make sure I was okay. I convinced him everything was fine, and that I'd see him today. Really, Douglas, the tires are simply bad luck. Dante will get me fixed up good as new."

Douglas did something then that shocked Jill speechless. He pulled her into his arms, hugging her tight. After a second or two, she returned his embrace, allowing his sense of calm and stillness to sweep through her, and she felt a wave of acceptance fill her that brought tears to her eyes. She blinked them back, hoping nobody noticed.

"I need to make that call, get hold of my brother." She gave him a final squeeze and stepped back, only then noticing the utter silence surrounding them. Everyone had stopped working and stared at them. Once again, she felt a wash of heat fill her cheeks. She wasn't used to being the center of attention, although nobody seemed all that surprised to find her in Douglas' arms. Ms. Patti smiled indulgently. Nica grinned from ear to ear. Serena gave her a surreptitious thumb's up.

"If you need anything," Douglas whispered in her ear, "day or night, you call me, you hear? I want your word, Jill."

She drew in a shaky breath, and nodded. "I promise."

Dipping his head once in acknowledgement, he walked over and put his arm around Ms. Patti, and surveyed everyone standing around. "Back to work, people. Walls ain't gonna paint themselves."

Paintbrushes slapped against the wall, and rollers began spreading paint at a rapid rate before he'd finished his sentence. He bent down and whispered something in Ms. Patti's ear, and at her nod, he placed a kiss against her cheek and walked out through the kitchen door.

"Jill, why don't you and I unload the food and drinks? By the time we're done, this crew is going to have worked up an appetite."

"Yes, ma'am. Give me a second to call Dante, and then I'm all yours."

Dante agreed to head over to her apartment and handle changing the tires on her old sedan as soon as he let Frank know what was going on. Said he could get a couple of retreads on and it wouldn't break the bank, which was a good thing because her savings account was on life support.

She'd get her final paycheck in a few days, which would help because the insurance company was paying her for all the vacation and sick time she had banked, which was a lot since she'd never taken any time off.

After getting his promise to have her car ready by later that afternoon, she turned around, and couldn't hold back her smile. Watching all her friends, and she'd come to think of all of them as friends, pitching in and helping out made her feel more like a part of the community than she'd felt in a very long time.

For the first time, she allowed herself to realize everything in her future looked bright. She crossed her fingers, and wished with all her might for her happy ending. With a contented sigh, she joined Ms. Patti and started laying out the sandwiches, cookies, and brownies.

Even with a rotten start, it was turning into a pretty good day.

CHAPTER FOURTEEN

"**S**on, you got a minute?"

Lucas rested his phone between his shoulder and chin while he continued typing on his laptop. "Sure, Dad, what's up?"

"I want to talk to you about Jill."

Lucas paused at the serious note in his father's voice. "Jill? What about her?"

"Your mother sent me over to Jill's apartment after church, asked me to help her with the food she was bringing to the bakery. When I got there, I found her standing in the parking lot staring at two flat tires."

"Two? Had they been tampered with?" As soon as the words left his mouth, Lucas winced, knowing his father would immediately pick up on his underlying suspicion.

"I'm not sure yet. I didn't see any outward sign of tampering, but I didn't want to spend too much time looking, because I didn't want to worry Jill. I also wanted to get her over where your mother and brothers could keep an eye on her, while I talked with you. Tell me what's going on."

"I'm not sure. Might be nothing." Lucas pushed the

laptop farther back on the coffee table, and leaned against the sofa cushions. "I talked to her last night. She mentioned she thought somebody was following her, and tried to make it seem like her imagination. Now I'm not so sure."

"She mentioned something about that when I pressed her. I don't like thinking somebody's messing with her. Think I should talk to Rafe about this?"

"I'll tell him, Dad. Is Frank going to tell you what he finds out?"

"She wouldn't let me call him. Her brother, Dante, is going to fix the flats for her. She mentioned something about getting a couple of retreads."

"What? Nope, not letting that happen. I know money's tight for her right now—"

"Why?"

Lucas wasn't sure how to answer his father's question, but knew if he asked, his father wouldn't tell anybody what he was about to divulge. "Dad, you can't tell anybody what I'm about to tell you. Jill's broke. She used every dime of her savings to pay off her brother's gambling debt. Wait...wait, before you say anything, Dante got in over his head and lost big in an illegal poker tournament. They beat the crap out of him, then took him to Jill and said they'd cripple him if she didn't pay."

Lucas heard his father's whistle over the phone. "I never suspected Dante had a problem. Where'd he even find a high stakes game around here?"

"I'll tell you all about that later. Matter of fact, that's the new story I'm writing, about the personal consequences of illegal gambling in Texas. Dante's been key in getting me introduced to the right people. He's been going to Gamblers Anonymous, trying to get his head on straight. But in the meantime, Jill lost everything she'd been saving for years to open her bakery."

"Got two choices here. You want to talk to Dante and tell him to put four new tires on her car, or you want me to?" Lucas could hear the smile in his dad's voice, knew he'd handle Dante the same way he'd done all his boys. Dante wouldn't know what hit him. It was almost tempting to sit back and watch his father handle Jill's brother, but he'd rather do it. He'd been working to build a relationship with the younger man, and pulling his dad into the mix might stir up more problems than it solved.

"I'll talk to Dante as soon as we hang up. Jill's at the bakery with Momma?"

"She's well protected, son. We won't let anything happen to your gal."

Funny how right that sounded.

"Thanks, Dad."

"I'm gonna want to hear everything. Plan on meeting me for coffee in the morning." Lucas knew an order when he heard one.

"Yes, sir."

"Right answer. Now I need to get back inside, because

I'm hungry and I want to grab something before your brothers eat everything but the wrappers. Call me when you hear something. Oh, and tell Frank to put those new tires on the family account." He hung up before Lucas could sputter out a response. Trust his dad to have the last word.

Pulling up his contacts, he speed-dialed Dante's number. He answered on the first ring.

"Hey, dude, what's up?"

"I heard Jill had a little mishap with her tires."

"Wow, word travels fast. She called me, asked me to get her fixed up this afternoon."

Afternoon already? Where had the day gone? He felt like he'd barely sat down to go over the info Heath had sent about his sister, and half the day disappeared. "Do me a favor. When you check out the tires on Jill's car, let me know if anything looks suspicious."

There was silence on the phone for a couple of beats before Dante asked, "What's going on? You wouldn't be asking me unless you're thinking—wait—are you thinking somebody's after my sister?"

"Calm down. I don't think anything." *Yet.*

"Yeah, right. Why don't I believe you?"

Lucas knew Dante was bright, and he'd figure things out fast, whether he told him anything or not. Couldn't hurt having an extra set of eyes keeping watch over Jill. "It's probably nothing, but having two flat tires at the same time seems a little…unusual. Maybe she ran over something in the road, and it's no big deal. I'm curious; it's part of my nature. It's why I became a reporter, because I get to ask all sorts of questions and get answers I might not otherwise get."

"And? Because I know there's more to this."

"Okay, and Jill might have mentioned she thought somebody followed her home last night. Wait, before you jump to conclusions, she checked and didn't see anybody. She thinks it's her imagination playing tricks on her."

"I'm guessing you don't, otherwise you wouldn't think twice about flat tires on somebody's car."

"Not somebody. Jill."

"Stop dancing around this, Lucas. Do you think somebody's after my sister? Is it my fault?"

"Why would it be your fault?"

"The gambling debts. I brought those guys right to her doorstep, man. If somebody's targeting my sister because I screwed up, I'll never forgive myself." Lucas heard the catch in Dante's voice.

"I don't think anything of the sort. What I think is you need to get Jill's car tires fixed. Put four brand new ones on. I'll settle up with Frank about the cost. And not a word to your sister."

"She's not going to be happy when she finds out. Monroe's aren't big on accepting charity."

"What charity? Jill and I are friends, have been since we were kids. I'm simply helping out a friend."

Dante's barely suppressed snicker was audible through

the phone. "You keep telling yourself that, dude. I've seen the way you look at Jill. Heard the way your voice softens when you say her name. I might be young, but I recognize love when I see it. And you're a fool if you let my sister slip through your fingers again."

"Dante, I—"

"Save it. I was going to take two tires over to the parking lot and change 'em there, but if I'm changing all four, I'm gonna tow her car into the shop, it'll be a lot faster."

"Don't forget to call me if you find anything odd."

"I will. Talk to you later."

Lucas disconnected the call and leaned forward, looking at his laptop but not really seeing it. Dante's words kept ringing in his ears, repeating over and over he was in love with Jill. Before he could think any more about it, his phone rang again. It was Dante.

"What?"

"I thought of something. Might be nothing, I don't know. Remember when you first got back, and stopped by Jill's place to take her out for a drink, and I was there?"

"Yeah, it's not like it was that long ago."

"When I got to Jill's apartment, there was a rose lying in front of her door. A single rose with no card or anything. A long-stemmed red rose. She didn't know who left it either, and then you showed up and I kind of forgot about it. With her thinking somebody's following her, and the thing with the tires, I'm not sure if the flower is significant or not.

Figured I'd tell you anyway, you know, just in case."

"Thanks. I'll ask Jill about it. Maybe she found the card later, or somebody told her they sent it." Strangely enough, Lucas didn't like the thought of somebody sending Jill anonymous gifts, especially roses.

"Or she's got a secret admirer who's afraid to talk to her, like in the movies."

"Maybe."

Lucas almost wished he was naïve enough to believe that might be the case, but he was too cynical and world weary, and had seen far too much ugliness to believe in something some innocent.

"Anyway, I thought I'd mention it, what with everything else going on. I'll call you. Later, dude."

After Dante hung up, Lucas pulled the laptop closer, and stared at it intently. After a few minutes, he knew any attempt at getting work done was futile. He couldn't concentrate, couldn't focus on anything but Jill and the possibility of her being in danger. Right now, he had too many balls in the air, and he'd never been great at juggling. Worrying about Jill, the possibility of finally locating his sister, and his meeting with Junior at the gaming club tonight all fought for priority in his head. Splitting his focus like this could spell big trouble, which he couldn't afford.

For now, Jill was safe. He shot a text to Rafe, asking him to keep his eyes open. Then a follow up e-mail to Heath, thanking him for the info on Renee/Elizabeth.

Glancing at the clock in the corner of his screen, he winced. He had one more stop before he headed over to meet up with Junior. Time to get his head on straight, and dig up a little juicy gossip on Texas's dirty little secret.

Standing in the shadows, he watched a cavalcade of people traipsing in and out of the storefront on Main Street. The site had stood vacant for months, yet now it was a hive of activity all centered around one woman. Jill Monroe. He wasn't sure when it happened, but somehow, she'd become enmeshed in his every thought until he couldn't eat. Couldn't sleep. Business slumped because he'd become obsessed with being near her. Now here she was, starting a business right in the heart of Shiloh Springs. A business he didn't have a personal stake in—at least not yet.

He'd considered renting the space for one of his legitimate business ventures, but had hesitated at dealing with Patricia Boudreau. The woman was squeaky clean, with an unsullied reputation, and he doubted she'd have dealt with him anyway.

The rumor mill reported Jill planned to open a bakery. The slightest smile curled his lip at the thought. Perfect. He'd have an honest-to-goodness excuse to see her every day, without hiding in the shadows like some lowlife stalker. Maybe he'd become a patron of her business. The thought of her slaving away in a hot, steamy kitchen wasn't ideal, but he couldn't demand she quit. The place hadn't even opened yet.

Maybe it wouldn't. A few discreet accidents would at least delay the bakery's opening, along with the added bonus of making Jill feel vulnerable. Accessible to being comforted, and he'd be ready to step in and play the gallant rescuer.

Lifting his cell phone, he tapped a few keys and put it to his ear. "Here's what I want you to do."

CHAPTER FIFTEEN

Jill stretched, feeling the muscles pull slightly in her lower back. But it was a good ache, because they'd accomplished so much. Who have thought one afternoon of painting could make such a difference?

"Anything else you need us for?" Serena glanced around the bakery, her smile matching Jill's. "It really looks great. Simple colors, yet not too girly, you know? I can't wait to see the sign you mentioned. You said a friend's designing and painting it for you?"

Jill nodded. "It looks like a large chalkboard, only instead of being black, it'll be the same sage green color as the trim color we used. She's using chalkboard paint, and then drawing or painting on different sweet treats like cupcakes, macarons, and cookies. The name and logo will go in the center, and then the whole thing will be sealed, so it doesn't get smudged or erased." Grabbing her phone, she scrolled through to the example she'd discussed with Harper. "It'll look similar to this, but without the fancy swirls and curlicues. I think simpler is better."

"Wow, I love it." Serena studied the picture. "It's going

to be perfect."

"Thanks."

Serena slung her arm around Jill's shoulder. "Well, if you don't need me anymore, I'm going to head home and take a long, hot bubble bath. I've got the feeling I'm going to be feeling this in every muscle tomorrow."

"I can't thank you enough for everything you've done to help."

"That's what friends are for. Especially around here. Throw in the Boudreaus, and you'll find you're never alone or without an extra set or two of hands when you need them."

"I'm starting to realize that. I've lived here all my life, and all of a sudden it's like I've been swept away into this world I never knew existed."

Serena's smile grew brighter. "Welcome to the club. Although I should warn you. Once you're in, they're never turning you loose, kiddo. It's kind of like the mafia, but in a good way."

Jill's sudden burst of laughter had heads turning toward her and Serena, and she put both hands in front of her mouth to stifle her mirth. When she had regained a bit of control, she turned back to Serena. "You did not compare the Boudreau family to the mob!"

"Sheesh, not in a horse head in your bed way. I mean, being part of their inner circle is hard to explain. They don't care about things like blood ties or your past. They care about the person you are and your character. But heaven help you if you ever hurt one of their own. Not something you'd ever do."

Jill turned over Serena's words in her mind. She'd never intentionally do anything to hurt one of the Boudreaus, although she might find herself a little heartbroken when Lucas went back to Dallas-Fort Worth. Even though she'd seen him several times since he'd been back, and they'd spoken on the phone, she'd done her best to keep from letting her heart get involved. It would be far too easy to tip over the edge, head over heels, all the way in love with Lucas. She couldn't let that happen. Not again.

"Thanks again, Serena. I know you'd rather have spent your weekend with Antonio, but I appreciate everything you've done to help me."

"He had to stay in Austin over the weekend. The FBI has them working overtime on some big case, so I haven't gotten to see him nearly as much as I'd like. I'm going to drive to Austin on Tuesday, so I'll see him then. Helping you out here kept my mind off how much I miss him."

Ms. Patti walked over and studied both women, before grinning. "Let me guess. Serena's bending your ear about how much she's missing Antonio."

"Sometimes I really do believe you're psychic or something." Serena pointed her finger at Ms. Patti. "You keep your woo-woo to yourself. I'm going home and call your son, then soak in the tub until the water turns to icicles."

Ms. Patti hugged Serena. "Thanks for your help the last couple of days. Tell my son to give me a call."

"Will do. I'll see you at the office tomorrow morning. I've got back-to-back appointments, so it's going to be a busy day."

"Need a lift?" Nica flung her arm around Serena's shoulders. "I can drop you off on the way."

"No thanks, I've got my car outside. How long are you in town for?"

"I have to head back tonight. I need to get back for classes Monday."

Something about the way she spoke tickled at the back of Jill's mind, but she couldn't figure out what seemed off. Before she could think about it further, Nica rounded on her. "How about you? Dad said he gave you a ride after church. Want me to take you home?"

"Thanks, but I'm waiting to hear back from my brother. He's fixing my tires. He'll probably be bringing the car around any time, so I'm good."

"Alright, then I'm heading out. Unless you need me for anything else?"

"I don't think so, but I appreciate all your help."

"No problem. I'll expect my weight in free cookies next time I'm home."

"You got it."

"See you at home, Momma." Nica placed a quick kiss on Ms. Patti's cheek and hustled out the door, avoiding

Chance's playful grab for her arm. Rafe and Tessa gathered the tarps off the floor, while Chance started pulling the plastic covering off the windows. The gleaning sunlight through the cleaned windows glistened, and the newly-painted walls gleamed, giving the whole space a feeling of peace and calm.

All the painting supplies and empty cans were neatly stacked against one wall, and Jill shook her head, amazed once again at how much the whole team had accomplished in a matter of hours.

"Can you be here early tomorrow, Jill? One of the equipment suppliers from San Antonio is supposed to deliver the tables and racks in the morning. Sometime between nine and noon."

"Of course, Ms. Patti. I'd planned on getting here early. There's some stuff I wanted to bring over from my apartment. I've also got some calls to make about setting up a time to meet with the distributors. I'm thinking of putting a couple of gluten-free options on the menu, too. I've made appointments to deal with wholesale suppliers for all our ingredient needs with a company out of Austin who'll deliver."

"That's good, dear." She grinned. "It's getting closer to opening day. Is it starting to feel real yet?"

"It's still a bit surreal, although it's finally sinking in. Now that I'm actually doing something tangible, ordering supplies, getting the physical space ready, I'm starting to believe this is really happening."

"How Sweet It Is will be the best bakery in Shiloh Springs. Mark my words."

Jill felt a thrill of excitement sweep through her at Ms. Patti's words. Knowing the Buchanan matriarch believed in her, trusted her to make the bakery a success, gave her a sense of accomplishment she'd never experienced before. And a sense of acceptance, and for somebody who'd never felt like she fit in, it was a heady feeling.

"If we're done here, Tessa and I are going to head out." Rafe wrapped his arm around Tessa's waist and pulled her against his side.

"Go ahead, I think y'all pretty much finished up everything I could ask for." Jill flashed him a grin.

"Got your car back from Frank's? We can..."

"Everybody, stop worrying about me. Dante should call any minute and let me know that he's put tires on my old junker. I'll have him drop it by here. You don't have to wait."

"We don't mind staying," Tessa objected.

"I know, but the weekend's almost over, and you need to spend time with your fiancé." Jill made a shooing motion. Her cell phone rang, and she checked the caller ID, noting it was her brother. "See, it's Dante."

"Okay, but it you need anything—"

"You'll be the first person I call, I promise." Turning away with a smile, she answered her phone.

"Hi, bro. What's the damage?"

"You're all good. Frank said he'll let me take the cost out of my paychecks, and he's giving me a pretty good employee discount, so it's not all that much. I owe you big time, so I'm taking care of the tires."

"Dante, no, you don't have to do that. I can—"

"You can let me do this. It's the least I can do, after all you've done for me. No argument."

"But…"

"I said no argument. That's final." Dante's tone brooked no further discussion, and she decided for once to give in.

"Thank you."

"I'm leaving Frank's garage now. Want me to swing by the bakery or drop the car off at your apartment?"

Jill glanced up as Tessa and Rafe walked out the door, waving at them. "If you don't mind, bring it by the bakery. I'm almost done here, and I can run a couple of errands before I head home. Thanks."

"No problem. See you soon."

Hanging up, she noted Chance and Douglas talking quietly by the large front window, and whatever Douglas said had Chance frowning. Ms. Patti watched them, and from the look on her face, she didn't have any more of a clue to what they were talking about than Jill. She had a sneaking suspicion Ms. Patti would have the information from Douglas before they were halfway home.

"Everybody can go home now. Dante's on his way over

with my car. It's all fixed. Thanks again for all your help."

"We can wait with you, if you'd like."

"Ms. Patti, I appreciate the offer, but I'll be fine. It'll only take him a few minutes to drive here from the garage."

"Alright, hon. I'll have one of the boys pick up all these painting supplies tomorrow. Give me a call if you need anything."

"I will. You have been an absolute godsend, Ms. Patti."

"Nonsense. You deserve this. Besides, I'm going to be watching, keeping an eye on my investment, so I know you're going to do fine."

Jill looked up with the front door opened, and Dante strode through, her keys dangling from his fingertip. "She's all ready to rock and roll, Sis."

Grabbing the keys from his hand, she gave him a swift hug. "Thanks for getting it done so fast. Any idea what happened?"

He shook his head. "We couldn't see any reason for the tires to go flat. Maybe it was a slow leak. Anyway, you've got four new tires on your old jalopy, so you're good to go for years."

"Four? Dante, that's way too much."

"I told you, Frank's cutting me a sweet deal, and taking the cost out of my check. Trust me, it's the best price you're gonna find around here."

Jill studied her brother's face, wondering if he was telling her the truth. She wouldn't put it past him to overextend himself, trying to make up for her bailing him out of his debt. After a few seconds, she simply shook her head, and tossed her keys in the air, catching them one-handed.

"You heard my brother, I'm all set to go with brand new wheels. Y'all can head home with my heartfelt thanks."

After another minute or two of goodbyes, Jill was alone in the bakery with her brother. "You really didn't find anything wrong with those two flats?"

It took a few seconds before Dante met her gaze, and she instinctively knew he was about to tell her a whopper. She'd grown up her whole life with him, and he had a habit of not looking you in the eye right before he was about to lie, and he was doing it right now.

"Hand over my heart, Sis, there was nothing. No nails. No punctures. No glass. I even had Frank take a look at one of them, to see if I missed anything. Why two of them went flat at the same time? Your guess is as good as mine."

"It seems strange they were fine when I drove to and from church, and then went I came out again, both were flat. Guess it's simply bad luck."

"Who knows? The place looks great, by the way. I like the accent wall. Have you picked a name yet?"

"How Sweet It Is."

Dante chuckled and chucked Jill under the chin. "I love it. Remember all those old black and white reruns Dad used to watch of the Jackie Gleason show? I remember him using that line all the time."

"I'd forgotten all about that. I was thinking more about the Marvin Gaye song. You know, *How Sweet It Is To Be Loved By You.*" She couldn't resist teasing him. "You should have seen Ms. Patti and Douglas dancing to it, right here in the kitchen. Said it was their song."

"Cool. Which makes the name work on multiple levels, because your sweets are gonna be legendary. Bet you sell out every day."

Jill leaned her head against her brother's shoulder, and he slid his arm around her waist. Standing here with Dante, she realized how truly blessed she'd been in the last few months. Things had started looking up when Tessa moved to Shiloh Springs, and now look—she was starting her own business. Such a dichotomy from the day-to-day drudgery of her nine-to-five at the insurance company.

"I almost want to pinch myself, to make sure this is all real and not some fantastical dream. One I'm going to wake up from, and everything will go back to the way it was before."

"I promise, Jilly, it's not a dream. Well, maybe, but only because it's the dream you've always wanted. You deserve every single minute of happiness, Sis."

"You do too, Dante. I want everything for you. I want you to be happy."

"Things are looking up every day. I've got a new job. I'm staying away from Junior and his gang. I'm even helping Lucas with—"

"Lucas? What are you helping him with?"

"Nothing! I...it's not anything big. He had some questions, research stuff from a story."

Jill's narrowed her eyes, and took a step back, until she could stare into Dante's eyes. Oh, yeah, he had guilt written all over his face.

"What kind of questions?"

"Sheesh, Sis, give me a break, will ya? He asked me a couple of questions for a story he's thinking about writing, that's all."

"You wouldn't know anything that Lucas might be interested in writing about. You've never even left Shiloh Springs. What in the world kind of questions could you possibly...did you tell him about your gambling?"

Please, please don't have told Lucas. Especially about me using my savings to pay off your debt. I'll never be able to look him in the face again.

Dante's shoulders slumped before he turned to face away from her, which told her everything she needed to know. She almost wished a hole would open and swallow her, because there was no way she'd be able to face Lucas again. Not if he knew she'd lost everything on a lousy poker game.

"Yeah, I told him. Every stinking, cowardly thing I've done because I couldn't stop sinking further and further into a hole I dug, and couldn't pull myself out of. I had to have my sister pull me out, because I'm such a fool. The thing is, Jilly, he got it. Didn't judge, didn't tell me what a loser I am, he listened. Course, I didn't need him to tell me I'd sunk lower than a snake's belly, I already knew that."

"Dante—"

"Don't try and make excuses for me. I've heard every one of them. Spouted them myself. Easy platitudes to cover up the fact that I'm an addict. A gambling addict who craves the thrill, the excitement, the adrenaline rush I get when I win. Even the disappointment of a bad hand can have its own kind of thrill, because the tension and anticipation have a unique sensation that adds to the whole mystique. But I'm not going back."

"Good."

"Things have changed, Jilly. I've changed. It took me a while, but I'm finally growing up. One day I'll be able to give you back everything."

"Stop it. I don't ever want to hear you talking about giving me the money back. It's gone. You're okay. As long as I never have to see you like that again, we're even." She hugged her arms across her middle, remembering his bruised and broken body hanging between the two men, enforcers or whatever they were called, blood streaked across his lip and down his chin, eyes nearly swollen closed.

"I promise. I've been going to Gamblers Anonymous." He held up his hand when she started to interrupt. "I'm still learning, in the beginning phase, but it's a start. I've learned that I'm an addict, and I have to own it. Admit I have a problem that's never going to go away, and that I'll need to fight the temptation every single day. But giving in to the temptation will not only hurt me, but it'll hurt those around me who love me. I won't do that to you ever again, Sis. I'd rather you shoot me than let me hurt you again."

Jill raced forward into her brother's arms, and he pulled her close, his chin resting on her head. She could feel him trembling, and squeezed him tighter. It seemed like forever since he'd opened up to her like this, spilling forth his secrets and his emotions, flooding from him like he couldn't keep them bottled up a second longer.

"I'm glad you're getting help. I'm here for you, no matter what. You know that, right?"

He sniffled and she hoped he wasn't crying, because if he was, she'd start bawling right along with him. "Yeah." He straightened and gave her a shaky grin. "Anyway, your car's done. Want to give me a ride back to the garage? I need to pick up my ride."

"Sure. Let me grab my stuff."

Locking the bakery doors took seconds. She dropped Dante back at Frank's and headed to her apartment, her mind whirling with everything he'd said. Something seemed fishy about his reaction to her flat tires, but she'd give it a couple of days and press the matter later, when he wasn't expecting it. Catch him off guard, and maybe she'd get the truth out of him.

In the meantime, she needed to get home and go over the list of things she needed to do in the morning. One day closer to opening. She crossed her fingers, and wished for smooth sailing going forward. No more surprises.

CHAPTER SIXTEEN

"Hey, Lucas. What's up?"

"Good to hear your voice, Shiloh. Things have been a little crazy. I wanted to ask you for a favor."

"Depends. What kind of favor? Small, medium, or you're-gonna-owe-me-big-time sized?"

Lucas chuckled. This was their standing joke, because when they'd been growing up, favors came with varying degrees of payback.

"It'll probably end up being the latter. This favor involves you heading out of town. I wanted to check and see if you had a couple of days free."

"Actually, baby brother, your timing couldn't be better. I gave the client the results from my latest case, and I'd planned to take a week off, and go lie on the beach and drink a few beers."

"Feel up to a trip to Portland, Oregon?"

"Okay, I'll bite. What's in Portland?"

Lucas held his breath for a few seconds before answering. Every time he'd gotten this close to finding Renee, his leads fell apart, and he didn't want to get his hopes up. As much as he'd rather go himself, he didn't want to leave Shiloh Springs. Not yet. Especially if there was the possibility Jill might be in danger.

"My sister," he answered.

"Son of a—seriously? Renee's in Portland? Why aren't you already on a plane?" He could understand Shiloh's shock. Maybe he was making a mistake in not jumping at the chance to follow up Heath's lead himself, but his gut told him he couldn't leave. Not yet.

"Long story, and I'll fill you in on the details later. I can't leave now, which is why I called you. Heath got in touch with me, told me he'd got a lead on my sister. Dad's info turned out to be a bust, because the woman going by the name of Elizabeth Reynolds in Cincinnati had been gone a year. No forwarding address, nothing to tie her to the city. But, get this. Heath gets a newbie to train. Guy's from Portland. Heath said he was on a stakeout with this kid when he started talking about this girl he knew. Pretty little redhead named Lizzie Reynolds. Even showed Heath a picture."

"You saw the picture?"

"Yeah." Lucas still remembered the gut-punched feeling the second he'd seen the photo. There'd been no doubt the woman in the picture was Renee. "Check your e-mail."

He heard Shiloh typing, knew he'd seen the picture because his brother's gasp was audible.

"Dude, she looks like you."

"I think so, too."

"Lemme call the airport, I'll leave on the next flight out."

Lucas breathed a deep sigh. Just like that, no more questions, his brother simply canceled his plans, ready to help. All of his brothers would do the same if asked, drop everything and rally the troops. It's what Boudreaus did.

"Thank you."

"Send me everything you've got on Renee or Elizabeth Reynolds. Did Heath's newbie have any idea clue how she'd ended up in Portland, or why she was running?"

"Heath didn't want to push him too hard for details. He was subtle, or as subtle as Heath gets, and got me the last known address in Portland. This guy, Chuck, said they weren't seriously dating, just friendly. I haven't been able to check out much since I got the information. This stinks. I need to be the one looking for her. She's my sister. I've spent years looking for her, trying to find her. Except I can't leave, because Jill might be in trouble."

"Seriously? What's going on? Last time I was home, Jill was fine."

"It might be nothing, and I'm blowing things out of proportion, but..."

Shiloh stopped him. "You don't make those kinds of mistakes. You're probably the most intuitive guy I know. If your instinct's telling you something's wrong, chances are good it is. I'll deal with Renee. When I find her, you'll be the first to know, bro."

"Thank you."

"No thanks needed. In a roundabout way, she's my sister, too. If she's in Portland, I'll find her. You take care of Jill. I'll call you as soon as I'm on the ground."

With that, Shiloh hung up. Lucas shot him an e-mail containing all the facts Heath had given him, along with the information from his trip to Cincinnati in his search for Elizabeth Reynolds. Running a hand through his hair, he closed his laptop and glanced at the clock. If he hurried, he'd have enough time for a shower before heading out to meet Junior.

Driving toward the gaming club, Lucas' phone rang, and the caller ID showed Dante. He'd known the younger man would call, if for no other reason than to check in with him before he headed into Junior's club.

"Hello."

"Yo. Wanted to give you a head's up. Did your dad tell you about Jill's car?"

"He did. I'm trying to wrap my head around what happened."

"She's fine. Only problem she's had all day was two flat tires. Your dad asked me to let him know if there was anything odd about them, coz it's strange to have two flats on the same day."

Lucas squeezed his phone tighter, wishing Dante would spit out whatever it was he'd found, instead of dragging things out like this.

"What did you find?"

"Somebody definitely tampered with the valves. There were definite scratches and evidence somebody had deliberately let the air out of her tires. Who'd do that?"

"I don't know, but I intend to find out. Where's Jill at now?"

"She dropped me off at the garage to pick up my car, and she was headed back to her apartment. Probably there by now."

"Okay. You got plans for tonight?" Lucas hated to ask Dante for a favor, but if he missed this chance to get a behind-the-scenes look at Junior's operation, he'd never get another shot, and he'd have to start over from scratch.

"Nothing I can't cancel, why?"

"I want you to stake out your sister's apartment. Park far enough away she won't notice you, but still close enough you can see if anybody else is hanging around. If anything arouses your suspicions, you call Rafe immediately. Think you can handle it?"

Dante's scoffing sound was all the answer Lucas needed.

"I think I'll be able to keep watch."

"I'm trusting you, Dante, to have my back here. If I didn't have to meet Junior tonight, you can bet I'd be sitting inside your sister's apartment right now."

Dante's chuckle unnerved Lucas, though he'd never admit it. Somehow the younger man read him like the Sunday newspaper, no matter how he tried to hide his

KATHY IVAN

feelings.

"I told you, you have it bad. For what it's worth, you've got my blessing, as long as Jill wants you, too. If not, I'll personally kick you to the curb. Understand?"

"I hear you. Don't hesitate to call Rafe or my dad if you can't get my brother. Tell them what you've told me, and they'll show up. Don't, under any circumstances, try to be a hero, Dante. We might be imaging things, or grasping at straws. Maybe it's coincidence."

"Do you honestly think so?"

"No."

"Me either. Go, do your job and get the information you need. I'll keep an eagle eye on my sister."

"Have you called my dad yet, and told him what you suspect?"

"No, I was gonna call him after I talked with you."

"Don't worry about it, I'll call him. Dante, thanks again for your help with my story."

"No problem. Oh, I told Jilly about me going to Gamblers Anonymous. She said she's proud of me."

Lucas' lip curled up at the sound of awe in Dante's voice, as if he'd expected a different response. "We're all proud of you. What you're doing takes guts, standing up to a problem and facing it like a man. I've gotta go, talk to you later."

Lucas hung up the call from Dante, and immediately dialed his father. He wanted to make sure his dad knew what Dante had found regarding the tires, and to keep his ears open in case Dante called.

"Lucas. Everything okay?"

"Yes and no. I just got off the phone with Dante. He suspects somebody tampered with the valves on both of them. Said there was clear evidence someone deliberately let the air out of both tires. Which makes Jill's claim she thought somebody was following her carry more weight, don't you think? Dante also told me somebody left a single red rose on Jill's doorstep without a note."

"When'd that happen?"

"The day after I got back to town. I think Jill's attracted the attention of somebody. Might be a love-struck fool, but letting the air out of her tires is kicking things up a notch."

His dad was silent for several long seconds, before he responded. "What are we going to do about this?"

Trust his dad to get right to the heart of things with an offer to help. His father's protectiveness extended to all his sons, and by extension to the women they cared about. His father had an especially soft spot for women, a throwback to times when women were treated with respect. He never considered women the weaker sex; after all he was married to Ms. Patti, and there wasn't a stronger, more capable woman anywhere. But Lucas and his brothers had been taught by a man who didn't brook a woman being mistreated or threatened in any way. Douglas, Gator, and Hank all instilled in their sons a sense of duty and honor, which included protecting those who were threatened or mistreated. That umbrella of protection now extended to Jill.

"Dante's going to stake out his sister's apartment, keep his eyes peeled for anything that looks abnormal. Unfortunately, I've got someplace I have to be tonight, and there's no getting out of it. I told Dante if he sees anything, he's to call you."

"Good. If I'm at the Big House when or if Dante calls, I'll have Rafe or Chance head over to help him, since they're closer. Hopefully, it won't be necessary."

"I wish she'd said something to me about what's going on."

His father was quiet for a moment before answering. "Son, don't take this wrong, but you've been gone for a long while, and from things your momma told me, Jill didn't handle it well when you left. Makes it not surprising she wouldn't immediately trust you."

Lucas bit back a sigh, knowing his dad was right. They hadn't exactly ended on a bright and shiny note. Instead, he'd told her he was leaving Shiloh Springs, blurting it out of the blue, without ever having told her what he'd planned. Somehow, in his youthful ignorance, he'd expected her to want to come with him. Like she didn't have a life of her own. Dreams she wanted or needed to follow. He'd simply assumed because he wanted to live and work in the Dallas-Fort Worth Metroplex, she'd automatically want the same.

"I was young and stupid. I knew what I wanted, and nothing and nobody was gonna stand in my way. If I wanted to follow my dream, I needed to be in a city bigger than Shiloh Springs. Guess I'm still stupid, because I thought Jill and I were making progress, that she'd forgiven me."

"Have you talked to her? I don't mean having conversations. I mean really talked with her. Explained why you went, what you've learned about yourself since you've been gone. Why you're coming home."

Lucas started at his father's words. How had he known?

"Dad?"

Douglas chuckled, and the sound warmed something deep inside Lucas' chest. "You're my son. I know how you think, sometimes before you do. You needed to figure out who you are for yourself, not be pigeonholed by your family's expectations. Course, it wouldn't matter whether you stayed up in DFW or moved back to Shiloh Springs, we're gonna love you regardless."

Lucas fought the lump that suddenly formed in his throat, grateful beyond words he'd been placed with the Boudreaus. That he'd been given the chance of forming bonds with a family who loved and understood him, and let him find his own way to becoming the man he was now.

"I've been thinking about coming home. Now that I've established myself in the journalistic community, have enough knowledge and experience, I can pretty much work from anywhere as long as I've got a computer, printer, and phone."

"I'll let your momma know she can finally show you the

places she's picked out for you. Apartments and houses."

"Momma knows, too?"

"Son, there's nothing your momma doesn't know, and usually a long time before I figure it out. You need to tell her soon. It's gonna make her happy. I think she wants all her kids close. It's her mother hen instinct. Now, you go investigate whatever it is that can't wait. I'll keep my phone close in case Dante calls. And, son, if things get too hot with whatever you're looking into, call me and I'll be there ASAP."

"Thanks, Dad. I really do have to go to this meetup, otherwise, I'd be the one parked in Jill's living room, sleeping on the sofa and keeping an eye on her."

"I know. You're a fine man, Lucas. I'm proud of you."

"I've never been prouder to be part of your family. I wish—"

"Don't," Douglas interrupted. "I know what you're gonna say, and I understand. Your mother and I have always understood. You need to remain an O'Malley until you find your sister. She wouldn't recognize the Boudreau name. Though to be honest, she might not remember the O'Malley name, either. She was a little tyke when you were separated, and she got placed with a different family. Just because you haven't changed your name doesn't make you any less my son. I love you."

"Love you too." Lucas barely got the words out past the lump in his throat, and his gaze landed on the clock. "I really do have to go, I'm already late. I'll check in with you tonight."

"I'll expect your call. Take care of yourself."

Lucas ended the call, shoved his cell in his pocket, and grabbed his keys and the envelope containing the cash he'd be using at the club. He needed to look flush, a potential big spender, so he'd taken ten grand out of his savings account. No way was he walking into this meeting with chump change. He simply needed to make sure Junior knew he had access to a ready supply of cash, a large enough wad to interest the big boss.

The drive to the strip mall seemed interminable, though it was really only about twenty minutes. He parked and watched silently for a few minutes, saw a handful of men and women heading inside. It didn't surprise him to see most of them looked like they could ill afford to risk money they didn't have inside this snake pit. Only it was their choice what they did with their cash, no matter how much it irked him.

"Well, it's now or never." He gave a self-deprecating snort when he realized he was talking to himself.

Climbing from his car, he strode across the parking lot, making sure he exuded an air of confidence, a man who was used to getting what he wanted. Tonight, he wanted to play poker with the guys Dante mentioned as being the high rollers, the regulars. He had names and descriptions to match.

Show time.

CHAPTER SEVENTEEN

She was being an idiot. Staring down at the photo album in her lap, Jill looked at the picture of Lucas, smiling and laughing at something somebody must've said. His head was thrown back, his smile wide and unbridled. Running a fingertip across the picture, she thought back to the day the photo had been taken.

It had been a Saturday afternoon, and a whole group of locals from the high school decided to head to the big public pool over at the community center. The temperature had been blazing hot, she remembered, and they'd packed a big cooler full of ice, sodas, and water. They'd had a blast, but all she could recall from that day was Lucas.

The memory felt as fresh and vibrant as if it had been yesterday, instead of years earlier. She remembered it with such detail because it was the day they'd had their first fight. Of course, now that she was older and hopefully wiser, she wouldn't even classify it as anything to get all hot and bothered about. Back then though, she'd just turned seventeen and she'd had a giant crush on Lucas Boudreau. Between that and raging teenage hormones, she'd been a walking, talking hormone bomb ready to explode at the slightest provocation.

Cue in Lisa Giardino, her high school nemesis. Not that Lisa knew or cared what Jill thought about her. She was the school bad girl, and she loved living down to her reputation. Lisa was the one all the boys flocked to when she crooked her little finger, and left them panting like pups in heat chasing after her.

All except Lucas. Somehow, he seemed immune to all her charms, and Lisa had definitely been blessed in the physical endowments department, though not so much in the mental acumen area. Things had been going great at the pool party, until Lisa showed up with her gal pals, trolling for their Saturday night conquests. For whatever reason, that sweltering hot afternoon, she set her sights on Lucas.

Jill shook her head, trying to escape the memory and turned the page in the photo album. A squeezing in her chest made her gasp. She'd forgotten about this photo. One she'd taken with her cell phone years ago, when she'd been a senior in high school. She'd printed it out, and stuck it under her pillow. Later on, she'd started an album with all his pictures and hidden it away, so nobody could find it or discover her secret crush.

Strange, but she hadn't drug out these photos since Lucas left Shiloh Springs to head for the big city life. Right after he left, she'd been accepted at Duke in North Carolina. She remembered how excited she'd been, getting that letter of acceptance. Money would be tight, but between student loans, scholarships, and the small amount her parents had put aside, she could make it work. She'd left Shiloh Springs and headed to Durham.

Turning the page, she smiled at a picture of Lucas, Rafe and Dane standing outside the high school. Rafe had graduated, she remembered, and Lucas and Dane were one year apart. All three men looked so different, yet even then the bond between the brothers was evident.

A knock on her door startled her. She laid the photo album on the coffee table and picked up her phone, checking to see who was outside. Dante had insisted on installing one of those camera doorbells, so she'd always know who was on the other side of the door.

Only there wasn't anybody there. She'd heard a knock, she was sure of it. Shrugging, she walked over and eased the door open, looking down the hall in both directions, but didn't see anybody. As she started to close the door, she glanced down and spotted a small white box sitting on the ground. Atop it was a pink ribbon, with frilly little curlicues at the ends.

Kneeling, she picked it up, carried it inside and closed the door. Curiosity piqued, she sat on the sofa and held the package in her hand. It didn't weight much, and she didn't see any kind of card or label.

It must be for me. It's in front on my door. But who would drop off a package and not check and make sure I'm home?

She carefully slid the ribbon off the box and tossed it onto the coffee table. Opening the white box, she realized that it was really an outer box, with another one inside, this one a vivid red. Taking the red box in her hand, she looked at it from all angles, before finally giving in and opening the lid. She gasped when she spotted the bracelet inside.

Diamonds. Each stone seemed to catch the light, reflecting back a prism of colors as the bracelet spilled across her fingertips. It had diamonds all the way around, resembling a tennis bracelet, but these stones were bigger than any she'd seen before.

Springing from the couch, she raced over to the door and flung it open, once again looking for anybody who might be in the hallway. Nobody was there, and there was nothing to indicate who might have left the gift on her doorstep.

Locking her front door, she slumped down on the couch and studied the bracelet. It couldn't hurt to try it on, right? She wouldn't, couldn't keep it, but there wasn't any rule that said she didn't get to have a bit of a thrill somebody wanted to shower her with expensive gifts.

Clasping the catch of the bracelet, she turned her wrist, watching the play of colors and sparkles against her skin, the diamonds catching and refracting the light. It was stunning. Too bad she couldn't keep it, because it had to be some kind of mistake. Nobody she knew would've left something this expensive on her doorstep.

"Alright, you beautiful thing, who do you really belong

to, and what am I going to do with you?"

Shrugging, she picked up her cell phone and dialed Lucas' number. Maybe he'd know what she should do about her mysterious gift. When the call rolled over to voicemail, she hung up without leaving a message, and decided to call someone who could tell her what to do, because she didn't feel safe having something this expensive laying around her apartment, especially since it was obviously a mistake, and had been delivered to the wrong address.

"Evening, Jill." Rafe's deep voice came through her phone. "What can I do for you?"

"Hi, Rafe. I'm hoping you can give me some advice, answer a question I've got."

"I'd be happy to. What's your question?"

"There was a knock on my door a few minutes ago. When I answered it, there wasn't anybody there, but I did find a package on the floor in front of my door."

"Was there a card or note, anything to indicate who might have left it?"

She shook her head before it sank in Rafe couldn't see her, since it wasn't a video call. "Not that I found. I checked the hallway again, and the floor around my apartment, but there wasn't anything."

"Did you open it?"

"Um, yeah. Rafe, it's a diamond bracelet. At least, they look like real diamonds. But who'd send me something like that? And leave it out in the hall, where anybody could stumble upon it? It doesn't make any sense."

"You're right, it doesn't make sense. Has anything like this happened before, somebody leaving things for you?"

"Not that I remember...wait, somebody did leave a red rose once. But that's not the same thing."

She heard Rafe sigh. "It sounds like you've got an admirer, one who's stepping up his game. Have you noticed anybody hanging around? Any calls where somebody doesn't speak on the other end of the line?"

"No calls. I haven't seen anybody hanging around." She bit her lower lip, wondering if she should tell Rafe about thinking somebody was following her home from the bakery. She probably should, because if she didn't, somebody else would. "I did have a weird feeling the other night, when I was walking home from the bakery. It was the night everybody came and helped with cleaning the place. Anyway, I was walking home and thought somebody was following me. You know that feeling you get when it seems like somebody's watching you? It was like that, only I didn't see anybody."

"Has that happened before?"

"Not that I recall. It was probably nothing, except—"

"Except what, Jill?"

"There's also two of my tires were flat this morning. I drove home from church, and stopped at home to change my clothes and pick up some food I was taking to the bakery. Everybody was going to be there, and we'd be painting all day, so I volunteered to bring food and drinks. I came out to the car and two tires were flat."

"Yeah, I know about that. Dad mentioned it while we were at the bakery this afternoon. Said you thought you might have run over something on the way home from church."

"Dante said they didn't find any reason for the tires to go flat. Figured it was a slow leak or something. He put four brand new tires on my old junker."

"It makes me wonder, because it's a few too many coincidences in a relatively short time frame. Have you met any new people recently? Anybody make your internal radar go off?"

"Not that I can think of off the top of my head. Anyway, what should I do with this bracelet? If these are real diamonds, and they do look legit although I'm no expert, I don't have a safe place to keep them."

"I'm gonna stop by and pick it up. Did it come wrapped or anything?"

"There was a jeweler's box inside of a plain white box. There was a pink ribbon."

She could hear Rafe moving around, and she knew he was on his way. "Do me a favor. Put everything into a plastic bag, one of those zipper kind if you have it. I'll be there in a few minutes."

"Thanks, Rafe. I hated to bother you, but I wasn't sure how to handle something like this. I tried to call Lucas, but got his voicemail."

"It's no problem. This is my job. We'll figure out who might be leaving you tokens of their affection, and let them know to knock it off. Unless you want them to keep sending you stuff?"

She shuddered at his words. "Thanks, but no thanks."

Rafe chuckled at her response. "Got it. See you in a few."

She disconnected the call and got up to do what he'd asked. Of course, that took all of a minute. Now she had to wait for Rafe to show up and take the diamonds off her hands. Each tick of her kitchen clock seemed to reverberate throughout the apartment, the incessant sound echoing in her ears.

When the doorbell rang, she nearly jumped out of her skin, then called herself all kinds of an idiot, because she knew it was Rafe. Still, she checked the camera before opening the door. He stood on her doorstep, dressed in jeans and a button-front shirt with pearl snaps, and his ever-present cowboy hat. Grinning, he reached for the baggie she didn't even realize she held in a stranglehold in her right hand.

Rafe whistled when he looked at the bracelet. "Those are some rocks. If they're real, they cost somebody a good chunk of change." Without waiting, he walked into her apartment and sat on the couch.

"I don't understand any of this. I can't think of anybody who'd send something like that. It's over the top, and while it's beautiful, I'd never wear anything like that."

"Sit down, Jill."

Uh oh. From his serious expression, she knew whatever he was going to tell her wasn't good news. Her insides tightened, waiting for him to tell her she was in trouble. Wracking her brain, she couldn't figure out a single thing she'd done or said that might cause Rafe to be upset.

"Rafe, what's going on?"

"I talked with Dad a few minutes ago on my way here. Seems like your brother didn't exactly tell you everything he found when he fixed your tires. Somebody tampered with the valves on two of them, letting out all the air. You wouldn't have been able to drive on them, and with the valves damaged, they'd have to be replaced. Not an expensive fix, but I find it suspicious that you'd have two of them occur spontaneously. Plus, Dad said there was evidence of scratches around the valves."

"What are you saying, Rafe? You think somebody deliberately flattened my tires? Why?"

"That's what we're going to figure out."

Jill felt physically ill at Rafe's implication. It couldn't be possible. Nobody wanted to hurt her. There had to be another explanation.

"I'm going to take this in to the sheriff's office and lock it in the safe. I'll see if we can get some prints off of the box or ribbon in the morning. Can you stop by sometime and give me your prints, so we can eliminate yours from any we might get off the box?"

"Of course. I'll stop by tomorrow afternoon, if that's okay. I've got deliveries to the bakery in the morning."

Rafe stood and held his hand out to Jill, helping her up. He squeezed it gently, his eyes filled with compassion and a touch of concern. "Lock up tight after I leave. I'll have the on-duty deputy do a ride by a couple of times to keep an eye on things. If you need me for anything, you've got my number. Use it."

"I will, I promise. Do me a favor? Don't tell Lucas about this. He's got enough on his plate right now, with this story he's working on and trying to find his sister."

Rafe studied her intently, and she barely resisted the urge to squirm under his perusal. Too bad she wasn't great at hiding her emotions, and with his job Rafe was an expert at reading people.

"I won't go out of my way to say anything—yet—but I'm not gonna lie to him if he asks."

"Thank you."

"You're welcome, Jill. Get some sleep." Rafe pulled her close and gave her a hug, then headed for the door. "Lock this behind me."

"After what you told me, I'm liable to stick a chair under the knob." She gave him a cheeky grin, and he returned her smile.

She turned the deadbolt, made sure it engaged, then sank onto the couch with a pillow clutched to her chest. After finding out about the suspected deliberate damage to her tires, and the possibility somebody might actually be watching her, she doubted she'd get much sleep.

Too bad Lucas wasn't around. He always made her feel safe, being by her side. Right now, she could use a little of his calming influence, because she had the feeling her life was about to become a roller coaster ride, and the bottom of her world was about to fall out from beneath her.

CHAPTER EIGHTEEN

"Luke, glad you made it."

Lucas barely made it through the front door before Junior raced to his side, a big grin on his face, acting like they'd been friends for years, instead of meeting for the first time. The guy exuded a certain charisma, which probably smoothed the path for bringing in a patsy, and suckering them into gambling way more than they could afford. Lucas stuck out his hand.

"You must be Junior. Dante mentioned you're the man I should talk to, that you'd show me the ropes."

Junior looked around before asking, "I thought Dante was coming with you. When I talked to him yesterday, he said he'd be escorting you to our establishment."

"He planned to come, but apparently there was some kind of problem with his sister, so he probably isn't going to make it. Might be able to get here, but it'd be late if at all. His sister's a bit of a prude, if you know what I mean. She's putting on the pressure to keep Dante away from here."

Saying the words left a bad taste in Lucas' mouth, but he was playing a part, and needed to convince Junior he was a man on a mission, and that was to find a high stakes game.

Junior laughed and clapped Lucas on the back. "Yeah, I've met his big sister. She's a real piece of work. She's one of those butter-wouldn't-melt-in-her mouth type broads. Always riding his case about spending time with us. Doesn't seem to understand Dante and I have been friends for a long time."

"Exactly. Women don't get it. We need to be able to blow off a little steam now and then. It's harmless fun, am I right?"

"That you are, dude. You ready to play? Hope you're feeling lucky."

Lucas rubbed his hands together, and gave Junior a cocky grin. "Lady Luck is gonna be on my side tonight, I can feel it."

"There's one thing you have to do before I let you through, dude. Follow me to the office." Without another word, Junior turned and started walking toward a door to the right of the entrance. He followed, wondering what the other man was up to, and whether he'd be tossed out before he ever got started.

Once inside the office, Junior leaned against the desk, his arms folded across his chest. Standing there, dressed in dark jeans and a T-shirt, his dirty blond hair a little scraggly around the edges, he appeared your typical All-American boy next door type from a small town. Nothing about him gave away the fact he was running a small empire of illegal activities. His posture appeared relaxed, like he had all the time in the world, and wasn't afraid of anybody or anything.

"So we're clear from the start, I gotta ask. You wearing a wire?"

"A what?"

Junior shrugged. "Unfortunately, can't trust anybody. You might have a referral from a regular, but I don't know you. Too many people want to shut us down, or want a part of the business, so we can't be too careful."

"I'm not wearing a wire."

"Open your shirt. Not that I don't trust ya—but I don't trust anybody." Junior said this with a huge grin, and crossed his arms over his chest. That's when Lucas spotted the gun tucked into his waistband. He wasn't surprised; he figured the bodyguards and hierarchy would all be carrying. After all tens of thousands of dollars, maybe more, passed through the gaming club almost every night, and these men weren't about to be caught by surprise.

"Guess you run a pretty strict place," he muttered while unbuttoning his shirt. He held the flaps open wide, and turned in a circle, showing Junior that he didn't have anything taped to his chest or back. He wasn't stupid. Hopefully, he'd be able to turn on the recorder on his phone, if they didn't confiscate it, which was a possibility. Lots of folks tried to cheat the system with any number of devices. He'd forgotten to ask Dante about whether they'd let him keep his phone.

"Alright, you're clean. There're a few rules you have to follow if you want to play here. First one, no phones or electronics allowed. You can turn it in to Rocky, he's the tall dude at the door. He'll give you a ticket, and you want to pick it up on your way out. You're not wearing glasses, otherwise we'd have to check them out for cheats. Now, please turn your head."

Lucas knew why—Junior was looking for listening devices, small hearing-aid type earbuds whereby a second party could feed information to the player. He'd done his homework, hopefully knew all the tricks and tells Junior and his boys might be looking for, and prepared for anything they might look at.

"Excellent. You got any questions?"

"I'm mostly looking for a good poker game. I'm not so much into the slots or electronic stuff. I like a good old face-to-face with your opponent, high stakes game. Did Dante tell you I'm from out of town? Since my sister's living here now, I'll probably be coming here several times during the year, and I'd like to establish someplace for a good game. Something similar to what I have at home."

Junior nodded while Lucas spewed out the details of his fabricated story. "Dante mentioned you were from somewhere back east. If you're wanting in on one of the high stakes games, that can be arranged if you can afford the buy in."

"How much?"

"Three grand minimum."

Lucas made a scoffing sound at the amount Junior mentioned, as if it were a piddling amount. "Not a problem, buddy. I spend more than that on a pair of shoes."

He could almost see the avarice in Junior's eyes, thinking he'd caught himself a big fish with deep pockets.

"Excellent. Let me take you to the back, and introduce you to the players at your table."

"Can I say, I'm impressed with what I've seen so far. You run an efficient place, your staff has done everything exactly how we do it back east. As a matter of fact, I'm one of the owners of two gaming clubs in North Carolina. Do you own this club yourself, or are you part of the management team?"

Junior's eyes opened wide when Lucas mentioned owning two clubs. Guess he hadn't figured Lucas for having that kind of clout, and the corner of Lucas' mouth kicked up. If only Junior knew he was spinning a tall tale, lying through his teeth. But he needed to get a stable foothold into this club, if he wanted to get all their dirty little secrets for his article, and maybe bring them down in the process.

"I'm senior management with a profit share in the business. The boss trusts me to keep everything running smoothly. Everyone knows you don't cross the line here. If you rack up a debt, you're encouraged to pay it as soon as possible." Junior almost preened as he outlined his importance. Pretty much what Lucas expected: he was a blowhard who liked to brag about how he was a big wheel instead of a minor cog in the machinery.

Lucas' smile was brittle, because Dante had told him how they'd strong-armed Jill into covering his debt. They hadn't hesitated to beat the stuffing out of Dante, stopping short of doing any permanent damage. That was the good thing about gambling debts, rarely were they fatal. You can't get money from a dead man.

"We've got the same policy. Like I said, I'm very impressed with what I've see. Any chance the owner's here tonight? I'd love to meet him."

"He may come by later tonight, depending on his schedule. The boss is a busy man, with fingers in lots of different pies around the area."

"Understood. If he happens to drop by, and I'm still here, I'd like to meet him. Professional courtesy, you might say."

"Sure. You ready to play? I'm assuming you've got the cash with you?"

Lucas pulled out the envelope containing the ten grand, and showed the contents to Junior. His eyes followed Lucas' every movement, reminding Lucas of a cobra, mesmerized by the shiny object before him. Ah, the lure of temptation affected everyone, and Junior was no exception.

"If you'll follow me, let's get you set up. Do you prefer five card draw or Texas Hold 'Em? We also have a hot blackjack table, if you prefer."

"Texas Hold 'Em is my game," Lucas answered. Fortunately, he'd played enough games with his brothers and the guys on assignments he was pretty savvy.

Junior opened the door and led him to the guard by the front door, and had his cell phone confiscated. He was then directed through the center of the gaming club, past all the electronic machines with their bright flashing lights, vivid colors, and the jingle of coins. The whir of the electronic spins filled the air, along with the sounds of laughter from the patrons partaking of their games of chance. Too bad the house always won, and those machines were finessed to rarely pay out the big bucks.

Junior opened a door and the first thing that hit him was the overwhelming stench of cigarette smoke. He waved a hand in front of his face, his eyes watering from the fumes. It hadn't occurred to him, being used to smokeless buildings, that nearly everybody inside the confined space would be puffing away.

"Gentlemen, we've got a new player, Luke. He's not from around here, so take it easy on him," Junior quipped. He turned to Luke, and pointed to the table. "This is the Texas Hold 'Em table. This here is Joey, Dennis, Two-Step, Weasel, and Pauly. Guys, try not to clean Luke out in one hand, okay?"

Two-Step gave a huge belly laugh at Junior's warning. "Ain't making no promises." He studied Luke, his eyes squinted against the cigarette smoke. "You know how the game's played?"

"I'm familiar," Lucas responded, taking the empty chair. "Buy in's three grand?"

"Yeah."

Lucas pulled some money from the envelope, and put it on the table. "I'll take five grand."

Two-Step's eyes widened slightly, but he passed the chips across the table, and handed the cash off to the guard standing close by. "Ante up."

Everyone tossed their chips into the center of the table, and Joey was handed a new deck. Apparently he was the dealer, the rest players. Lucas knew it would take a couple of hands to get the feel of the other men at the table, assess any tics or quirks, any giveaway tells.

"What ya doing in Shiloh Springs, Luke?"

Lucas glanced at Pauly, a short, skinny balding man of indeterminate age, with thinning salt and pepper hair. He wouldn't have suspected Pauly of being a high roller, and suspected that he might be a plant at the table, somebody who encouraged the others to keep playing and digging deeper into their pockets for the next hand.

"My sister moved here, and she's getting married. Chances are good I'll be traveling here several times a year, since she's going to be living here."

"That's cool. You married?"

"No. Guess I haven't met the right woman yet." The minute the words left his mouth, a picture of Jill sprang forth. He shook his head, knowing he couldn't think about her now. This wasn't the time or the place to consider his feelings for Jill. He needed to concentrate, and Pauly was doing a darn good job of trying to distract him.

He lost the first hand when Weasel had a full house to his two pairs, queens over fours. The second hand he lost again, this time to Two-Steps' four deuces. He folded. On the third hand, he drew to a straight flush, and won the pot. The men chatted, tossing digs and barbs back and forth, and he listened closely, trying to figure out who these men were, and how high up in the club's hierarchy they stood, because a couple of these guys weren't casual Saturday-night regulars.

They'd played around an hour and a half, when the dealer called a ten-minute break, for people to head to the bathroom or handle whatever other business they might need, like getting more cash. Lucas suspected Weasel needed to slip outside and smoke some weed. Dennis hadn't said much for the last hour and a half, but he'd had shifty eyes and Lucas suspected there was more to Dennis than he'd uncovered. African-American, tall and well-built, he carried himself like an athlete, but he definitely knew how to play Texas Hold 'Em. He'd won a few hands, lost a few, always watching everyone. Kind of like him.

Standing up, he stretched his back, and Junior walked up to him. "I heard from the boss. If you're gonna be here a while, he's coming by in a couple of hours. Might be closer to midnight."

Lucas smiled and slapped Junior on the back. "No problem, I'm having a good time, though I'm down a couple grand. Gotta see if I can win it back."

"Who knows, maybe your luck will turn."

"It might. I should tell you, I spotted Pauly as a plant right off. You might want to tell him to cool it with the third degree, he's a little too obvious. Though it's a good idea to have at least one guy at the table as a distraction."

"Stupid punk. He's in deep with the boss, and he's working off the debt by steering the table. You've got a good eye."

"It's more like experience. I'm not exactly a newbie at the poker table."

The big grin on Junior's face was all the answer he got. "I'll come get you when the boss arrives, if you're still around."

"Thanks."

Grabbing a bottle of water, Lucas walked back to his seat, noticing Dennis had already returned to the table. Time for a little chit-chat before the rest of the gang got back. Insight into the players would add depth to his story. Besides, there was something about the way Dennis carried himself that reminded him of his brother, Antonio. Wait, that was it! He reminded him of a fed. Almost every single FBI agent he'd dealt with carried themselves with a certain air of confidence. No matter how hard they tried to hide it, unless the agent was adept at undercover work, the federal training showed. *Wonder what he's doing out in the middle of small-town Texas at an illegal after-hours gaming club?*

"You from around these parts, Dennis?"

"I moved to Santa Lucia about six months ago. Original-ly from Oklahoma City."

"I've never heard of Santa Lucia. Is it close to Shiloh Springs?"

"Next big town over the county line."

The more Dennis talked, the more convinced Lucas became there was more to the man than a poker player. From his speech to his mannerisms, he screamed fed. Which piqued his curiosity even more, making him wonder if he'd stepped smack into the middle of an undercover operation to take down the clubs in the area, or if the dude really was simply a guy who liked to gamble his paychecks.

"I'm not from around here, so I have no clue where all these places are. I know Shiloh Springs, because my sister lives here now, and I know Austin. Dallas-Fort Worth too, but everybody's heard of them. Won't take me long to find my way around, I'm thinking."

By now, the other players were making their way back to the table. Lucas immediately noticed that Joey was no longer their dealer, and an Asian woman slid into the vacant chair. Lucas couldn't help noticing that she was a lovely woman with flowing dark hair, huge brown eyes accented with mascara, and a beautiful white smile. She expertly shuffled the cards with a skill he couldn't help admiring. Meeting his gaze, she smiled, then moved on to Dennis. Seeing him, her smile dimmed the tiniest bit, before she regained her practiced composure, but not fast enough for Lucas not to notice. She'd recognized Dennis, and hadn't expected to see him here. *Interesting.*

"Are you gentlemen ready to resume play? I'm Lucy, your new dealer. Please ante up." Her voice was a low husky caress, professional and polished, exactly what he'd expect from someone in her position.

Lucas tossed his chips into the pile on the table, and glanced at his hole cards. King of Clubs and Queen of Clubs. Pretty good start. She quickly performed the flop and dealt the community cards in the center of the table. King of Hearts, Queen of Diamonds, and Ace of Clubs. He called the bet. The dealer then dealt the turn card, or the fourth card in the community cards. It was the Ten of Clubs. If the dealer uncovered the Jack of Clubs, Lucas would have a royal flush.

His heartbeat sped up as a shot of adrenaline raced through him. Even though he'd come for information, there remained an air of excitement he couldn't quash at the thought of a royal flush. Although not impossible, it was a difficult hand to get.

The dealer turned over the river card, and he deflated. It was the six of clubs, which meant although he hadn't achieved the elusive royal flush, but he did have a flush. Deciding to push his luck, he raised the bet by two grand. Dennis immediately folded, tossing his cards face down onto the table. Pauly tugged at his collar, a sign Lucas picked up

LUCAS

on, which meant he was about to bluff. He called. Weasel looked at Pauly and then at Lucas, and tossed his cards onto the table.

"I'm out."

"Raise it another two grand." Lucas grinned when Pauly gulped, the sound audible even in the noisy back room. Looking at the stack of chips in front of Pauly, he had enough to cover the bet, but barely. If he folded, he could play a few more hands. If he called and lost, Pauly was out of the game.

"I—I fold."

Lucas turned over his hole cards, and watched Pauly grin. Guess his hand hadn't been that good after all. Surreptitiously, he glanced at his watch, wondering how long it would be before the big boss got there. It was already eleven thirty, and he was down about half the cash he'd brought with him. The loss would be worth it, if he managed to get enough info to help Rafe nail these jerks to the wall.

For now, he'd keep playing, waiting for Junior to take him to meet the big boss. The thought filled him with a sense of urgency, because Lucas had the feeling something big was in the air. Nothing he could put his finger on, but his gut instinct never let him down.

With an inward sigh, he picked up his cards and started the next hand.

CHAPTER NINETEEN

Jill had barely pulled the T-shirt and pajama bottoms on when the doorbell rang. She'd planned to take her e-reader to bed with her since she felt wide awake and knew sleep wouldn't come easily. Looking at the doorbell's camera, she took an automatic step back in shock.

The doorbell sounded again. This time, knowing who stood on the other side, the sound resonated with an eerie sense of foreboding. Fleetingly, the thought raced through her head to pretend not to be home, but she got the feeling her unwanted guest already knew she was cowering behind the door. She wondered if he was amused or irritated by her delay in answering his summons.

"Can I help you?" she asked through the intercom on the doorbell.

"Ms. Monroe? It's Emmanuel. Emmanuel Benevides. I'd like to speak with you."

Jill felt a shiver race through her at the sound of his voice. Did he think she wouldn't recognize the man who'd had her brother beaten bloody? Not likely. "Mr. Benevides, is this something that can wait until tomorrow? It's late, and

I'm really not comfortable opening the door to a stranger this late at night."

"Ms. Monroe…or may I call you Jillian? Such a lovely name for such a lovely woman. I'm only asking for a moment of your time."

"I'm sorry, Mr. Benevides—"

"Please, call me Emmanuel."

Jill shook her head, unable to believe she was having a conversation after ten o'clock in the evening with a known thug. Was thug even the right word? No matter how he tried to pretty up the circumstances, he ran a gambling ring, and she wasn't about to open her door to a man like him—especially when she was alone.

"Mr. Benevides, it's late, and I barely know you. Unless this is some kind of emergency, I'd really like you to leave."

"*Querida*, I heard you had some difficulty with your car. I wanted to see for myself you were alright. I hope it was nothing serious."

An eerie sense of dread spread through her with each word he spoke. How could he possibly know about her tires? She doubted it was the hot topic around Shiloh Springs. Jill knew she was a tiny fish in her small town, and didn't warrant any kind of attention or notoriety.

"Everything's fine, Mr. Benevides. It wasn't serious. My brother, Dante, fixed the problem right away." Instantly she regretted mentioning Dante's name, bringing up the reminder of what the other man's actions had done to her brother.

"Ah, yes, your intrepid brother. I haven't seen Dante is a while. He's doing well, I presume?"

"My brother is fine. Is there anything else, because I'd like to turn in. It's been a long day."

"Very well, *querida*." I'm going to leave my card with my number." Jill watched a small white business card appear beneath her front door, and picked it up with two fingers, not wanting to touch it.

"I have it."

"Excellent. I look forward to hearing from you."

Eww, why does the thought of talking to him make my skin crawl?

"By the way, did you receive the gift I sent you?"

"Gift? What are you talking…do you mean the brace-let?"

"*Si*, the diamonds. I know it will look beautiful on you, though not even their brilliance compares to your beauty, Jillian."

"I got your gift, although I had no way of knowing it was from you, Mr. Benevides, since there wasn't a card. I turned it over to the police. I'll make sure that Sheriff Boudreau makes sure it's returned to you. I can't possibly accept such a gift. It's far too expensive."

"I insist. I'll personally notify Sheriff Boudreau to return it to you. Please, call me tomorrow. I look forward to getting to know you. Good night, my dear. Pleasant dreams."

"Ah, good night, Mr. Benevides."

She kept her eyes glued to the camera, watching until he was out of sight before leaning against the door and drawing in a ragged breath.

That was weird. I've barely spoken to the man, and he's acting like he wants to—what—go out with me? Date me? I wasn't very pleasant the only time we've been face to face. What in the world is he thinking?

"Well, guess that confirms it. No way am I sleeping tonight."

She'd barely taken two steps before her phone rang, and she jumped. During the whole conversation with Mr. Benevides, she'd held her cell in her hand, and once he'd walked away, she'd forgotten she still held it. She was surprised to see her brother's name on the caller ID.

"Dante? What's wrong?"

"You tell me. What was Emmanuel Benevides doing at your apartment?"

"How'd you know he—"

"Never mind how I know. Sis, you need to stay away from him, he's bad news."

Jill walked over to the couch and sat back against the cushions, tucking her legs beneath her. Something in her brother's voice had goosebumps popping up on her skin. Guess her instincts were right about Benevides. He was trouble, the kind she didn't need to get involved with. She had enough on her plate, and didn't need to attract the unwanted attention of a psycho.

"It's not like I invited the guy over, Dante. He showed up at my door, saying he heard about my car trouble. I have no idea how he found out about my flats, but he gives me the creeps, so I didn't open the door. He did admit he's the one who sent me the bracelet."

"What bracelet?"

"That's right, you didn't know about that. It's been kind of a crazy night. Somebody left a diamond bracelet outside my front door. There wasn't anybody outside, because I checked. I called Rafe and he came over and took the bracelet to the sheriff's station, because those diamonds looked real, and I didn't know what to do with something that expensive."

There was a long pause before Dante asked, "Emmanuel Benevides sent you a diamond bracelet?" Each syllable got louder than the last.

"Yep. Of course, I told him I'd given it to Rafe, and I'd have it returned. Mr. Benevides insists I keep it. Said he'd talk to Rafe and have it given back to me. Which seems really odd, don't you think? I don't know the man. Only met him one time, which I'm sure you remember?"

"Yeah, it's kinda permanently etched into my brain. A beatdown like that isn't something you forget."

"He left me his number. He wants me to call him tomorrow."

"Jilly, you stay as far away from Emmanuel Benevides as

you can. You aren't part of his world, and if I have anything to do with it, you'll never be."

"I've got no intention of calling him. Now how about you answer my question? How did you know Mr. Benevides came to my apartment?"

When her doorbell rang, it startled her enough she almost dropped her phone.

"It's me, Jilly. Open the door."

She slid open the deadbolt and the door lock, and found her brother standing in the hall. He wasn't alone.

"Douglas, I mean Mr. Boudreau, what are you doing here?"

"You can call me Douglas. I think we'd better talk."

Pulling the door wider, both men walked into her apartment, and she found herself nervously pulling on the edge of her T-shirt, tugging it down to cover the gaudy sleep pants she'd put on. She hadn't expected company, so she'd grabbed a pair or bright yellow bottoms with rainbow-hued unicorns dancing on them.

"Okay, somebody tell me what's going on. First, I've got the local gambling lord showing up on my doorstep, sending me diamonds. Then the two of you show up immediately on his heels. What aren't you telling me? Oh, by the way, what's the big idea not telling me the tires were tampered with? I had to hear it from Rafe."

"My son's got a big mouth." Douglas took her arm gently and steered her to the couch, taking a seat beside her. "I wasn't convinced you'd rolled over something when I looked at your flat tires earlier, so I asked your brother to give them a once over. He spotted some scratches and damage around the valves."

Jill nodded, understanding what he was saying. It had finally sunk in, though she still didn't have a clue why. "I'm still not sure why I was kept out of the loop. Shouldn't I have been the first person to be told?"

"Sis, we didn't want you to worry."

Jill rolled her eyes, before giving her brother a disgruntled glare. "I'm a whole lot more worried now than I would've been if you'd told me the truth."

"I'm sorry. It won't happen again."

"Darn right it won't. You're not too big for me to wallop." She smiled sweetly to temper her threat. "Now explain to me why you and Douglas are here? Or should I simply assume you decided to watch my apartment, since you couldn't bother to tell me my tires were tampered with?"

"I was worried, okay? Lucas and I agreed—"

Jill stood up and slammed her hands on her hips, glaring at her brother. "You dragged Lucas into this without telling me? You are so dead!"

"Jill." She froze on the spot at the sound of Douglas' deep voice, filled with command. Fisting her hands, she turned to look at him. "Dante doesn't bear all the responsibility. I knew. Lucas knew. None of us were going to stand idly by while somebody threatened one of our own."

A feeling of warmth spread through her, displacing the icy chill which enveloped her for the last several minutes, ever since Benevides had knocked on her door. Something about the way Douglas said those words made her feel...cherished.

"While I appreciate the sentiment, guys, I'm a grown woman, perfectly capable of taking care of myself. From now on, include me in anything pertaining to me and my safety. Got it?"

"Understood," Douglas nodded as he spoke, and Dante's head bobbed in agreement. "Now that we've cleared that up, tell me about Emmanuel Benevides. Dante seemed very closemouthed when you mentioned him."

Jill's eyes met Dante's, reading the shame and regret filling his expression, before he nodded. "Let me tell him."

"Alright."

Jill moved back to sit beside Douglas, watching Dante pace back and forth in front of the coffee table. She agonized along with him, knowing he'd give anything not to have to admit his weakness to Douglas Boudreau. Yet she recognized her brother had grown up a lot in the last few months, becoming a man she was proud of.

"Emmanuel Benevides runs the local gaming club. He's got a place over on the county border. He's the big boss, rakes in tons of money from illegal gambling. I got sucked in with some of my buddies. It was easy money at first. We graduated from poker games in Junior's garage to informal back room poker tournaments for higher stakes. Benevides promoted my friend Junior to manager, because although Junior's my buddy, he's also ruthless when it comes to money and power—and Benevides tempted him with both."

Dante scrubbed his hands over his face, and not for the first time Jill wished her brother had never given in to temptation.

"I knew there was illegal gambling in the county, heard rumors about it for years, but had no idea where the club was located."

"Yeah, Douglas, these places aren't out in the open, because then Rafe could bust 'em. It's in a nearly deserted strip mall. Place is always packed. Heck, some nights there's so many people there, they could get busted for being over occupancy. You can't imagine the amount of money it pulls in on a nightly basis. Emmanuel runs the one here in Shiloh Springs, and another one in Burnet County. I'm ashamed to admit how much money I threw away, chasing after a pipe dream."

"I think I've got the picture. Your buddy Junior encouraged you until you got in over your head, right? Racked up a debt big enough you couldn't pay it back. That's what they do. At least, they did when I was young and stupid."

Dante's eyes rounded in surprise. "You?"

Douglas chuckled. "Son, none of us is perfect. I was something of a wild man when I was in the Army, both here and abroad. It's easy to get sucked in. People pay attention to you, make you feel important, especially when you're winning. Losing, on the other hand, sucks. You find yourself chasing the next hand, the next win. The fever, the rush, catches you by the throat and doesn't turn loose. Winning is a heady, intoxicating feeling. Makes you feel like you're on top of the world and nobody can stop you. Problem is, nobody stays on top for long, and the fall can be a killer."

"That's it exactly!" Dante's voice rose in excitement. "You feel like you're invincible. Nobody can touch you because you're the big man. Until reality slams you upside the head with a reality check. It certainly did for me."

"Dante, it's okay. It's over, we're past it." Jill walked over and wrapped her arm around her brother, giving him a gentle hug.

"No, we're not. I'm the one who brought Benevides to your door. You lost everything because I'm an idiot. Now that you're in Benevides' sights, I'm not sure what he'll do. He might carry himself like a gentleman in front of you, but I've seen the real man. Trust me, he's evil to the core. I want you to stay as far away from him as possible."

"I agree with your brother, Jill. I think we should have Rafe and Antonio find out exactly who Mr. Benevides is, and why he's suddenly sniffing around you."

Jill shuddered as she remembered Emmanuel's eyes, the soulless black void, and wrapped her arms across her chest, trying to ward off the sudden chill. "Excellent idea. I need to know who and what I'm dealing with."

"How about I spend the night on your couch, Sis? It'll make me feel better, especially since Benevides came sniffing around. In the morning, we'll talk to Rafe, and fill him in on everything."

"Yes, you can spend the night. I can't go see Rafe first thing in the morning, though. I've got deliveries and shipments coming in, and I have to be at the bakery. We can call him in the morning, and see if he can come by there."

Dante looked at Douglas, who gave a sharp nod. Jill bit her lip to keep from smiling at the way her brother deferred to the older man. He couldn't find a better role model and example to follow. She walked over and clasped his hand in between hers.

"Thank you, Douglas, for being concerned about me, and coming to watch over me with Dante. Since he's going to stay the night, you go on home. If anything happens, I promise we'll call."

"I'll hold you to that, Jill. I haven't told Ms. Patti much, because she tends to worry about you gals. Be prepared, because when she hears about this—and she will—you're gonna have to answer a million and one questions. Don't be surprised if she shows up on your doorstep. She might be a sharp businesswoman, but at heart she's a nurturer, and you're officially one of her baby chicks."

"I'm honored. Thank you again."

After he left, she twisted the deadbolt, locked the apartment up tight, and whirled on her brother.

"I'm too tired to deal with anything else tonight. Pillows and an extra blanket are in the hall closet. If you're hungry, help yourself to anything in the kitchen."

Walking the short distance between them, she grabbed her brother's face between her hands. "I appreciate that you worry about me, but next time, don't leave me in the dark, okay? I'm not a fragile porcelain doll. I won't break." She stretched up on her tiptoes and kissed his cheek. "Love you."

"Love you more."

Emmanuel Benevides sat in his Mercedes in the apartment building's parking lot, and watched the lights go off in Jillian's apartment. Dante showed up on her doorstep mere minutes after she'd turned Emmanuel away, along with an older man who looked very familiar. If he wasn't mistaken, and he rarely was, it had been Douglas Boudreau. Strange, his intel hadn't mentioned either of the Monroe's knowing the core family of Shiloh Springs, though he'd seen them traipsing through her new shop. Like everyone else in this tiny town, he'd heard of the Boudreau family and their foster sons. All of them held positions of authority, so-called honorable men, like their adoptive father. He doubted any of them would be darkening the doors of his clubs.

A few bad seeds had made their way through the Boudreau clan over the years, ones who'd managed to withstand the syrupy message spewed by the do-gooders. The Texas foster care system didn't always succeed in placing kids with an environment that matched their personalities, no matter how careful the selection process worked. One of the men who'd stayed for a short time with the Boudreaus worked with his big brother, Javier, down in Harris County.

Might be time to dig a little deeper, and see if these Boudreaus were going to be a problem. Emmanuel chuckled, the sound echoing inside the car. Luckily, he was very good at taking care of problems. Do-gooders like the Boudreaus might think they were pillars of the community, but Emmanuel knew how easy it was for the mighty to fall. To give in to temptation. Or to threats. When that didn't work, he wasn't opposed to physical displays to get his point across.

It irked his pride that Jill Monroe turned him away from her door, a thwarted suitor for her affection. She fascinated him, had from the second he'd seen her standing before him, unafraid for herself, her only concern for her brother. It had been close, because he'd almost decided to wipe Dante's debt clear, just to see her again. But business and pleasure didn't mix, as he'd learned the hard way. Still, he hadn't forgotten about Jillian.

Tonight, he'd heard the tremble in her voice, tinged with fear. Not such a bad thing, fear. People did a lot of things they'd never do, with a little motivation. She'd regret turning him away from her door.

Turning over the engine, he pulled out of the parking lot

and headed for his club. Time to get a little work done, then he could turn his mind toward pleasure. Winning the beautiful Jillian would be his greatest challenge, and possibly his greatest reward. Regardless of the cost, he would have her.

CHAPTER TWENTY

"Hey, Luke, you ready to take a break?" Junior walked over to stand behind his chair. Lucas winced, wanting to berate the idiot for a clear *faux pas*. Didn't he know better? You never take up a position behind an active player.

"Let me finish this hand."

At the turn of the next card, he folded, and stood, motioning to have his stack of chips cashed in, and headed toward the front of the club with Junior. Hopefully, it meant he was about to meet the big cheese. The noise from inside the main room was deafening, the place packed wall-to-wall with bodies, crammed into the space and playing the electronic machines, plunking down their money like lemmings.

"Got a call from the boss. He's on his way. He should be here in about ten minutes. Wanted to give you a head's up, though. It sounded like he wasn't in a real jovial mood, if you know what I mean. It's up to you, but if you want to come by another time to meet him, it might not be a bad idea."

"Thanks, but I think I'll stick around."

Lucas thought he heard Junior murmur, "It's your funeral" under his breath, and almost laughed out loud. Wasn't like whoever the big boss was would take him out back and blow his brains out. All anybody here knew was Luke was a dude from back east, who wanted to play whenever he was in town.

It was more like five minutes before the door swung inward, and a Hispanic male strode through like he owned the joint—which he obviously did. Employees and guards reacted like they'd been gigged with a cattle prod. Postures changed, from relaxed and slouched to military-style attention. Smiles got plastered on the faces of the women moving from area to area, taking drink orders and generally helping customers. Guy apparently commanded a hearty dose of fear and respect from those working for him. Good to know.

Lucas stood off to the side, watching, observing every movement, every nuance of the man's aura of control. From every movement, even his stance, it was apparent he held a tight rein on his workers. Whether through fear and intimidation or excellent pay was yet to be determined. Junior rushed over, words spilling from his mouth a mile a minute. He practically genuflected, and Lucas fought the urge to roll his eyes at the display.

Focus. Watch. Figure out who this dude is, what's his angle, and the best way to take him down.

Junior gestured toward Lucas, and motioned him over. He took his time crossing the distance separating them, calm and casual, but with a 'don't mess with me' attitude. For now, he'd cede control to the newcomer, the boss, and learn how to read him. Figure out his weakness, because men like Junior's boss always had one. Pride, greed, corruption of others, a need was always there beneath the surface to display their superiority. He needed to figure it out.

"Luke, this is Emmanuel Benevides. He's the proprietor of this fine establishment. Emmanuel, this is Luke—what was your last name again? I forgot."

"Stewart."

"Yep, that's right. Luke Stewart. He's the friend of Dante Monroe's I told you about. His sister moved to Shiloh Springs, and Luke's visiting. He wanted to meet you, because he's got his own club back home."

Benevides listened as Junior rambled through the introduction, his gaze laser focused on Lucas, appraising and weighing him. Lucas couldn't help wondering if he'd pass muster or be found lacking.

"Welcome to my club, Mr. Stewart. Where exactly are you from?"

"North Carolina. Charlotte to be precise. Nice place you've got. I'm impressed."

"You're very kind. I hope Junior's been giving you the VIP treatment." Benevides' voice held no hint of an accent, and Lucas figured he'd probably been born and raised in the

U.S. Benevides' gaze caught Junior's, and Lucas saw the other man turn pale. Uh oh, looked like Junior had done something his boss wasn't too pleased about.

Without a word, Junior spun and raced toward the back room, the one Lucas spent the evening playing poker. Within minutes, he reappeared, holding a glass of what looked like whiskey in one hand, and a bottle of beer in the other. He gave a brief nod and handed the whiskey to Benevides, and passed Lucas the beer.

"Mr. Stewart, perhaps you'd join me in my office. I'd like to hear a bit more about your club in North Carolina. Junior said you own your own place."

"I don't own the entire club. I'm merely a silent partner. I have two others who run the day-to-day operation. You might call it an…investment in my future."

Benevides' smile sent a chill up Lucas' spine. "A profitable one, I hope."

"I do well."

Benevides opened an unmarked door, and stood aside, waiting for Lucas to precede him into what appeared to be an office. Though the furnishings were sparse, the one thing that stood out was the large freestanding safe off to the side. He could only imagine the amount of cash socked away inside. With the crowd outside, he'd wager it held upwards of six figures. Probably more after they closed out the night's activities.

"Junior told me Dante referred you?"

Lucas nodded, ready to embellish his tale. "Yes. His sister is a friend of my sister. It's a crazy story how she ended up here, but she's happy and that's all that matters. I mentioned to Dante I missed my poker games, and he recommended your club."

He hadn't missed the strange expression that crossed Benevides' face when he'd mentioned Dante's sister, even though he hadn't said Jill's name. Something in his eyes made Lucas twitchy.

"You've met Dante's sister, Jillian. Such a lovely woman."

"Sure. I've met her once or twice, when she's been with my sister. I didn't pay her much attention. I've always made it a point not to get involved with any of my sister's friends. Did that once. Things got ugly. It's easier to avoid that particular complication."

Good thing I'm lying through my teeth. I don't want this dude getting any ideas about Jill. I'll have to get Dante a head's up to keep Jill away from Benevides.

"Tell me about your club, Mr. Stewart."

"Luke. It's a little smaller than this one. The setup is on the outskirts of Charlotte. We've found too close to the city tends to draw more unwanted attention than we're comfortable with. Most of our clientele prefer card games. Less poker than here; we run more toward blackjack. Although we have seen an uptick in selling lottery tickets, our own of course. Prizes vary from televisions to large appliances, automobiles, and of course, cash."

"Lottery tickets? Texas does a huge business selling lottery tickets, and they are legal. I can't see spending the time or effort on something with little monetary return."

Lucas shrugged, and took another drink of his beer. "It's legal in North Carolina, too, but people find the temptation of winning a prize without the requirement of giving Uncle Sam a portion of their prize is tempting. A temptation most of them are willing to indulge. I'll be honest, probably a third to a half of our profits come from those private lottery ticket sales."

"Interesting." Benevides leaned back in his chair, his fingers steepled above his chest. "I may look into something like that, if the profits are as good as you claim."

"Trust me, they are. You might spend a thousand bucks on an enormous flat screen TV, then sell ten or fifteen thousand chances to win it for a dollar a pop. Fourteen grand profit, and your winner goes home ecstatic because they got a huge prize. Same thing with other prizes. Your return on investment can be astronomical. We've got a guy who regularly prints up scratch off tickets for cash prizes and the like. His work is impeccable. Looks exactly like something the state would have, at a fraction of the cost."

A soft knock on the door stopped Lucas from concocting even more elaborate lies. Reading the greed in Benevides' eyes was easy, and he seemed interested in what Lucas alluded to, almost like a cobra watching the snake charmer.

"Come in," Benevides barked.

Junior walked in, hold several money pouches. A slight smile curved the corners of Benevides' lips when he spotted them. Junior moved past them, headed directly for the safe, and entered the combination, depositing the bags inside. Lucas felt the bottom of his stomach drop when he spotted the stacks of cash inside. Looked like he'd underestimated the amount.

After Junior closed the door behind him, Benevides stood and offered his hand. "I've enjoyed hearing about your endeavors on the east coast. Perhaps we can talk further, if you're going to be in Shiloh Springs for long?"

"I'm not sure how long I'll be around. I know I'll be traveling to Shiloh Springs several times in the upcoming months, both for business and to visit her." Lucas tried to be as vague as possible. Having spent several hours in the club, he had a good chunk of information for his story, notwithstanding all the dirt he'd gotten from Dante. Yet something kept him from burning his bridges completely. He needed access to Benevides, to the club, to give to Rafe and Antonio. It was imperative they got enough evidence to shut them down. It might be only one club in a slew of many, but it was in his own backyard, which meant he knew a lot of the people who'd be tempted to indulge. Understood the lure of quick cash, the enticement of winning, making the big score.

"Feel free to come back anytime."

"Thank you."

"If you'll excuse me, I need to get some work done. You know how it is."

"Of course. I need to get back to my sister's place anyway."

Lucas stepped out of the office, again being hit with the scent of stale cigarette smoke and alcohol. With a quick glance around, he spotted Dennis, the guy he'd played poker with, walking out the front door. Increasing his pace, he decided to take a chance and see if he could catch up with the guy.

Hot air smacked him in the face when he walked outside. The day had been a scorcher, and the humidity still hung in the air. Dennis leaned against his car with his arms crossed over his chest, a speculative look on his face.

"You seemed to have a good night."

"Not bad, though I pretty much broke even," Lucas answered. "Feel like talking?"

Dennis chuckled, his laugh deep and filled with mirth. "I've been killing time, waiting for you to get out of the boss man's office. But not here, too much chance of somebody noticing us."

"Do you know Juanita's?"

"Yeah. Meet you there." Without another word, Dennis climbed into his car and sped away, leaving Lucas to stare at his taillights. With a weary shake of his head, he slid behind the wheel of his car and followed. Ending up at Juanita's parking lot was becoming a habit.

Pulling into the nearly deserted parking lot, he spotted Dennis' sedan parked in the first row, close to the building. Glancing at the clock on his dash, he knew Juanita's would be closing soon, so they'd have to make this quick if they didn't want to be spotted.

Dennis climbed into the passenger seat, and swiveled to face Lucas. "Who are you?"

"I think that's my question. You asked me to meet you."

"Like you didn't have a million questions, sitting in Benevides' place. I beat you to the punch."

Lucas admitted what Dennis said was true. He'd still bet the guy was law enforcement, though he wasn't sure what type.

"So, you a fed?"

The right side of Dennis' lip quirked up and Lucas spotted the deep dimple in his cheek. *Glad he finds me amusing.*

"Not exactly."

"Lemme guess. This is personal."

Dennis slumped in the seat, and heaved a sigh. "Yeah. These clubs might not seem to be a huge deal for a lot of people, but the people that run them are a blight. Did you know in Texas, gambling is only a misdemeanor, carries a five hundred dollar fine? These leeches rake in hundreds of thousands of dollars at a time, and barely get a slap on the wrist."

"So I've heard. The laws need changing, but it takes time."

"And in the meantime, these so-called gaming bosses take their profits and use them to transport women and children across the border in record numbers, filling the pipeline of human trafficking until it's become a multibillion-dollar business. Between that and funding the cartels in Mexico and South America, supplying illegal guns and drugs, it's like a cesspool of corruption, yet law enforcement's hands are tied, because the laws don't consider this a big enough crime. What's it going to take to open the Texas legislature's eyes to the massive amounts of money changing hands? Of course, some of that money is being funneled straight into corrupt politicians' pockets."

"You seem to know a lot about what's going on with the illegal clubs. Something or somebody put you on their scent. I've got my own reasons for being at the club tonight. If this is personal for you, I want to hear your story, get all the facts. If this is about vengeance, getting even through some kind of vigilante justice, I'm out."

Dennis met Lucas' eyes, never once backing down. "Oh, there's a measure of vengeance in my quest, but I'm not planning on heading inside one of these places and shooting up the place. I'm not going to hunt down Benevides or Junior in a dark alley. I want them behind bars. Payment due for what they did to my brother."

Lucas wanted to bang his head against the steering wheel. Frustrated at another person dragged into gambling's wretched stranglehold, leaving behind family to pick up the pieces and try to comprehend why.

"Looks like we both want the same thing."

"I knew it! Took me a few minutes once you sat down at the table, but there was this gleam in your eyes, like you were sizing up everybody at the table, wanting to dig deep enough to know their story. What's your deal?"

He could be making the biggest mistake of his career, but his gut told him to trust Dennis. Lucas believed he was telling the truth, and he might have actual intel, enough to go to Rafe and Antonio. Regardless, at the very least, his story would shed light on an insidious disease buried in the legal system, allowing its cancerous reach to spread throughout the state. Might open the eyes of people who could get things done, maybe get the penalties increased. If nothing else, he'd shine a light on the devastating consequences the impact of gambling had on each individual who succumbed to its lure.

"Before you decide whether to tell me anything else, I'm going to be straight with you. My name isn't Luke Stewart. I'm Lucas Boudreau. I'm an investigative reporter, doing research for a story about illegal gambling."

"I didn't peg you for law enforcement, unless you've been undercover for a long time. You're too smooth. You've got eyes like an eagle, studying and cataloging everything around you."

Lucas nodded, before answering. "I figured you for a cop. You move like one."

"Closest I ever got to being a cop was being raised by one. Dad served in Chicago for twenty years. When he retired, said he wanted to move where it was warmer. Said he was sick of the snow and ice. Picked Texas."

"Good choice."

"He always claimed it was the best decision he ever made. Lost him a couple of years ago to cancer."

"I'm sorry." Lucas glanced at the clock on the dash and winced. It was already after one. Interviewing and getting details from Dennis would probably take a couple of hours. Besides, he wanted to get his recorder, to document everything, and have a record of the conversation and the facts.

"Listen, I really want to talk with you and find out more about your brother's story. Can you meet me tomorrow? We can start fresh. Plus, if you don't mind, I'd like to tape our conversation, have the facts on the record."

"I've got to work in the morning, but I can meet you after."

"Great. Why don't we meet here? We can grab a bite and then work on the story."

"Works for me. Say six o'clock?"

"Sounds good. Oh, one more question. Who's Lucy?"

Lucas watched Dennis's eye widen at the woman's name, knew there was a story there. "Caught that, huh? She's my sister-in-law—was my sister-in-law. She ended up working at the club because she was broke. Woman's too proud for her own good. I offered help, but she wouldn't accept any. I didn't know she'd started working there until I saw her at the club a few months ago. Tried to get her to stop, but she won't. She's up to her neck in debt from Jimmy's death."

"Gotcha. She wasn't expecting you to be there tonight, was she?"

He shrugged. "Lucy doesn't run my life. She's pretty much cut me out of hers."

Oh, yeah, there's definitely a story there.

"Sorry to hear that. I'll see you tomorrow."

Dennis climbed out and Lucas watched him walk across the parking lot. He waited until the other man drove away, then realized he hadn't gotten his number. Guess he was tired to have forgotten something like that.

Looked like tomorrow was going to be an eye opener, as long as Dennis showed up. Time would tell.

CHAPTER TWENTY-ONE

It was late, but Lucas couldn't sleep. After talking with Dennis, he headed home, planning to grab some shut eye before meeting him the next day. Everything was falling into place, and he could almost feel the story taking shape in his mind. The initial night at Benevides' club went well, better than he'd hoped.

Benevides had been open to the whole line of baloney he'd practically spoon fed him about his "club" in North Carolina, and the counterfeit lottery winning tickets. Between his poker table observations and the information he'd gleaned from Junior and Benevides, he had a much better handle on where the story led.

He'd written up notes, documented more facts, and transcribed the recording of his interview with Dante. For somebody so young, he had a mind like a steel trap, remembering minute details about places, people, even the type of electronic machines used at the gaming club.

Yet it was hard concentrating on his story, something that never happened, because his focus shifted to Jill. This trip home felt different. Usually he'd drop in, spend some time with the family, and then he'd be itching to get back to his place in Dallas-Fort Worth. He wasn't sure what had changed, but he wasn't in any particular hurry to go back to an empty apartment in the heart of the city, eating takeout and watching baseball.

Being back in Shiloh Springs, surrounded by his family felt right. He didn't believe the old idiom you can't go home again. Deep in his soul, he'd always known someday he'd end up back here, where he'd spent his formative years, rough as they'd been. Shiloh Springs had given him something he'd never expected—a family and a home. Maybe it was time he considered coming back where he belonged.

He wasn't sure what prompted his next action. Some imp on his shoulder, or a deep-seated, almost overwhelming desire to talk to her, but he gave in to temptation, picked up his phone and texted Jill.

ME: You awake?

A few seconds passed, before he heard the text alert.

JILL: Yes.

ME: Want to talk?

JILL: Okay.

He quickly dialed Jill's number, suddenly desperate to hear the sound of her voice.

"Hi."

"Hey. Did I wake you?"

"No, I wasn't sleeping. Mostly tossing and turning." He

could almost hear the laughter in her voice.

"I haven't been to bed yet. Working on the story, and needed to unwind before trying to grab a couple of hours. Sorry I didn't get to see you tonight, though. It's been nice getting to spend time with you since I've been back."

He heard cloth rustling, and he couldn't help picturing her leaning against the pillows, a bedside lamp sending a soft glow through her room. She'd have her hair down, spread across the pillow, and he swallowed. *Stop, dude. The last thing you need is to be picturing Jill in bed. Looking all tousled and mussed, like she's just waking up, her soft skin lightly flushed and her lips so kissable, soft, begging for yours.*

"I've missed you too, Lucas."

"Do you ever miss us? The way we used to spend every spare minute together? We couldn't keep our hands off each other. Some days I'll hear something, a voice or a song, and I'll think of you."

He heard her sharp inhalation, and wondered if his admission startled her.

"I miss us, too. You were my everything. My first real boyfriend. My first taste of puppy love. My first kiss."

"I remember, too. I'd told you about Renee. How we'd gotten separated by child welfare, and ended up with Douglas and Ms. Patti." He closed his eyes, thinking back to that day. Young, stupid, filled with raging hormones, angry at the unfairness of a system who'd basically stolen his baby sister away. At least, that's how he looked at it through teenage eyes.

"We started eleventh grade. I came up to the Big House to work on homework. I'd needed help with algebra, and you'd wanted help with chemistry."

Lucas chuckled. "You were such a sucker. I told you I wanted help with chemistry, but my mind was strictly filled with biology. Especially the man/woman kind."

"Perv."

"What can I say, Jill? I was a teenage boy, and you were pretty."

Jill's rich laughter sounded sweet, and he smiled at the sound. He'd missed talks like these, where they'd share their days. Back in school, they'd talk almost every day, filling the other in on everything they'd done. It became almost a nightly ritual to wait for her call.

"I remember that was the first time you took me to your mother's secret garden. The gazebo. If I close my eyes, I remember every detail, every smell. It was the perfect afternoon."

"Close your eyes, Jill. I'll close mine. I want to remember it with you."

"Lucas…"

"Please, indulge me. Close your eyes, sweetheart."

After a beat or two, he heard, "Fine, they're closed."

"Tell me what you're thinking, standing in the gazebo. I remember how I felt. I was nervous. I'd never taken anybody there. Momma's secret garden is exactly that—secret. We were supposed to get her permission before we took anybody there. She always claimed it was a magical place, and only to be shared with somebody we really cared about."

Her heard Jill's indrawn breath. "I didn't know that."

"Momma's very private when it comes to her special spot. Always claimed there was a fae-like quality to it, like it held the magic of love. All us guys would laugh, because we didn't care about silly girly stuff like falling in love. In the years since, I've learned she was right."

"The first thing I remember is the scent of roses. Roses and pine trees. Not a combination you'd expect, but it comforted me. I looked at the white structure, which should have been out of place in the middle of all those trees, on a ranch in the middle of Texas, but it wasn't. It fit in a way I couldn't comprehend, but it felt right."

"Exactly. She worked on her garden for years, striving to make it perfect. I used to see Rafe trailing along behind her, ready to dig in the dirt. I always wondered if it was because he fell in love with gardening, or if it was because it meant he got to spend quality alone time with Momma."

"Probably a bit of both." Lucas could hear the smile in her words. "Tessa said Rafe still likes gardening. He's constantly planting things at his house."

"He's got a green thumb, that's for sure. Not something I can boast having."

"Unfortunately, I didn't get the gardening gene, either," Jill admitted softly.

Lucas chuckled. "Something else we have in common. What else do you remember?"

"We kissed." The words were so low, he almost wondered if he'd heard them or if he imagined them.

"We kissed," he repeated the words, letting them sink in.

"It was my first kiss."

"I wish I could say it was my first, but I swear it was the most special kiss I've ever gotten."

"Maybe then, but since—"

"The. Most. Special. Kiss. Ever. There's nothing that compares with a kiss given in love."

"Lucas—I…"

"I'm not trying to embarrass you. Simply stating the truth. What else do you remember, sweetheart?"

"We talked about Renee. I remember you swore to find her, no matter how long it took. Though you hadn't seen her in over a decade, your love for your sister brought me to tears. I remember you telling me about your Aunt Hattie, who'd raised you after your mother died. I'm sorry about what you went through, Lucas. No one deserves to be treated like—"

"Sometimes life deals us a lousy hand, sweetheart. I'm thankful Renee was too young to realize or remember a lot of what happened."

"But you do."

"Life's not always fair. I never knew who my father was. Kind of hard when your mother is a hooker. The state felt

Aunt Hattie would be the best place for us when my mother OD'd. Little did they know we'd have been better off on the streets, scrounging for food like rabid wolf cubs. She was a mean, nasty drunk, without an ounce of compassion or love in her heart, but she wasn't about to lose out on the checks she got once a month for taking me and Renee into her home. I don't like thinking about my life before Douglas and Ms. Patti. I thank God every night for placing me in their home. I hope Renee ended up with people who loved and cared for her."

"Lucas, have you heard anything about her recently? I know you haven't given up looking for her. Ms. Patti kind of keeps me in the loop, because she knows we were friends."

"Are. We *are* friends. Because I was an idiot doesn't change the fact you were and still are my best friend." Lucas' voice caught in his throat after he said the words, because the truth of what he really wanted to say struck him in the heart.

He loved Jill. A wave of emotion rolled over him was like a tsunami, threatening to drown him with the reality of what he'd carelessly tossed aside. He realized the cost had been too high. The cold, hard fact he'd thrown away the best thing that ever happened to him slammed into his brain, and hit him with the realization he might never get it back.

No, that wasn't something he'd allow. He wouldn't accept Jill was lost to him forever. He'd found his way back to her. Back to Shiloh Springs. Back home, to his heart. The realization this might be his last chance shook him to his core, bringing with it the knowledge he'd better not blow it.

"I'm glad we're friends, Lucas."

He needed to tell her how he felt, but not like this. Not over the phone. He needed to look into her beautiful eyes when he said the words. Once he'd finished this story, he'd tell her. Make her realize he wanted to spend the rest of his life with only her.

"I did get a new lead on Renee. Heath actually came up with one. She's supposedly in Portland, Oregon. Shiloh's headed up there, hopefully he's already in the air. If it turns out to really be Renee, I'll be on the next plane out."

"Lucas, that's wonderful!"

"Yeah, I'm excited, but I've been burned too many times to get my hopes up. This lead seems legit, though. Heath even managed to grab a picture of her. Wanna see?"

"Of course!" The excitement in Jill's voice fed his. Pressing the button, he texted her the photo.

"This is her."

There was silence for the longest time, before she whispered, "She looks like you."

"That's what everybody says. It's close to how I remember her. The hair's a little darker, but her eyes are the same."

"I pray your search is almost over, and you find her."

"Me too." Lucas wished he was there with her, instead of in his lonely bedroom, staring at the walls. It was late, but he was reluctant to hang up. He knew he should let her go. He had the luxury of sleeping in in the morning, then working some more on his notes. Jill probably a host of things to get the bakery set up to open on time, and here he was keeping her from getting any rest.

"It's late. I guess I should hang up and let you get some sleep. I needed to talk to you. Hear your voice."

"I'm glad you called. This was nice, reminiscing about old times. We've got a lot of good memories. After all, we shared a lot of our growing up years together. You're right, though, I probably should get some sleep. Good night, Lucas."

"Night, Jill. See you tomorrow."

Swiping the button the end the call, he closed his eyes, letting the wave of exhaustion sweep over him. Talking with Jill relaxed and calmed him. Gave him a sense of peace missing from his life for a long time. Probably since the day he'd left Shiloh Springs behind in his rearview mirror.

He didn't regret leaving. How could he, when he'd learned and grown both as a person and a reporter. But things change. Coming to Shiloh Springs, he hadn't intended to make any life-altering decisions. It had simply been a chance to visit and recharge before starting his next assignment. Instead, he'd realized something was missing from his life and like an epiphany from on high, he knew what he needed to do, and it started and ended with Jill Monroe.

CHAPTER TWENTY-TWO

J ill wrangled Dante off the sofa and into the shower, though she wouldn't say he'd made things easy. Her brother slept like the dead, and was grumpy as heck when he didn't want to get up. It was like dealing with a toddler. Tough. She had a full morning of business meetings set up, between getting to the bakery for the deliveries, dealing with all the things currently on her to-do list, and making time to deal with yesterday's debacle. Plus, she still had to deal with Rafe, tell him about Benevides' little trip to her apartment.

There was one conversation she wasn't looking forward to.

"Got anything to eat?" Dante walked into the kitchen and reached for one of her brightly colored coffee mugs, filling it from the carafe.

"Breakfast will be ready in five minutes. Think you'll last that long, bottomless pit?"

"Maybe, as long as it's something tasty."

"Homemade cinnamon rolls with caramel icing."

"Mmm."

She refilled her cup, needing the extra jolt of caffeine.

Most of the night had been spent tossing and turning with little sleep. The events of the prior night had played through her mind over and over, like a movie on a loop. Everything linked back to Benevides.

A brisk rap on her front door interrupted her thoughts, and she glanced at her brother. He set his cup on the table and walked to the door. Without bothering to look at the video doorbell feed, he pulled the door inward. Rafe stood on the other side, and stepped through into Jill's apartment, removing his cowboy hat and holding it at his side.

"Morning, Dante. Jill."

"Hey, Rafe. I was going to call you this morning. Have you talked to your dad?" Jill stood with her arms folded over her chest, and nervously bit her bottom lip.

"Not yet, why?"

"She found out who the diamond bracelet came from. Emmanuel Benevides." Dante spat out the name, his expression twisted like it left a sour taste in his mouth. "I don't like him nosing around my sister. Dude is bad news."

Rafe looked between Dante and Jill, not saying a word. She could tell something was wrong and it didn't have a thing to do with yesterday's fun times.

"We'll need to talk about Benevides, but that's not why I'm here. Dusty worked the night shift last night, and called in a few minutes ago. Jill, somebody busted the front window out of your new bakery."

"What?"

"He's there now with the evidence team, but I thought you'd want to know. Especially after yesterday."

With infinite care, she moved over to the couch and slid onto the cushions, trying to process what Rafe said. None of it made sense. Who'd want to wreck all the hard work she'd put into the bakery?

"Do you know how it happened?"

"I'm withholding judgment until I have more information, but from first inspection, it looks like it was deliberate. Any idea who—"

"Benevides did it."

Dante crossed his arms over his chest, his stance antagonistic, and Jill knew he was about to do something stupid. Like go and confront Benevides. Not gonna happen, because his goons would wipe the floor with her little brother.

"You have proof, Dante? Because making wild accusations without evidence won't do anything except rile people up unnecessarily. I have to deal with facts, things I can prove."

"Rafe, you know who Benevides is, what he's capable of. I bet he's the one who messed with Jill's tires, too. Not him personally; he'd never get his hands dirty. He'd have his hired muscle take care of things. Can't you see, Jill did the one thing nobody's ever had the guts to do to Benevides. She told him no."

"Jill?" Rafe's raised brow made her shrug. What was she supposed to say? She had told Mr. Benevides she didn't want to see him, didn't want his gift. Wait, that happened after the flat tires, right? Maybe he wasn't connected after all.

"After you left last night, Mr. Benevides stopped by. Said he'd heard about the problem with my car and wanted to make sure I was okay. Which seems odd, since I've only met the man once." Her eyes darted to Dante, whose body seemed to slump at her words."

"How did you meet Benevides, Jill? I tend to agree with what Dante said, he's bad news. I can't imagine how you'd cross paths with somebody like him."

"She met him through me." Rafe turned to look at Dante, and waited for him to continue. "I got into trouble. You should know up front Jill had nothing to do with my actions. Everything I did was totally my own fault and my problem. Except my stupidity brought Benevides right to her doorstep. Something I'll never forgive myself for."

"I know what Benevides does, though I haven't been able to gather enough evidence to do more than raid his place. I'm guessing you got in over your head with gambling debts."

Dante nodded. "Like I said, I was stupid. Benevides demanded the money I owed, and when I couldn't pay, his guys beat the crap out of me. I ended up telling him my sister would bail me out."

"Rafe, I didn't have any choice. Benevides showed up with two men and Dante. He could barely stand on his own two feet; he'd been beaten to a pulp. I gave Mr. Benevides his pound of flesh, and Dante went into Gamblers Anonymous. This was weeks ago. Now, out of the blue, Benevides comes around? I don't get it."

"Sis, have you looked in the mirror? You're beautiful. Benevides is probably besotted with you."

"He's right," Rafe added with a soft smile, and Jill felt heat sweep into her cheeks. "Seems like more than a coincidence you start receiving gifts and Benevides pops up out of the blue. Didn't you say you thought somebody was following you?"

"Sis?"

"It could have been my imagination. Remember, I didn't actually see anybody or any sign I was being followed."

"Rafe, I wouldn't put it past Benevides to stalk her. If he wants something, he gets it. Oh, crud. I bet Benevides had one of his guys sabotage Jill's tires. He'd probably planned on swooping in and coming to the rescue, like a white knight."

"Only Dad thwarted his plans by stopping by and giving Jill a ride to the bakery. Makes sense in a kind of twisted way."

"Alright, guys, I'm getting confused. You think Mr. Benevides is what, stalking me? That he sent me the rose, the diamonds, and set up a scenario to rescue me from distress? That's beyond crazy." Jill's hands clenched into fists on her lap, because she actually could imagine him doing it.

"All questions I intend to ask Benevides. In the meantime, I need to deal with the window at the bakery. I'm heading there now; do you want to meet me there?"

"Of course. I've got equipment and supplies being delivered today. I'll have to make arrangements to have the window boarded up until the glass can be replaced."

"Let me handle that. I'll have Liam stop by with some plywood. He's already got the tools in his truck, and can get it boarded up faster than hiring it out."

Jill drew in a deep breath, trying to quell the trembling in her hands as reality sank in. Somebody was out to get her.

"Thanks, I'd appreciate his help."

Rafe grinned, and instinctively Jill relaxed under his aura of confidence and self-assurance. Rafe was a born leader, caring about everyone in his county. When she'd been approached about signing a petition to have him removed from office, she'd vehemently defended him and his job, refusing to sign. Hopefully whoever was mean-spirited enough to try such underhanded tactics had backed down, because she hadn't heard anything about it since. She started to ask Rafe about it when he spoke.

"I'll meet you there, whenever you're ready. Don't worry, Jill, we'll get things sorted out. I'll deal with Benevides, and let him know you're not to be bothered."

"Rafe, I want—"

"Dante, you'll stay out of this. Men like Emmanuel Benevides won't back down from you. I'm not trying to be mean or hurt your feelings, but he already had you hurt once. Benevides and I've had dealings in the past, and he knows I won't be intimidated. I don't have a problem tossing him in a cell if he tries anything. I hope I get enough evidence soon so I can arrest him. I really want put him in a cage for a long time."

"Might happen sooner than you think," Dante muttered softly. So soft, Jill almost missed it. Did her brother know something the sheriff didn't?

Rafe left, and Jill grabbed her purse and keys. Dante argued he wanted to go with her, but Jill shooed him away, telling him he needed to get to work. Frank was depending on him. He'd reluctantly agreed after she promised to call if she needed him.

She ended up parking in front of the coffee shop across the street from the bakery, because all the spots directly in front of it were occupied. Ms. Patti's white Escalade took up two spaces, and Douglas' red Ford truck took up the space beside it. The sheriff's cruiser sat front and center, and she watched Dusty walk out through the front door.

"Good morning, Dusty."

He looked up at her greeting and gave her a weary smile. "Morning, Jill. Sorry you have to deal with this mess. Techs are almost finished."

"Any idea what caused the damage? Like a rock flew off the road and hit the glass?"

Dusty studied her without saying a word, and she tried reading him. They'd become friends when he'd moved to

Shiloh Springs, and discovered he was a pleasant, easygoing man with a quick smile. He took his job seriously, and most people in the town trusted him. This morning he looked tired, and she remembered Rafe saying Dusty had worked the night shift. He probably hadn't been home yet.

"Don't think so, Jill. We'll know more when we've had a chance to examine the evidence, but on first glance, it looks like somebody took a baseball bat to it. Thing shattered into a million pieces. The metal framework around the casing is bent all to heck, which makes me lean toward a bat or maybe a tire iron."

"Why would anybody smash my window?"

Dusty reached out and squeezed her shoulder. "We aren't sure when this happened. Might've been teenagers out causing trouble. Doesn't happen a lot, but once it a blue moon, kids get antsy. We had a bunch of mailboxes knocked down by hooligans driving up and down the street with baseball bats, smashing them for fun. Might be the same ones."

"Do you really think so?"

"Yeah. Some kids like to run a little wild on the weekends. But I'm spit-balling here. Rafe has the crime scene tech guys all over this. We'll figure out who did it."

"I understand. Thanks for getting things handled so quickly, Dusty. Go home and get some rest."

"That's the plan."

She headed for the front door, watched people milling

around inside through the glass front door. *Guess it's a good thing they didn't break that, too.*

"Jill, honey, are you okay?" Ms. Patti rushed over, enveloping her in a hug. The scent of her perfume wafted around her, as familiar as the smell of fresh-baked cookies with its vanilla undertones. An almost immediate sense of peace welled up inside her.

"I'm fine. Trying to figure out who'd do something like this."

"Don't worry. My son will find the culprit and throw the book at him. Stuff we can fix or replace. I'm happy you weren't here when this happened."

"Me, too. I came as soon as Rafe told me. It's too late to have the deliveries delayed. We can make them drive around the back, and come in the entrance in the alley, while we deal with getting everything cleared away."

"Liam and Douglas already headed to the hardware store to get plywood to cover the hole. They should be back any minute."

Even as she spoke, Liam and Douglas carried a huge piece of wood onto the sidewalk and leaned it against the wall. She watched them move in synchronization, lifting the heavy panel and screwing it into place. In no time, the gaping hole was covered, shrouding the interior in dim light. Enough lights shone from the light fixtures to see clearly, but it wasn't the same cheerful, homey atmosphere Jill loved.

The crime techs left soon after that, and Ms. Patti fol-

lowed, citing an appointment she couldn't cancel, and Jill
shooed her out the door. Afterward, a whirlwind of people
seemed to rotate through the bakery nonstop, and she found
herself swept off her feet with deliveries, supplies, and
equipment. Directing the delivery people where each thing
went kept her occupied and her mind off everything that
happened over the last several days.

It was midafternoon before she finally stopped and
looked around at what she'd gotten achieved despite the
early morning disruption. She had one more delivery
coming. She smiled. This particular delivery was one she'd
been anticipating ever since she'd chosen the name of the
shop. Today, Harper was bringing the bakery's sign.

When she heard the front door open, she'd looked up
smiling, expecting to see her friend. Instead, Lucas walked in
scowling, and pointed toward the blocked window.

"Why didn't you call me? I had to hear about this from
my brother."

"Which one?"

"Liam. Don't change the subject. The minute you found
out, you should have called me."

"Lucas, you're working. I wasn't about to disrupt your
day with something that's been handled. Rafe is dealing with
figuring out who did this. Your dad and Liam boarded up
the window early this morning."

Lucas pulled her close, as if compelled to touch her, feel
her, convince himself she wasn't hurt. "Jill, you don't know

how terrified I felt when Liam called. If anything happened to you, I don't think I could handle it. I can't lose you again."

"You're not going to lose me, I promise. They're pretty sure it was teens out late causing mischief. Really, I'm fine."

He shook his head and softly cupped her face in his hands. Slowly, he lowered his head and kissed her. Shock and desire warred deep inside her, and she gave in to temptation, returning the kiss. Her lips parted under the urgent demand of his. It seemed like an eternity since Lucas had kissed her, and with every brush of his lips against hers, she felt like she'd found her way home again.

"I told myself to wait, to court you, make you realize you wanted me as much as I want you," he whispered. "But the second Liam said you were in danger, nothing else mattered except getting to you. Holding you. Keeping you safe."

"I'm not in danger, Lucas," she protested. "A broken window isn't the end of the world."

"It isn't only the broken window. When were you going to tell me about all the other stuff? The rose left at your doorstep? The bracelet? Even the flat tires. I had to find out about everything from somebody else. You should have told *me*."

I guess whatever one Boudreau knows, the rest do, too.

"I only started putting the pieces together last night."

"Jill, we talked last night. Why didn't you tell me then?"

She drew in a long breath before answering him, debat-

254

ing exactly what to tell him, and decided on the truth. "Last night, it seemed like we'd stepped back in time. We talked like we used to, when we were a couple. Revisiting old memories, things we did together. I…I didn't want to ruin it."

Lucas rested his forehead against hers, and she closed her eyes, wishing he'd pull her into his arms again. Kiss her like he never wanted to stop. Why was life so unfair, giving her everything she thought she wanted—a new job, one she'd craved and dreamed about forever, and yet not let her have the man she'd loved for her whole life?

As if he'd read her mind, his lips captured hers again, sending need coursing through her. This kiss was unbridled, passionate, and she melted into his embrace. Wrapping her arms around his neck, she responded, pouring all of her unrequited love into their shared kiss.

She ignored the niggling of doubt in her head, wanting to share and yet keep this moment forever. Wrap it in cotton-wool and store it, like a golden treasure she'd take out and cherish when she was alone. And she would be alone. This wouldn't last because Lucas would return to DFW, and she couldn't be, wouldn't be, his part-time girlfriend. Somebody he spent time with when he came to Shiloh Springs to visit family. Her heart would wither and die. She had too much self-respect to accept anything less than his whole heart.

"Lucas, I…" She trailed off when he pulled her against

him, and she could feel the slight tremble of his body against hers.

"We need to talk. There's so much I need to tell you."

Before she could answer, the front door opened and Harper walked through, clad in overall shorts, a bright red T-shirt, and a pair of steel-toed boots. Jill eased out of Lucas's embrace, hoping her friend didn't notice how flustered she was. "Jill, what happened?"

"Long story, I'll fill you in later."

Harper looked at Lucas, and gave him a cheeky grin. "Hello."

"Hi."

"Lucas, this is my friend, Harper. We work together at the insurance company. I mean worked. It's still hard to realize I'm not there anymore. Harper Westbrook, this is Lucas Boudreau."

"Nice to meet you, Lucas. Jill's mentioned you a time or two." The look she shot Jill said that Harper would have a ton of questions once they were alone. Not that she was sure she had many answers. Her head felt like she'd been riding a Tilt-A-Whirl at top speed, and it kept getting faster.

"Mr. Boudreau, would you mind giving me a hand? I brought the sign for the back wall of the bakery."

"Be happy to."

Lucas followed Harper out to her beat-up van and Jill watched, thrilled and excited, as one more of the final pieces fell into place. Next to having her ovens delivered, installing the sign had become her touchstone, kind of like decorating one of her cakes. The sense of accomplishment she felt blossomed inside, and she did a little booty shake, excitement flooding her like bubbles in a champagne bottle. She'd agonized over all the fine details, worked with Harper on every nuance, every confection choice, and every color. This sign was her baby; well, hers and Harper's, since she'd done all the actual artwork. But Jill planned on getting a portion of the credit.

Lucas carried in one end, while Harper handled the other end, a painter's tarp draped over the signage. Leaning it against the wall, Harper slapped Jill's hand away when she tried to peek.

"You ready to hang this baby? Let me grab my tools, and we can get started." Harper glanced at Lucas and added, "Don't let her cheat. She's going to try and sneak a look the second I'm out the door."

Jill huffed out a breath, and crossed her arms across her chest, sticking out her lower lip in an exaggerated pout. Harper's laughter floated behind her as she sprinted out the front door, returning with a maroon-colored tool box. Grinning at Jill, she yanked the tarp off the sign in a dramatic fashion.

Jill's hands covered her mouth as she struggled to hold back happy tears. The photos Harper had e-mailed her hadn't done it justice. The stunning colors and artwork went above and beyond everything she hoped for, and she couldn't stop staring at the concrete evidence her dream was about to become reality.

"Harper, it's perfect."

"She's right. You've done an amazing job. The vibrant colors and artwork are so realistic, it makes me want to reach out and take one of the treats right off the sign. Good job." Lucas slid his arm around Jill's waist, and pulled her against him. "Let me give you a hand hanging it, Harper."

"Give me a sec, I need a couple measurements to make sure I put the bracings in the right places. Don't want this baby falling off and knocking somebody on the noggin."

With practiced ease, Harper climbed onto a countertop and whipped out a tape measure, marking spots on the wall with a pencil. Tucking it behind her ear, she turned and motioned to Lucas.

"Do me a favor, hand me that toolbox."

Lucas' hand slid from around Jill's waist, and he grabbed the toolbox and handed it to Harper. She dug deep inside the toolbox and pulled out a small cordless drill, and drilled four pilot holes into the sheetrock.

"Darn it, I left the braces in my car. I'll be right back."

"Wait. If your car's unlocked, I'll grab it."

"I never lock it. Jill, don't go getting any ideas about raising my insurance rate. You didn't hear that."

Lucas headed out the front door, and Harper shot Jill a look. "Girl, we're going to have a long talk about keeping secrets. You never told me Lucas was so fine."

She chuckled. "Wait until you see his brothers."

Harper's eyes sparkled, and she waved a hand at her face, fanning herself. "Brothers? That dude's got brothers? Holy hotness, where's the list and how do I sign up?" Harper lowered herself to sit cross-legged on the countertop, the cotton-candy pink highlights in her hair glistening under the lights. "How many brothers are we talking about?"

"Nine brothers and one sister. Four of them are taken, but that still leaves a smorgasbord of Boudreaus to choose from."

"Lucky me." Harper grinned and clamored to her feet when Lucas came through the door, holding the wooden brace. "This won't take long," she added, "since I predrilled the pilot holes.

"What can I do?" Lucas watched Harper's every move. Jill knew it was the old-fashioned chivalry Douglas drilled into his sons. She'd never see one of the Boudreaus treat a woman as anything but an equal, yet they immediately threw themselves into action if even a whiff of danger arose.

"Give me a second to get this last bolt in place—and I'm done. If you'll hand me the sign, it should slide into place. This wooden brace has a groove in it, and the one attached to the sign will simply notch right into it."

Jill's breath caught when Harper lifted the sign high, and heard the slight thunk when it slid onto the brace. Without a word, Harper whipped a small level from her pocket, and placed it atop the sign, then let out a whoop.

"Level on the first shot. Awesome." She jumped down from the counter, and walked over to Jill. "So, what do you think?"

Jill flung her arms around Harper, squeezing hard enough the other woman let out a squeak. "Can't breathe, woman."

"It's perfect. Beyond perfect. You read my mind and then gave me even more than I asked."

"Sounds like a ringing endorsement. I concur, you did an amazing job." Lucas moved to stand at Jill's side, examining the signage. "I like the font you used for the lettering of the bakery's name. It's bold, but with a touch of subtleness that ties in with the vibe of the place."

"As long as Jill's happy, we're all good." Harper ran a hand through her hair, the curls springing back in blonde and pink ringlets. Her green eyes sparkled, and she grinned. "I put a couple coats of lacquer over the chalk, so it's not going to rub off. Oh, oh! Wait, I brought you something else."

Spinning on her heel, she raced out the front door, and was back within minutes with a brightly wrapped package. She shoved it into Jill's hands.

"What's this?"

"A little something I made you. Call it a combination congratulations-on-making-your-dream-come-true and a housewarming, or should that be business-warming gift?"

"Thank you."

"Open it. It's not much, but..."

"Stop. Whatever it is, I know it came from love." Jill ripped the red, yellow, and orange wrapping paper off and shoved it toward Lucas, who smiled.

"What's that look for?" Jill handed him the ribbon, which he added to the wadded-up paper.

"I never pictured you as the rip the wrappings off kind of girl. I imagined you'd carefully peel back the tape and fold the wrapping paper neatly before opening the present type."

"Ha! If I did that, it'd take me too long to get to the good stuff."

Lifting off the lid, Jill turned to Harper, her eyes watery with tears. "It's beautiful."

"I thought maybe you'd find a place where you could use it." Her fingertip ran along the small chalkboard that she'd decorated to mimic the sign she'd hung. The smaller plaque had the words 'Daily Specials' written across the top in the same style and font as the larger sign.

"It's perfect. I even have an easel I can stand it on." She hugged Harper one-handed, clutching her present to her chest. "I'm so glad you're my friend."

"Me, too. Anyway, I've got to skedaddle. Call me if you have any problems with the sign. I promise I'll be here opening day, Jill." Harper turned to Lucas. "Nice to meet you, Lucas. Take good care of my friend, or you'll be answering to me."

"You've got it, Harper."

Jill watched her friend until she was out the door, her hands still wrapped around the gift. Despite the horrible start to the morning, things had turned around. Opening day was close, and she felt a quiver inside. Those two words—opening day—made it feel real.

"Wish I could stay, but I've got a meeting at six, and I can't be late. You have your car? I can give you a lift if you'd like."

"Nope, I'm fine. Go to your meeting. I've got a couple things to do before I head home."

Lucas stared at her, his green eyes sparkling with an inner glow, like he carried all the knowledge in the world and wanted to share with her. The fire in their depths, usually so well hidden, seemed to blaze with desire. Without a word, he leaned closer, and brushed his lips against hers, the briefest touch.

She found herself responding, one hand sliding around the back of his neck, and pulling him closer, deepening the kiss. It felt like an eternity had passed since they'd kissed, and she lost herself in sensation. The touch of his lips lit a fire inside her, one she never wanted to go out. All too soon, he released her lips, and drew in a deep breath.

"I wish I didn't need to take this meeting. There's so much we need to talk about, but I don't want to rush this. Promise we'll talk later?"

"Alright."

He pressed another kiss against her forehead, and walked away, not looking back. Hugging the sign and the wrappings to her chest, she sighed.

"I am such a goner."

CHAPTER TWENTY-THREE

Lucas pulled into the parking lot right before six, excited about his meeting with Dennis. Hopefully, the man could provide him with more ammunition to use against Benevides. He needed Benevides put out of business and behind bars. Shutting down his operation might become his top priority, especially after he'd heard about his harassment of Jill. His over-the-top behavior bordered on stalking, but the guy apparently knew how close to the line he could get without crossing into prosecutable. Lucas felt in his gut this probably wasn't the first time Benevides had pulled his would-be hero-in-disguise act on another unsuspecting woman.

He spotted Dennis standing by his car, surprised to note he wasn't alone. Lucy from the club leaned her hip against the hood, her posture suggesting she might not be happy to be here. Sliding into a spot a few feet away, he climbed from his car.

"Evening, Dennis. Lucy."

"I hope you don't mind I brought Lucy along. She knows more about the ins and outs of Benevides' club than anyone. As long as you keep her name off the record, she's willing to answer your questions."

"You don't need to talk for me. I'm capable of answering Mr. Stewart's questions without an interpreter."

"Come on, Lucy, you know I didn't mean anything like that. I—"

Lucy suddenly grinned. "You are so easy. Dude, I'm busting your chops. Lighten up."

Lucas' eyes widened at her words. This was a completely different person than the polished and sophisticated Lucy he'd met at the club last night. This woman was witty and funny, her smile brightening her face.

"I appreciate you're joining us, Lucy. I take it Dennis explained what we talked about last night?"

"He didn't give me a lot of details, just he was meeting somebody who wanted dirt on the club. When he mentioned you by name, I'll admit my curiosity was piqued. So, tell me, what's your deal?"

"My name is Lucas Boudreau, and I'm an investigative reporter, working on a story about gaming clubs running illegal gambling through the state. I want to focus on a couple of individuals, highlighting their struggles, the impact these illegal gambling places have not only on them but how it affects their loved ones. The families picking up the pieces when things go wrong—which they inevitably do."

He watched her eyes close as she swallowed, agony written upon her countenance. Whatever she'd been through

LUCAS

hurt her on a gut-deep level. He tried to imagine what she
endured, having to go into the belly of the beast, work side-
by-side with the people who'd torn her life asunder. It
boggled his mind, and he wanted justice for people like
Lucy, Dante, and Dennis.

"Telling a story is all well and good, but it doesn't shut
the doors. The money flows into the hands of people like
Emmanuel Benevides. If you only knew…"

"I want to know. If there's a way to shut him down permanently, I'll jump all over it. I should tell you in advance,
my brother is the sheriff of Shiloh Springs. Another brother
is an FBI agent, working out of the Austin branch. A third
brother is the district attorney for Shiloh Springs. I don't
want you walking into this blind, or thinking after the fact I
tricked you or attempted to coerce you into talking. I'd
rather you be fully informed, so there's no misinformation,
no hidden agenda. I don't make up falsehoods for my stories.
I work in tangible facts. If I can produce the kind of evidence
that'll put Benevides and his ilk behind bars, and stop the
flow of money to the cartels, the human traffickers, and the
drug deals, I'm all over it. I'll gladly share my info with law
enforcement, unless I'm sworn to secrecy. Do either of you
have a problem with what I've told you?"

Dennis chuckled and held his hands up in front of him.
"I can't speak for Lucy, but I've been gathering my own intel
on Benevides for months. Wanted to have enough to take to
the feds, but this might work even better."

Opening the back door of the car, he reached inside and pulled out a large manila envelope and handed it to Lucas without a word.

Lucas studied it for a moment before asking, "What's inside?"

"Everything I've gathered on Benevides' operation. People I've seen him meeting with. Dates and times. Dollar amounts when I could get 'em. I buddied up to Junior about a week after I started visiting the club, got real chummy. That meant after a while, he started trusting me, and got more lenient about what he said and did when I was around." He shook his head. "That boy thinks he's a player, but he's nothing but cannon fodder. Benevides will use him, and then spit on his corpse when his usefulness is over."

"Which might be sooner than you think." Lucy pushed her dark hair over her shoulder, eyes narrowing as she continued to study Lucas. "Junior's getting sloppy. Benevides hasn't been around as often as he used to, because he's got some special project he's working on. Whatever it is, it's about a woman, that's all can tell you. When Junior asked him about her, Benevides backhanded him hard enough to draw blood."

"Benevides doesn't strike me as the type to let a woman distract his attention from business."

Lucy shrugged. "I wouldn't think so either, but he's been distracted for weeks. Whoever this Jillian person is, I pity her, because Benevides never takes no for an answer."

LUCAS

Every muscle in his body froze. "Did you say Jillian?" He could barely contain the flare of rage surging through him. Guess he sounded scary, because Lucy took a step back, her hip bumping against the car.

"Lucas, back off." Dennis took a protective stance in front of Lucy, and she shoved at his back. "Tone it down, or we're outta here."

"You said Jillian. Did Benevides mention a last name?" Lucas could barely contain the anger and adrenaline coursing through him. The combination was a heady cocktail, fueling his desire to head straight for Benevides and rip his head from his shoulders. Yeah, that could work, then he'd never bother Jill again.

"He didn't, but it sounded like Junior knows this Jillian. Mentioned that she was a total prude, which is when Benevides clocked him."

"When did this happen?"

"Couple of days ago, why?" Lucy's steely-eyed gaze raked him from head to toe. "Let me take a wild guess. You know this Jillian, right?"

"Yes."

"Takes things to a whole different level. Makes your story take on a different slant if it hits you from your own personal perspective." Lucy looked at Dennis' back, and gave him a gentle push. "Okay, you were right. I trust him. Let's get this interview over with. I want Benevides nailed to the wall. His head on a pike. I'll personally bring the horses if

267

you want to draw and quarter him."

"Bloodthirsty wench." Dennis' voice held affection and something Lucas was pretty sure was love. He'd heard that exact tone around his place often enough over the years it was unmistakable. Lately, as his brothers fell like dominos, he'd heard them use the same tone.

He started to speak when his phone alerted the text tone. When he saw Shiloh's name, he quickly displayed the message.

"I need to take this. Why don't you head inside and get a table, and I'll be right behind you."

Lucy shrugged and started toward Juanita's front door. Dennis jogged to catch up, and Lucas re-read the text.

SHILOH: I'm in Portland. Checked out Elizabeth Reynolds' apartment. It's empty. Manager said he didn't know she'd moved out, but he saw her yesterday. Something spooked her, or else she found out somebody's looking for her.

ME: You missed her by one day? I can't believe we're so close to finding Renee. I'm in the middle of a meeting, but I'll call you tonight. Shoot me an e-mail with anything you've got.

SHILOH: Will do.

ME: Thanks.

Shoving the phone in his pocket, he entered Juanita's, and spotted Dennis and Lucy sitting in a corner booth. It was early enough the place wasn't packed wall-to-wall, like it was on the weekends.

"Sorry, I had to take that. It was my brother." He scooted into the booth and laid the manila envelope onto the seat beside him. "He's looking into a personal matter for me, and wanted to update me on what he's found."

"Hope he had good news."

"Thanks, Lucy. Things are looking hopeful."

The waiter came and took their orders. Juanita's was one of Lucas' favorite Tex-Mex restaurants. The owners opened the place over twenty years ago, a husband and wife duo who ran the place and did all the cooking. Though DFW had some good Tex-Mex places, none of them held a candle to Juanita's in his heart.

"Lucas! I didn't know you were home." Juanita bustled over to their table, a bowl of guacamole in one hand and warm tortilla chips in the other. Lucas stood, giving the older woman a hug. She was like a favorite aunt, one who kept him in *carne asada* and guacamole whenever he hit town.

"Juanita, my lovely, you look younger and more beautiful every time I see you." Lucas pulled her into a hug. "Decided to run away with me yet?"

"Flattery will get you extra guacamole and salsa, *mijo*. But my Carlos will burn your supper if he hears you flirting."

"Carlos would never burn anything, but I'll take my chances, because you are a sight for this lonely boy's eyes. I hope everything is good."

"Can't complain. Business is doing well. Our daughter, Carolina, is around with our first grandbaby."

"That's wonderful, Juanita."

"Best news we've had for a long while. Carlos is over the moon, happy about becoming an *abuelo*."

"Where are my manners? My mama would have a fit if she found out I brought guests and didn't introduce them. Juanita, this is Lucy and Dennis."

"Welcome, welcome. Lucas' friends are welcome anytime. Now let me get back to Carlos, tell him you're here."

"It's good to see you, although I'm heartbroken you never say yes. We can elope, run away where nobody can find us."

She patted him on the top of his head like a schoolboy. "One of these days, I'm going to say yes. Then, we'll see how fast your legs will carry you out the front door." Chuckling, she headed for the kitchen.

"Guess you come here a lot." Lucy dug a chip into the guacamole and stuffed it into her mouth. Her eyes widened and she grabbed another. "I totally get it, if the food is anything like this. Wonder how I missed finding out about this place."

"I've been coming here forever. My folks brought us here, and I visit Juanita and Carlos every time I'm back in Shiloh Springs."

"It's a nice place. Owner seems to like you." Dennis swallowed down a large sip of his beer.

"You guys want to eat first, or go ahead and start?"

"Might as well get it over with," Dennis groused. "You might want to take a look at the info I gave you, in case you have any questions, we can get them out of the way first."

"Good idea."

Lucas picked up the envelope, and pulled out page after page of meticulous notes, detailing everything Dennis had overheard and observed at Benevides' club. He had to give the other guy credit: his information read like a police report, right down to the handwritten pages pulled from a small spiral notepad and stapled to the written summaries. Impressive.

He'd also printed out copies of photos he'd taken. Men meeting with Benevides, coming out of his office. Leather pouches changing hands, which he could only assume were stuffed with cash. A few of the names he recognized, some he didn't. But one photo among the rest had him straightening in his seat.

Reining in his growing excitement, he shoved the page at Dennis. "This! When did you take this pic?"

"Look on the back. I pulled the date and time from the metadata on my phone and documented it."

"Do you know who this is?" Lucas couldn't hold back his grin. He recognized the man instantly, because he'd written an article outlining every aspect of human trafficking across Texas and the surrounding states. Sex workers and slave laborers moved through the U.S. on a regular basis, the majority of them processed and delivered on the orders of this man.

"No clue. I remember security being pretty tight the

night he showed up. Dude brought his own security people, and Benevides amped his personal guards up, too. I figured he was a big shot from the way everybody acted." Dennis studied the picture intently, as if trying to memorize the face.

"I've seen him at the club twice," Lucy added. "This night and one earlier in the year—maybe end of February?"

"Would you guys mind if I invite my brother, Rafe, to join us? He really needs to hear about this, the sooner the better."

Dennis rolled his eyes before grinning at Lucas. "Which brother is Rafe? The sheriff, the fed, or the D.A.?"

"Sheriff. Rafe Boudreau is the elected sheriff of Shiloh Springs. I'm positive I recognize the man from the picture, but I want corroboration in case I'm seeing things I want to see, know what I mean?"

"I don't have a problem with your brother coming. Saves me having to tell my story more than once."

"I agree," Lucy added before taking a sip of her margarita. "You know, guys, I'd come here for the margaritas alone. Best one I've ever had."

"I'll be sure to let Juanita know. Her cousin, Hector, is the bartender."

"So this place is pretty much a family affair."

"Yep." Lucas whipped out his phone and quickly texted Rafe, who responded back almost immediately, saying he was close by and would meet them ASAP.

"Rafe should be here soon."

The waiter stepped up to their table, his hands loaded with plates. The aroma of the grilled meat, cheese, and spices filled the air, and Lucas felt his stomach growl, only then realizing he hadn't eaten for most of the day. His mouth watered and he grabbed his silverware. They dug into the food, the taste hitting his tongue in a symphony of delights. Almost half his meal disappeared in a matter of minutes, and he spotted Rafe walk through the door. He waved him over.

"You sounded excited, bro. What's up?" Rafe nodded to Dennis Lucy.

"Sit down and I'll fill you in. You want anything before we start?"

"No, thanks, I'm meeting Tessa after we finish up here."

"Take a look at this and tell me what you see." Lucas passed the photo across the table, and watched Rafe's eyes widen the minute he spotted the two men in the photo.

"When was this taken?" Rafe's voice hardened with command, and Dennis began chuckling.

"Oh, yeah, he sounds like your brother."

"Rafe, sorry, forgot to introduce you. This is Dennis and she's Lucy."

"Pleased to meet you. Now answer the question, Lucas. When was that picture taken?" Rafe's frown was pronounced, gaze glued to the photo.

Lucas grabbed the picture and turned it over, watched Rafe's eyes widen at the date. "I didn't know he'd come across the border. He's got nerve, I'll give him that. Williamson is gonna have a hissy fit when he hears about this."

"Will somebody please tell me who the dude in the picture is? The suspense is killing me." Lucy's balled-up fists landed on the table and she glared at Lucas. "The way you both reacted to the picture, I'm guessing Mr. Slick's bad news."

"This," Rafe flicked the edge of the photo, "is Javier Escondido. Runs the Escondido cartel, south of the Texas/Mexico border. Everyone, and I mean everyone, wants a piece of this guy. FBI, DEA, local and state cops all want to take him down."

"The bigger question is what's he doing with Emmanuel Benevides? Of course, Benevides might be funneling his money through Escondido's cartel."

"Probably true, bro. But this," Rafe tapped the edge of the paper, "seeing them together gets me one step closer to nailing his hide and tossing him behind bars. Anybody know where this was taken?"

Lucy grinned, raising her hand. "I know!"

"Gonna share with the rest of us?" Lucas watched Dennis bump Lucy's shoulder with his in a kind of go-ahead-and-tell-them motion.

"That's the back alley, behind the club. Emmanuel tends to do business there with the men he doesn't want to be seen with. Of course, he's not exactly subtle, and pretty much all the club's employees know what happens out back." Lucy pointed to Escondido's pic. "I got some really icky vibes from him. Man has dead eyes, if you know what I mean. Acted like he owned the world, and we'd better fall in line or he'd make us disappear."

Lucas and Rafe exchanged a glance, and Rafe nodded once. They'd talk once they were in private, because this case had turned on its head with the introduction of Javier Escondido.

"Anything else either of you know about how Benevides runs the two gaming clubs, something we might be able to connect him? Anything at all can help."

"Sheriff," Dennis met his eyes straight on, "I've been keeping tabs on Benevides for months, ever since my brother's death. I can't prove anything, but I think—no, I know—he was behind Jimmy's suicide. I gave Lucas copies of everything I have."

Lucas held up the manila envelope. "Dennis' father was a cop, and these notes are documented concisely. From what little I've looked at, it'll go a long way toward building a case against Benevides, and if we're really lucky, Javier Escondido, too."

"You said these are copies?"

"Yes, sir. I have the originals locked up tight." Dennis sat up straighter, adding, "There is a safe deposit box in Austin. Only ones authorized to open it are me and Lucy."

"Good. I'll take these and—"

"No. I'll scan and e-mail you copies, but I'm keeping those." Lucas slid the picture of Escondido and Benevides into the envelope. "Soon as I'm done here, I'm heading over to Jill's. Benevides has an unhealthy attraction to my girl, and I'm planning on watching her like a hawk until he's out of the picture."

Rafe chuckled. "Sheesh, bro, you're starting to sound like the rest of our brothers, going into overprotective mode. When are you going to admit you're head-over-heels in love with her?"

"Like you were any better with Tessa? The family was taking bets on how long it would take you to propose."

"I've had Dusty and Jeb doing drive-by checks of her apartment and the bakery. We'll keep a close watch on her, at least until we determine our next step."

"Thanks."

"Get me those copies tonight, bro. Dennis, Lucy, it was nice meeting you. I need to head in and make a few calls. Austin FBI office needs to hear about Escondido showing up in Shiloh Springs. Twice. It's time to rattle a few cages, because Border Patrol was supposed to take him into custody the second he stepped onto U.S. soil."

"You'll get 'em as soon as I leave here. I'll call if we come up with anything else."

Rafe nodded and headed for the door, giving Juanita a brief hug on the way out.

"You guys ready to get started?" At their nods, Lucas placed his cell phone on the tabletop and hit record, and wondered how many other surprises Dennis and Lucy might uncover as they talked.

Lucas wanted this ended, once and for all, because any hint of danger toward Jill needed to disappear—and it would. He'd make sure of it.

CHAPTER TWENTY-FOUR

J ill dragged her tired body across the threshold of her apartment, pausing long enough to turn the deadbolt, and click the lock in the door's handle. Exhaustion beat at her like a steady drumbeat. She hadn't realized how much work still remained to finish before opening day. Thinking about it made her brain hurt.

After the fiasco with the smashed window, and Lucas showing up worried about her, she'd finally convinced him to go to his meeting. Harper stuck around for a while after he left, and in between deliveries of equipment, she'd unloaded a ton of boxes filled with baking supplies, sorting and stacking all the ingredients for making incredible pastries. Harper turned out to be a huge help, bouncing around with energy to spare. Who knew her friend raced around like the bunny in that commercial who never stops?

Several people dropped by, mostly Boudreaus, and Jill knew they were keeping a protective eye on her. To be honest, it made her feel special, knowing she had so many people who cared about her. Even Dante called enough times she'd finally told him she'd quit answering the phone if he didn't stop. It was kinda nice to have her overprotective brother watching over her, even if she didn't need it. She was a big girl, more than able to take care of herself.

Tossing her purse on the hall table, she eased her tired, swollen feet out of her shoes and slid them under the table, too. With a sigh, she slumped onto the couch, and leaned back against the comfy cushions. She needed a hot bath and a cold drink, not necessarily in that order, but couldn't rouse the energy to get off the sofa.

When her phone rang, she groaned. Like a dolt, she'd left the stupid thing in her purse. Climbing to her feet, she snatched her purse up and dug until she found her phone. The ringing stopped right as she swiped to answer, switching over to voicemail.

"Well, if it's important, they'll leave a message or call back."

Headed toward the kitchen, she wasn't surprised when it rang again, showing Dante's name on the caller ID.

"Hey, Dante. Yes, I'm home. No, I'm not planning on going out tonight. You can take the night off babysitting and go have some fun."

"Good evening, Ms. Monroe. I'm afraid I'm not your brother. He was kind enough to loan me his phone, since I assumed you wouldn't answer if I called."

A shiver of unease crept up Jill's spine at the sound of Emmanuel Benevides' voice. Where was Dante? She doubted he'd simply handed his phone over to Benevides without a qualm.

"What do you want, Mr. Benevides?"

"I think we should talk, Jillian."

The way he said her name made her skin crawl. Why hadn't this guy gotten the message she didn't want to see him?

"I guess I'm going to have to be blunt. I'm not interested in talking to you or seeing you. There is no scenario where I want to spend time with you."

"I'm aware you don't have a high opinion of me, *querida*, but that's because you don't know me. I tend to intimidate most people—except you. I'm not asking much, just a few hours of your time, getting to know one another."

"I'm sorry, but I'm already seeing someone." *Okay, maybe that's a little half-truth, but I kinda, sorta been seeing Lucas.*

"Perhaps I can dissuade you, show you I'm not the person you think me to be. I believe we have a strong connection..."

"Where's my brother?" She'd had enough of Benevides' innuendos and serious lack of comprehension. There wasn't a chance in Hades' handbasket she'd get involved with him. He was a criminal, to say nothing of what he'd already done to her brother. The chances were higher she'd jump into a live volcano before she'd date him.

"Please, Jillian, before you decide, I'm outside with your brother. Won't you allow us to come up?"

Something about the way he enunciated the words, devoid of any emotion, told her she didn't have much of a choice. She couldn't risk harm to Dante because she refused to see Benevides.

"Fine."

She ended the call and wiped her sweaty palms, feeling icy tendrils of fear spreading through her. In less than two minutes, the knock sounded on her door. The camera showed Benevides standing beside her brother. Taking a deep breath, she undead the locks and opened it.

"Dante, are you alright?"

He shot a glare at Benevides, and then pulled her into his arms. "I'm fine, Sis. Let's talk."

Dante steered her toward the living room, leaving Benevides to close the door. She heard the soft snick, followed by footsteps. Standing with her arms crossed, she didn't offer Benevides a seat. She wanted him gone, because her ingrained Southern hospitality wasn't up to the challenge of being nice to an uninvited guest. If he didn't like it, he could show himself out.

"Okay, you're here. Now what?" Try as she might, she couldn't quite keep the hostility out of her tone.

The corners of his mouth twitched. With Dante at her back, she felt a modicum of safety, though she couldn't help wondering if Benevides had his ever-present goons close by. Probably. He didn't strike her as the type to go anywhere unprotected. Dante's hand squeezes her shoulder, a not-so-subtle signal to ease back on the antagonism.

"Sis…"

"I know. I apologize, Mr. Benevides. I've had a long day, and I'm tired. What is it you want from me?"

"I thought we might have a civilized conversation. Get to know each other a little better. I'm sorry you had a tough day. I hope there weren't any…difficulties."

She knew it! She'd speculated all day long about whether Benevides was behind the damage to the bakery. The gloating tone in his voice convinced her he was behind the vandalism.

"Nothing I couldn't handle with the help of my friends."

"Ah, I presume you mean the Boudreaus. Such fine up-standing citizens." Derision peppered his words, almost mocking, and she wouldn't stand for it.

"The Boudreaus are the finest, most generous, kindest people I know. They're didn't hesitate to step in and offer assistance when something happens to one of their own."

"And are you considered 'one of their own'?"

"Yeah, she is," Dante answered before Jill even opened her mouth.

"Dante, I think it's time you left. Jillian and I have much to discuss, and your presence is no longer required."

Dante's glare should have peeled the paint off the walls, yet Benevides appeared unmoved by the other man's ire. Jill's glance bounced back and forth between the them.

"I'm not going anywhere."

"Dante—"

"Don't argue with me, Sis. I'm not budging from your side. I wish I'd never dragged you into this mess, that you'd never met Benevides."

"Leave. Now." The steely edge in Benevides' voice brooked no argument, and Jill felt her brother waver, indecision warring with fear. She felt the tight grip of terror squeezing deep in her chest. She couldn't let anything happen to Dante.

"It's okay. I think Mr. Benevides and I need to clear the air." Shooting daggers at the older man, she squeezes Dante's forearm. "He won't be staying long."

"Jilly—"

"I promise I'll call you in thirty minutes. If you don't hear from me by then, call 911 and Rafe."

"Really, Jillian? Surely you don't see me as a threat."

"Since you apparently won't take no for an answer, Mr. Benevides, I clearly need to take precautions. Dante, go. I'll be fine."

Dante hesitated for several seconds, before his shoulders slumped. She knew a bitter inner battle raged within him, but he acquiesced.

"Thirty minutes. Not a second more."

"I promise."

With a hate-filled glare at Benevides, he left. Jill felt in her gut that he'd be sticking around outside, but at least she got him out of the immediate line of fire, though she doubted Benevides would have taken things to that extreme.

Not here, where any number of witnesses might pop out of their apartments at the sign of a struggle, or heaven forbid, the sound of a gunshot.

"Jillian, I don't intend to harm you. Far from it. The last thing I want is for you to fear me. I simply want to get to know you better. We met under unfortunate circumstances, which I truly regret. Perhaps we could start over."

She wrapped her arm across her waist, trying to figure out what game Benevides was playing. He couldn't possibly think she'd be interested in anything but him leaving her alone. Yet his eyes, his entire expression, shone with…hope?

"I'm afraid our first meeting left an indelible impression, one not easily dismissed. You brought my brother to use as collateral to recoup his gambling debts. Your demand for repayment wiped out my savings. I barely had enough money to cover my rent. It's kind of hard to look past that."

She watched warily when his hand reached inside his jacket pocket, and he pulled out a check and handed it to her. When she noted the amount, her mouth dropped open, shock riveting through her. The amount was ten times what she'd given him to obliterate Dante's debt.

"I can't take this."

"Jillian, I assure you, there are no strings attached. I admit I haven't always been a good man. Since I met you, even under those inauspicious circumstances, I've changed. You've changed me."

"Mr. Benevides—"

"Emmanuel, please."

"I'm sorry, Emmanuel. I applaud you wanting to change, become a better person, but I had nothing to do with your transformation."

Especially since I don't believe for a minute you've changed your ways. Your heart is still a lump of coal in your chest, and you're really creeping me out.

"I understand your hesitance to accept my words at face value. I'd like the chance to change your mind, *querida*."

"Are you asking me to *date* you?"

"Yes. I believe we will be perfect together."

"I told you, I'm already involved with somebody else."

"I can make you forget this person."

"I don't want to forget him. I love him with every beat of my heart. I always have and I always will. My feelings aren't capricious or foolish. I chose him long ago, and have stayed loyal and true."

Her front door reverberated under a pounding fist. Benevides' scowl showed he wasn't happy with the interruption either. When she started toward the door, he grabbed her forearm, his grip tight enough it hurt.

"Do not answer."

"Jill!" Lucas' voice swept over her like a wave of tranquility. He was here, an old-fashioned white knight, riding to the princess' rescue.

Benevides frowned at the sound of Lucas' voice. "This man's voice sounds familiar. Who is he?"

"Lucas Boudreau, the man I love."

"Boudreau! I am becoming exceedingly tired of all your Boudreaus foiling my attempts to woo you."

"Jill, if you don't answer me, I'm breaking down the door."

"Your friend is going to attract unwanted attraction. Perhaps you should open the door." He released her arm and she darted across the space, her hands fumbling with the locks, they trembled so badly.

"Lucas!" She flung herself into his arms, feeling them wrap around her like bands of steel. In his embrace she felt welcomed. Cherished.

"Please come in, Mr. Boudreau."

Jill felt Lucas tense beneath her hands at the sound of Benevides' voice.

"What are you doing here, Benevides?"

"Why don't you come inside, and we'll chat. I must admit, you certainly fooled me. You played your part exceptionally well. I'm not normally so careless when meeting new people. Let's chalk it up to being distracted, my thoughts on the lovely Ms. Monroe."

"Leave Jill out of this."

"How can I? Here I am, trying to court the lovely lady, only to find out she's besotted with a double-crossing liar. Don't tell me, you only visited my club because it's part of a job. Which Boudreau are you again? I know you're not the sheriff, I'm all too familiar with him. Are you the FBI agent?

Maybe the private investigator?"

"Close," Lucas answered. "Investigative reporter."

"Looking for an interview? You could have simply asked."

"I'm sure you'd love seeing your face splashed across the internet, playing the benevolent do-gooder, helping out the helpless and downtrodden masses by providing entertainment."

Benevides' smile sent a chill down Jill's spine. She couldn't fathom why he toyed with Lucas like a cat who'd spotted a big, juicy mouse, but icy fear struck her square in the chest. He was up to something sinister, but what?

"People come to my clubs to have a good time."

"And lose every dime they have. I guess that's secondary to having fun, right?"

"Luke, Luke, Luke. I'm a simple businessman providing a service."

The sound coming from Lucas didn't sound remotely human. It was more of a predatory growl. Her eyes widened, and she stared at him. What she saw had her taking a step back, but his arm tightened around her waist, pulling her against his side, anchoring her in place.

"The service you provide, Benevides, is despair, anguish, and heartache. Siphoning away every penny from people until all their options are gone. Right now, though, I don't care. All I want is for you to leave Jill alone. She doesn't need somebody like you in her life."

"Somebody like me? Mr. Boudreau, what she doesn't need is a person like you, pretending to be someone they're not. You entered my establishment, pretending to be somebody you weren't. Lied to make my manager believe your intentions aligned with mine. While all along you intended to set me up for alleged criminal activity—which you cannot prove."

"Lucas, please," Jill whispered, "let's get out of here."

He looked down into her eyes, and she read the concern in his gaze. "Okay, baby, I'm taking you home."

Jill let out the breath she'd been holding, because everything would be alright. Until it wasn't.

"I'm afraid I can't allow that, Jillian. Mr. Boudreau and I have unfinished business."

Jill spun around at Benevides' voice, ready to blast him once and for all, and get him out of her apartment. Only her mouth clamped shut at the sight of the gun. She zeroed in on his hand, steady, unwavering, the muzzle pointed at Lucas, who stood still as a statue at her side.

"Put down the gun and let her leave, Benevides, and you and I can handle our business like men."

"Seriously, Lucas? I'm not leaving you here with this man holding you at gunpoint. By the way, that was a very sexist remark. Don't do it again."

Lucas brought her hand to his lips, placing a brief kiss along her knuckles. "Yes, ma'am."

"Please stop. This maudlin display turns my stomach.

Jillian, step away from Mr. Boudreau."

"No." Jill couldn't have moved anyway; her feet seemed superglued to the floor. She wasn't about to give Benevides a clear shot at an unarmed man, especially the man she loved. Not happening.

"Jill, do what he asks. It'll be okay, I promise."

"I can't—"

Lucas put a finger to her lips. "Yes, you can. You can do anything. You're strong and brave. The bravest woman I've ever known."

"Exactly, Mr. Boudreau. Did you know Jillian stood up to me the first time we met? Looked me in the eye, her defiance a distinct change from the reaction I get from most people. She went toe to toe with me, defending her brother." Benevides glanced at Jill. "He doesn't deserve you defending him, by the way. Did you know he's already been back to my place? All those promises he made you, empty and worthless, just like him."

Jill's heart broke at his words. She'd believed Dante when he swore he hadn't been back. The promise he'd been attending Gamblers Anonymous. Had that been a lie, too? When her eyes met Lucas', the truth was evident. Benevides wasn't lying.

"Jill is an amazing woman, but she's not yours. Do you really want to drag her down in the slime with you, Benevides? She deserves better."

"I can give her the world, Mr. Boudreau. Anything she

wants, I merely have to snap my fingers and she'll have it. Everything I have is hers."

"Everything paid for with blood money, right? Why don't you tell Jill where you get all your income? Oh, wait, she already knows. Illegal gains from dishonest gambling, leaving carnage and chaos and wrecked lives in your wake. Jill, has Benevides ever told you how the money he rakes in gets funneled to the cartels in Mexico? What's your specialty, Benevides? Human sex trafficking? Drug smuggling? Or do you deal in stealing little kids for dirty old men?"

Watching Lucas' face as he shot accusations at Benevides, Jill knew he was sending her a message, trying to make her understand, his eyes flashing. He gave a subtle jerk to the right, though his disdainful gaze never left Benevides, not for a second.

"Mr. Benevides, is it true?"

Benevides took a step toward her, his hand outstretched, and she retreated, not wanting him any closer.

"Jillian, *querida*, don't listen to this *idiota*. He spews hate-filled nonsense. Yes, I own clubs where gambling occurs. You know this, because of your brother."

"Where does the money go? Is what Lucas said true?" She couldn't keep her voice from quavering, because thinking about others in danger because of the man standing in front of her turned her stomach. Nausea rose to the back of her throat, and she struggled to keep from throwing up. Benevides truly was a monster if he did any of those things.

"Go ahead, Benevides, tell her the truth. You're gonna kill me anyway, might as well get it all out in the open."

Jill couldn't believe how Lucas taunted the other man. The man still holding the gun pointed straight at Lucas' chest. Did he have a death wish?

"I, personally, have no dealings with what happens with the money once it's out of my hands, my darling. It's true, I run the American clubs, but I'm not the only boss. The clubs are all co-owned with my brother."

"Go ahead, tell her who your brother is, Mister Big Man."

"Lucas, shut up."

"Mr. Boudreau, you are a hair's breadth away from disaster. Please stop talking." Benevides took another step toward her, and this time Jill stood her ground. "My brother is Javier Escondido."

Jill felt the air whoosh out her lungs. As naïve as she was about a lot of things, even she'd heard of Javier Escondido. Drug kingpin, head of the Escondido drug cartel south of the border, he was a legend among law enforcement for being as slippery as an eel.

"Javier Escondido is your brother?"

"Half-brother, actually. I promise, you'll have no contact with him."

"Of course I won't, since I'm not going to be dealing with you again. I want my life back, without drug cartels, gambling, or stalkers. I want my bakery to open. I want my brother to get professional help." She didn't add that she wanted Lucas safely away from the monster standing before her, but she wished it with all her heart.

"Jillian, you don't mean that. You are meant to belong to me. Not this—"

"Jill, hit the floor!"

Instinct kicked in, and she did exactly what Lucas yelled, landing so hard it knocked the wind out of her. She watched in stunned disbelief when Lucas dove across the space separating him from Benevides, reaching for the gun. Wrapping his hands around Benevides' wrist, the two men wrestled for control.

Everything seemed like a slow-motion black-and-white old-time movie, as each man battled for control, chest against chest. Struggling to gain the upper hand, Lucas pushed at Benevides, and she watched his foot skid across the hardwood.

At the sound of a gunshot, she pushed herself upright, eyes glued to the two grappling men. The gun tumbled to the floor, both men frozen in place. A grimace of pain flashed across Benevides' face as he slumped to the floor, his back landing against the leg of the table.

Lucas took a step backward and looked at his blood-soaked hands, shock written on his face, before he turned toward her. Without hesitating, she flung herself into his arms, her hands touching him everywhere.

"Are you hurt? Did he shoot you?"

Lucas shook his head. "I'm fine. Benevides is the one who took a bullet."

She leaned her head against his shoulder. "I almost lost you. I don't know what I'd have done if…"

"You're never going to lose me, sweetheart. Never." He glanced at Benevides, blood leaking through the hand he'd clamped to his shoulder, his body slumped in defeat. Reaching into his pocket, Lucas pulled out his phone and hit a button.

"Hopefully, the whole thing recorded, and he's gonna get tossed into jail. Let me call 911, get the police here."

"It's over?"

"Yeah, baby, it's over."

CHAPTER TWENTY-FIVE

Lucas' hands trembled, and his whole body shook while he held Jill in his arms. The ambulance pulled away from the apartment building, Benevides restrained in the back, headed toward the hospital. Jeb followed it, intent on making sure Benevides stayed put once he got there. Lucas glanced over at Dusty, who gave him a single nod, and continued interviewing Jill's neighbors, as they recounted everything they'd seen and heard in horrifying detail.

"Are you alright, sweetheart?"

"I can't stop picturing you and Benevides fighting over his gun. It was like watching a movie in slow motion. But I couldn't move. I froze in place. When I heard the shot..." She burrowed her head against his shoulder, and he pulled her closer.

"Everything's going to be fine. Benevides will live, and he's going to face charges. Chance will make sure whoever handles the case throws the book at him. Attempted murder. Attempted kidnapping. Probably a whole laundry list of charges once they've gone through all the evidence I handed over, along with the recording on my phone. His clubs are being closed down as we speak. Rafe's at Benevides' club now, and he called Burnet County to get their cooperation in shutting everything down at both locations. The money will dry up once Benevides is behind bars. Chance is hoping he'll roll over on Escondido in exchange for leniency.

"Have you heard anything about Dante?" Jill's voice broke on her brother's name.

"Benevides' men knocked him out and tied him up behind the dumpster at the end of the complex. EMTs are checking on him now. I caught a glimpse of him, and other than a bloody gash on his forehead, he looked fine."

"What happens now that everything's over?"

"The reign of corruption and terror Benevides held over the less fortunate people of Shiloh Springs is finished, yes. You and me—we're never going to be over."

Blue eyes widened at his words, and he smiled gently, tucking a strand of hair behind her ear. Benevides taunted her about taking out the man she loved, knew the only way he could've known how Jill felt was if she'd admitted as much. Still, he needed to hear the words for himself, and tell her how he felt, and hope it wasn't too late.

"Lucas, I—"

"It's my turn to talk. Sweetheart, I've been a fool. The biggest idiot to ever walk upright, because I couldn't see everything I've ever wanted, ever needed, stood right in front of me. I've been everywhere, seen more than I ever expected, but something's always been missing. A piece of my heart.

My soul. No matter how hard I searched, I've always known why I couldn't find contentment. Peace. Because the only time in my life I've ever truly known those was when I was with you."

His thumb smoothly slid over her cheek, feeling the dampness of her tears against his skin. Was it too late? She was crying, and it nearly broke him. He never wanted her to hurt ever again. Whatever it took, her happiness was his first and only priority—even if it meant his walking away from her.

"Even if you never want to see me again, and I wouldn't blame you, I have to tell you how I feel. What I've always known, even when I tried to run from it. I love you, Jill. With everything I am, every beat of my heart, I love you. If you don't feel the same, I'll walk away. I'll stay away from Shiloh Springs, if that makes you happy. Whatever it takes, baby, because you are my everything. I can't let you go on believing I don't care. You've always been my best friend, the center of my universe, I'll feel this way until I draw my last breath. Jill Monroe, I—"

"Lucas, shut up."

"What?"

Cupping his cheeks between both hands, her eyes filled with unshed tears, and she smiled. "How can I tell you I love you too, if you won't stop talking?"

"You love me?"

"Of course I love you. I have from the day we met when

we were kids. I never stopped loving you."

His lips crashed onto hers in a ferocious kiss, pouring everything he felt into this moment. When her lips moved against his, returning the kiss with equal fervor, a sense of belonging and acceptance swept through him, and he knew he'd finally come home.

The kiss turned gentle as he worshiped at her lips, and he finally pulled back to stare into her beautiful blue eyes. They shone with happiness and love. Her cheeks were flushed pink, and he moved closer for another kiss, but paused at the sound of a throat clearing behind him.

With a sigh, he stepped back, though he kept his arm wrapped around Jill, half-afraid if he let go, he'd wake up and find this had all been a dream. Turning his head, he spotted his father standing behind them, with his mother by his side.

"Son."

"Dad."

"Looks like everything worked out." At his father's indulgent smile, Lucas knew his dad already figured everything out, and approved.

"Seriously, Douglas? Everything worked out? Can't you see poor Jill's been through an ordeal? She needs to be—" Ms. Patti abruptly broke off what she'd been saying when she noticed Lucas' arm wrapped around Jill.

"Jill needs us to leave them be, so Lucas can finish what he started." Douglas steered Ms. Patti away, whispering to her as they walked away. She glanced over her shoulder, gave Lucas a smile, and wrapped her arm around Douglas' waist, leaning into him. Bless his dad, he understood him better than anyone, except maybe Jill.

"I don't think I've ever seen Ms. Patti speechless before."

"You'll probably never see it again, so enjoy it while it lasts."

"What happens now?"

"Now, I'm going to take you to the Big House. You can't stay here; your apartment is a crime scene. I'm going to pamper you and court you properly, the way you deserve. I'm moving back to Shiloh Springs. My career is established, and anywhere I can set up a computer and have Wi-Fi, I can work. I'm going to give you time to get over this night, then I'm going to bring you flowers and champagne, take you out under the stars, and ask you to marry me."

"I accept."

Lucas chuckled, and reached for her hand. "I haven't asked yet."

"You don't have to ask me. I know my own feelings. I've been in love with you my whole life. I don't need fancy surroundings or candlelit dinners. I only need you. Lucas Boudreau, will you marry me?"

The happiness bubbling up within Lucas swept over him, until he felt like he was drowning in the depths of her love, and he did the only thing he could.

He said yes.

CHAPTER TWENTY-SIX
EPILOGUE

H eath sat in the big open window of the hayloft, looking out at the grand vista before him. Though he'd seen it a thousand times before, it never ceased to make him feel a part of the whole that was the ranch, affectionately known as the Big House. There was something about looking out over the vastness of land as far as the eye could see that settled his soul, gave him peace he never felt anywhere else. Probably why he'd found himself gravitating back home more and more lately.

Life in the city held its own unique excitement, but it paled in comparison to the verdant pastures of the Boudreau homestead. He found himself hunting for excuses to come back to Texas, even though he loved his job in D.C. Yet something was missing, and he hadn't been able to work out why his instincts were rattled. A feeling of anticipation, like static electricity before a thunderstorm, coursed through him, and he felt a charge in the air.

He turned when he heard somebody climb the ladder to the loft, and wasn't surprised when his father's head appeared. His daddy had cornered him in the kitchen earlier, and mentioned they needed to talk. But with several of his brothers and their womenfolk around, there hadn't been a chance. Until now.

"Son. Thought I'd find you here."

Heath smiled. "It's my favorite place. You can see forever, and everything seems fresh and new from up here. Besides, it's quiet."

Douglas sat beside him, his legs dangling through the opening, and nodded. "A man can do a lot of thinking out here. Nobody to bother you except the horses, and they don't tend to talk much."

Heath chuckled at his father's words. "True. It's nice to see Lucas looking so happy. I always thought he and Jill would end up together."

"They hit a bit of a rough patch, but looks like things are gonna work out for them. I suspect we'll be having another engagement party soon." Douglas picked up a piece of straw and drew it between his fingers. "Lucas told me you gave him some news about his sister."

Heath leaned against the side of the opening, angling slightly to face his father. "It was the weirdest thing, Dad. If I didn't know better, I'd think somebody upstairs had a hand in getting me that info. I mean, what are the chances some wet-behind-the-ears newbie is assigned to me for training, and he happens to start talking about Lucas' sister?"

"It's the best lead we've gotten in a while, since the one I had turned out to be a bust."

"Not really," Heath protested. "You got us Renee's most recent alias, which matches with what the kid told me. I'm surprised Lucas didn't hightail it to Portland the second I gave him the info."

Douglas shook his head. "He couldn't. Everything exploded at the same time. He had his hands full with the gambling story, the investigation into Benevides, and keeping Jill safe. It was touch and go for a minute there, but it all turned out right in the end. The gambling clubs got raided and shut down. Benevides' obsession with Jill and his attempted murder of Lucas will keep him locked up hopefully for the rest of his life."

"Is Lucas planning on heading after Renee now things have settled down?"

Douglas shook his head. "Shiloh flew to Portland to check out the information. If it turns out to be Renee, Lucas will be out there on the next flight. In the meantime, he wants to stick close. Jill won't admit it, but this whole thing shook her."

"Does that mean my baby brother is moving back to Shiloh Springs?" Heath managed to instill a touch of humor in his words, and felt a pang of envy at the thought of moving back to the place he still considered home. Man, he missed it here.

"He's got a few loose ends to tie up, but yes, he's coming home. Your momma is over the moon. If she had her way, all of her chicks would be coming home to roost, preferably under the same roof." He raised both hands when Heath started to speak. "Don't look at me, she's your mother."

They sat in silence for a couple of minutes, and Heath allowed the tranquility of the ranch to seep into his soul. He'd be the first to admit he wasn't cut out to be a rancher, but he still worked the land whenever he was home for more than a day or two. There was something soothing about climbing on horseback and riding through the fields, looking for strays. Getting up hours before the sun peeked over the horizon to feed and water the cattle wasn't such a hardship when it was only for a couple days.

"Want to tell me what's weighing so heavy on you, son?"

Even to his own ears, his chuckle sounded hollow. "Wish I could point to one thing and say, 'Here's my problem, Dad.' It's like I've got an itch I can't scratch. I'm restless. It's not work—everything's fine there. Maybe I'm homesick."

Douglas' large hand landed on his shoulder, squeezing gently. "Maybe you're not homesick. You're heartsick."

Heath started at his words. "What do you mean?"

"I saw the way you reacted to Camilla when she visited Beth. Don't bother denying it. The chemistry between you two nearly set the foreman's house on fire. Have you seen her? Talked to her?"

Why wasn't he surprised his dad noticed his attraction to the beautiful blonde? The moment he laid eyes on her, he'd felt like he'd been hit in the chest with a sledgehammer. She was the opposite of everything he looked for in a woman, and yet he couldn't seem to stay away from her. Went out of his way to tease and torment her, and she rose to the bait so easily.

"I haven't seen her since I went back to D.C., though I've thought about her. A lot. It wouldn't work anyway. Long distance relationships are nothing but a pain in the keister, and rarely succeed. Besides, I'm not looking for a relationship."

Douglas studied him closely, giving him the same intense stare he'd used his entire life, and Heath knew his dad had more to say, but weighed his words carefully. While he cherished his father's knowledge and wisdom, talking about women and relationships wasn't something they shared often. *Because, face it, what grown man is comfortable talking to his dad about sex?*

"Distance doesn't matter if it's the right woman." His father stood and held out his hand, and helped Heath stand. "You might not think you're ready, but your heart may have other plans."

Slapping Heath on the back, Douglas climbed down the ladder and Heath followed, contemplating his father's words. Maybe his dad was right, and he was fighting a losing battle, because he thought about Camilla Stewart every day. Even when he slept, she invaded his dreams, teasing him, taunting him, and making him ache.

Stopping in the middle of the barn, he made a decision.

When he got back to D.C., he'd get in touch with Camilla. See if maybe there was a chance to fan the spark between them and let the flames burn.

The minute he stepped through the kitchen door, Heath knew something was wrong. Beth was on the phone, her eyes filled with tears, and Brody had his arms wrapped around her. The kitchen was silent, all attention focused on Beth until she disconnected the call.

"Honey, what's wrong?" Ms. Patti reached out a hand to Beth.

Beth drew in a deep breath, her eyes searching the kitchen until they met his.

"Camilla's in the hospital. She's been shot."

Thank you for reading Lucas, Book #5 in the Texas Boudreau Brotherhood series. I hope you enjoyed Lucas and Jill's story.

Want to find out more about *Heath Boudreau* and the excitement and adventure he's about to plunge headfirst into? Will he win Camilla's heart? Keep reading for an excerpt from his book, Heath, Book #6 in the Texas Boudreau Brotherhood. Available at all major e-book and print book stores.

Heath
(Book #6 Texas Boudreau Brotherhood series) © Kathy Ivan

"Officer Dandridge, I'm Heath Boudreau. I got your number from one of the nurses at the hospital. I'm calling regarding Camilla Stewart."

"Mr. Boudreau. Are you a relative of Ms. Stewart's?"

The man on the other end of the line sounded like a no-nonsense officer, so Heath got right to the point.

"No, I'm a friend. Her emergency contact, Beth Stewart,

305

informed me Camilla had been shot. Since Beth knows I work for the ATF, she asked me to see what I could find out."

"Understood. Mr. Boudreau, there's not much I can tell you. I've talked with Ms. Stewart, although briefly, because the hospital needed to do some tests and perform a CAT scan. From what I've discerned thus far, through her statement and via witness accounts, Ms. Stewart was the apparent victim of a botched carjacking."

"Carjacking?" Heath hadn't expected that answer. But then, what had he expected?

"Ms. Stewart received a superficial GSW to her upper arm, which required stitches, as well as an injury to her forehead. I haven't heard back from the doctor as to whether the head injury was caused by a second bullet or as a result of her fall."

"Fall?" Heath was beginning to feel a bit like a parrot, repeating Officer Dandridge's words. "How'd she fall?"

"According to the witness, he stated when Ms. Stewart was hit in the arm or shoulder, she spun and tripped, hitting the asphalt in the parking area."

"Do you know if her car was stolen?"

"When I spoke with Ms. Stewart, she stated she didn't own a car."

Heath huffed out a breath, frustrated that he wasn't getting a straight answer from the cop. "They why are you saying it's an attempted carjacking? Most carjackings I know of happen when the owner is inside the vehicle or getting ready to enter or exit said vehicle. Since Camilla doesn't own one, the facts don't jibe."

"I agree, Mr. Boudreau. Like I said, I didn't get to talk with Ms. Stewart for very long yesterday, because the doctor took her for a CAT scan, to see if there was any concussion or other brain injury. Also, she was having some difficulty remembering the events surrounding the incident."

His gut tightened at those words. "She's got amnesia?"

LINKS TO BUY HEATH:
www.kathyivan.com/Heath.html

NEWSLETTER SIGN UP

Don't want to miss out on any new books, contests, and free stuff? Sign up to get my newsletter. I promise not to spam you, and only send out notifications/e-mails whenever there's a new release or contest/giveaway. Follow the link and join today!

http://eepurl.com/baqdRX

REVIEWS ARE IMPORTANT!

People are always asking how they can help spread the word about my books. One of the best ways to do that is by word of mouth. Tell your friends about the books and recommend them. Share them on Goodreads. If you find a book or series or author you love – talk about it. Everybody loves to find out about new books and new-to-them authors, especially if somebody they know has read the book and loved it.

The next best thing is to write a review. Writing a review for a book does not have to be long or detailed. It can be as simple as saying "I loved the book."

I hope you enjoyed reading Lucas, Texas Boudreau Brotherhood Book #5.

If you liked the story, I hope you'll consider leaving a review for the book at the vendor where you purchased it and at Goodreads. Reviews are the best way to spread the word to others looking for good books. It truly helps.

BOOKS BY KATHY IVAN

www.kathyivan.com/books.html

TEXAS BOUDREAU BROTHERHOOD
Rafe

Antonio

Brody

Ridge

Lucas

Heath (coming soon)

NEW ORLEANS CONNECTION SERIES
Desperate Choices

Connor's Gamble

Relentless Pursuit

Ultimate Betrayal

Keeping Secrets

Sex, Lies and Apple Pies

Deadly Justice

Wicked Obsession

Hidden Agenda

Spies Like Us

Fatal Intentions

New Orleans Connection Series Box Set: Books 1-3

New Orleans Connection Series Box Set: Books 4-7

CAJUN CONNECTION SERIES

Saving Sarah

Saving Savannah

Saving Stephanie

Guarding Gabi

LOVIN' LAS VEGAS SERIES

It Happened In Vegas

Crazy Vegas Love

Marriage, Vegas Style

A Virgin In Vegas

Vegas, Baby!

Yours For The Holidays

Match Made In Vegas

One Night In Vegas

Last Chance In Vegas

Lovin' Las Vegas (box set books 1-3)

OTHER BOOKS BY KATHY IVAN

Second Chances (Destiny's Desire Book #1)

Losing Cassie (Destiny's Desire Book #2)

ABOUT THE AUTHOR

USA TODAY Bestselling author Kathy Ivan spent most of her life with her nose between the pages of a book. It didn't matter if the book was a paranormal romance, romantic suspense, action and adventure thrillers, sweet & spicy, or a sexy novella. Kathy turned her obsession with reading into the next logical step, writing.

Her books transport you to the sultry splendor of the French Quarter in New Orleans in her award-winning romantic suspense, or to Las Vegas in her contemporary romantic comedies. Kathy's new romantic suspense series features, Texas Boudreau Brotherhood, features alpha heroes in small town Texas. Gotta love those cowboys!

Kathy tells stories people can't get enough of; reuniting old loves, betrayal of trust, finding kidnapped children, psychics and sometimes even a ghost or two. But one thing they all have in common – love and a happily ever after).
More about Kathy and her books can be found at

WEBSITE: www.kathyivan.com

Follow Kathy on Facebook at facebook.com/kathyivanauthor

Follow Kathy on Twitter at twitter.com/@kathyivan

Follow Kathy at BookBub bookbub.com/profile/kathy-ivan

DISCARD

Made in the USA
Las Vegas, NV
26 February 2021